Harlem Angel

Book 1 of the Circle

Brenda M Hardwick

authorHOUSE®

AuthorHouse™
1663 Liberty Drive
Bloomington, IN 47403
www.authorhouse.com
Phone: 1 (800) 839-8640

© 2018 Brenda M Hardwick. All rights reserved.

No part of this book may be reproduced, stored in a retrieval system, or transmitted by any means without the written permission of the author.

Published by AuthorHouse 02/28/2018

ISBN: 978-1-5462-2429-7 (sc)
ISBN: 978-1-5462-2428-0 (hc)
ISBN: 978-1-5462-2495-2 (e)

Library of Congress Control Number: 2018900521

Print information available on the last page.

Any people depicted in stock imagery provided by Thinkstock are models, and such images are being used for illustrative purposes only. Certain stock imagery © Thinkstock.

This book is printed on acid-free paper.

Because of the dynamic nature of the Internet, any web addresses or links contained in this book may have changed since publication and may no longer be valid. The views expressed in this work are solely those of the author and do not necessarily reflect the views of the publisher, and the publisher hereby disclaims any responsibility for them.

DEDICATION

Ivan and James, thank you for always believing in your Mom!

ACKNOWLEDGEMENTS

Thank you, Divine Creator, for blessing me with the gift of storytelling. Thank you to Carolyn Fritz, for reading, Angie Hodapp for your tears, Michelle Dupuis, for giving your time, talent, gifts, and everyone else who listened to me talk about this book over the last twenty-five years!

ONE

Two heavyset men sidled down the sidewalk taking turns looking over their shoulders as if afraid someone was following them. Each time they turned to look, Soraya ducked, sweating and breathing a sigh of relief when they didn't see her. They seemed to look through her, like she wasn't there. She didn't understand that but brushed those thoughts aside to concentrate on the two thugs, what they looked like and what they were doing.

They spoke in whispers. "Is he in there Bro-Man? I can't see in," the tall one said as they reached the shop and looked through the grimy windows.

"Yeah, he's in there Cuddy. Light's on."

The shorter of the two, Bro-man, seemed very nervous; he fidgeted with something under his coat. "You think anybody seen us?"

"Naaah, Bro-man. Mos these folks round here is havin supper or watchin the tube by now. 'Sides, we *fit* down here."

"Yeah. Guess you right Cuddy. We do *fit*," his laugh sounding like a muffled bicycle horn.

"Shhhhh now, c'mon! Let's be done wi'this."

Soraya watched the scene unfold with mounting apprehension. The *Hearth Shop* was on a quiet street; not much traffic on it at all. She didn't recognize any of the buildings around it either and wondered just where she was. It was getting late; darkness was already covering the city in its blanket of inky black.

The men were suspicious by the fact that they were there. The hour was really too late for any foot traffic because the shops along the street were all closed.

Soraya's breath caught in her throat. She knew something terrible was about to happen; she could feel it. As the men opened the door into the shop, that feeling clouded her mind making her feel like she was wading through clear Jello.

The two thugs were being overcautious and their movements seemed exaggerated, like a scene shot in a slow-motion video. The man called Cuddy had to stoop to walk through the doorway; and being the taller of the two, he grabbed the tiny bell over the door in a black-gloved fist to keep it from ringing when they stepped inside. Trying desperately to think of something she could to do help, Soraya followed them in, tiptoeing quietly on bare feet, wearing only the nightshirt she'd worn to bed. The men closed the door behind themselves, trying not to let it squeak on its hinges.

Somehow Soraya knew that the shopkeeper, Zacharias, never locked the door because all were welcome at the *Hearth Shop*. He wouldn't have locked those doors even if he knew they were coming; but he would have been prepared, which he wasn't. And Soraya felt he should have been ready. She felt that he should have been expecting them. The events scrolled before her like a Saturday matinee movie across a theater screen, except the audience consisted of only one... her. Everything except her body was vividly clear, like it was etched in crystal. She vowed to remember every detail as she watched Cuddy and Bro-man quietly shuffle across the floor. Soraya tried to press her back carefully against the dirty front windows but it was as if they weren't there so she had to try and not fall through them. Wanting to blend in with her surroundings, she cupped her hands over her mouth to help quiet her breathing which was so loud in her own ears she just knew they would hear her.

"Hey, should we cut out the lights?" Bro-man said still talking in whispers.

"Naaah, them windas so dirty nobody can see in here," Cuddy responded.

"You sure bout that?"

"Think man! *WE* couldn't see in here, so nobody else can either!" Cuddy growled.

"Okay, okay, I got it!" Bro-man whined.

Cuddy, who was obviously the leader, whispered again, "He's in the back. You hear'im?"

"Yeah, I hear'im. Hope he don't yell or nuthin."

"Won't matter if he do. We'll stick'im like a pig and git outta here quick."

As they started towards the shuffling noise coming from the back of the shop, Bro-man pulled on brown leather gloves. Cuddy had a long, jagged-edged hunting knife in his hands, like the ones they always used in slasher horror movies. Bro-man carried a short club, kinda like the ones the police use.

Soraya screamed, "Zacharias!" But he couldn't hear her and neither did his attackers. She felt hot, then cold and clammy as fear-soaked sweat beaded her brow and coated her body. She needed to *DO* something, say something, but nothing she thought of or tried seemed to help.

Soraya reached for the bell to make it tinkle but couldn't touch it. There was no substance to her hands. All she could do was watch, helplessly terrified, as the two thugs went about their work.

"Come on old man, we ain't got all night," Bro-man said as he struggled with the wirey old man. Soraya could tell from the look on his face that Zacharias was very surprised as they dragged him from the back room. Bro-man grunted under the strain of trying to hold the old man's flailing arms. "Too bad there ain't enough room t'do you back there."

Cuddy said, "Will you quit squirmin old man! It ain't gonna help you none."

Soraya could hear frustration in the big man's voice, but it was no match for her own feelings of inadequacy.

Zacharias looked up briefly and then straight into Soraya's eyes. Then, as if in response to the thug's request, the old man just went limp. She was shocked as she realized, "He can see me!"

"Let's finish this," Bro-man said.

The thugs took turns swinging their weapons and Soraya cringed with each blow as they methodically beat and stabbed the old man to death. It was almost as if she could feel his pain. Her heart beat rapidly and she felt her body tense as she watched their arms go up and down, up and down, delivering death with each swing. They stepped away from his battered body, admiring their handiwork, and Soraya was sickened by what she saw. They left a bloody mass, almost unrecognizable as once being human.

"Do we take anything? You know, make it a robbery?" Bro-man asked.

"No! Don't take nuthin. Boss said jus off the old dude an leave."

"Okay, okay, but we's leavin' some pretty good stuff here. Could fetch a few extra bucks on the market."

"Hey man, I ain't one for crossin the boss. I don't like it when he gets mad, ya' know what I mean?"

"Yeah man, you right Cuddy, Ray be mean when he's pissed. Let's get outta here before we gets too tempted."

Soraya stood by feeling stupid and completely useless as the two men stepped across the body and opened the door to leave. This time the bell did tinkle, sounding tinny and mournful as she moved to stand in the doorway. Her stomach clenched as she watched two tiny runnels of blood streaming across the floorboards to drip between the slats into the dirt below, making hollow thuds that seemed to echo like the blows on a kettledrum. She imagined what the mud it was making would look like and wretched.

Stepping back, out of the doorway, she turned away from the scene as Cuddy reached towards her to shut the door and she jumped back, fear taking complete control. Soraya started screaming again, and this time she couldn't stop.

"Soraya! Soraya! What is it? Wake up baby!" Soraya Rawlings woke to her own screams mingled with her mothers' pleading voice. Constance was rocking her again, like when she was a child and woke up with night terrors. Her mother was shaking and Soraya was sweat soaked and tangled up in the knots her thrashing had tied into her sheets.

"I'm okay Mama; really, I'm okay," she croaked. Soraya's throat was dry and the words came out strangled as she tried to push her mother away to get unsnarled from the sheets.

"Soraya, oh my Soraya. You gonna have t'see her; this cain't keep happenin!"

"See who Mama, and nothing keeps happening, I just had a nightmare."

"So you sez, so you sez. But they worse now than eva', girl."

Soraya shuddered, her mother's *ghetto* English always made her want to slip back herself, all her education for naught. She finally loosed herself from her mother's grip, stood up and started untangling the mess that her bed had become. "Mama, they're just dreams. Dreams don't hurt anyone."

As she said the words, they almost caught in her throat, remembering the look on the old man's face when his eyes met hers before he died.

"Don' say that!" her mother screamed.

Soraya jumped when her mother suddenly grabbed her by the arms with more strength than she would have believed Constance Rawlings still had in her whole body. She pulled Soraya down close and spoke just above a whisper.

"You was marked girl, from birth! They all tol me you was special, got somethin to do special. I didn't believe, still ain't sure I do, but them dreams you have. Somethin bout them dreams bothers me; always did. Now's worse. You gotta go see her. You gotta go *now*! We ain't gon git no sleep in dis here house til you do!"

Constance shook Soraya's arms once more then dropped her hands to her sides and left the room, shaking her head. A definite *tsk, tsk* could be heard as she shut the bedroom door behind herself. Soraya just stood there for a moment, surprised. She'd never heard such conviction coming from her mother. Constance had always been a *middle of the road* type of person. Never giving in strongly to one idea or another, waiting to see which would be the prevailing one and jumping onto that *side* when the contest was over.

It also dawned on Soraya to whom the *her* she was referring to was. It had to be Iona Mabutu, the old shopkeeper at the *Home Shop* on 118th. The Witch, as Soraya and her friends had called her when they were kids.

As sure as she was that her mother was talking about Miss Iona, Soraya also became sure that her mother was right. "Mama says I need to go see Miss Iona… What can that old woman do about my dreams? They're just bad dreams!" she mumbled.

On impulse, or intuition, Soraya dropped the tangled mass of sheets and picked up the jeans and t-shirt from the chair where she'd tossed them before going to bed, and put them back on. After dressing, Soraya looked in on her mother. She saw Constance roll from one side of the bed to the other, like she was trying to get comfortable. Soraya watched as her breathing slowed, and Constance was finally sound asleep, whistling a little as she exhaled. "You'll get to sleep now Mama," she whispered.

Soraya was halfway to the shop when she realized she could have driven her car. Shaking her head, she kept walking. Although Harlem, like any other big city in the middle of the night, could be called anything but safe, somehow the thought of adding another sound to the wee hours of this night was just too much. Besides, the shop wasn't that much farther away and this *was* her neighborhood. She'd walked these streets many a night when she was a teenager.

Darting a look over her shoulder, she adopted that *don't fuck with me* attitude, and continued on toward the shop. Even though she knew the neighborhood, and most of the thugs would be asleep themselves at three in the morning, it was always smart not to look like a victim.

Soraya arrived at the corner of 118th and Lenox Avenue. She stood there shivering in the darkness, toes perched on the threshold of the pool of radiance that poured from the streetlamp to sparkle in the black of the night. Bathed in that pocket of white light, the small shop was nestled between an old tenement and Corney's restaurant at the end of a block full of brownstones. Set back from the street, slightly off line from the rest of the buildings, the shop was shrouded in the shadow of mystery, and the glow from the streetlamp was in stark contrast to the building's aura of foreboding.

The shop belonged to the old woman. The old folks in the neighborhood all said she came over on one of *the* ships. Soraya shook her head in old disbelief, "Old woman would have to be more than four hundred years old", she snorted. "Nobody lives that long!"

The stories had to be an exaggeration, like the stories of her being a witch. Soraya stood there thinking, "But what if she really is that old?" Harlem would have still been young and clean when she came here. And where was she before she came to Harlem? Soraya couldn't recall ever hearing anyone say exactly when Miss Iona arrived or how, just that she did. The old woman was just… here. Both she and the *Home Shop* showed up on the same day, according to stories. As far-fetched as that sounded, Soraya knew that even the wildest stories usually had a grain of truth in them or the story couldn't grow.

Constance used to tell Soraya the story of the first day she remembered someone going to visit the shop. The story was only from the past eighty years or so, from her mother Constance's lifetime. If Iona was really that old, she would have been ancient even when it happened! Soraya shivered again, automatically cinching her coat tighter as she recalled her mothers' voice.

"Yeeeah Soraya, I remember. Funny you should ask bout old Iona... I remember. It was ol' Miz Cheever who went in fust. My Mama used to say they told ever'body t'leave that ol' woman lone, but Miz Cheever had a mind'a her own and wouldn't listen, even t'the Elders in church, let lone her neighbors. Anyways, Miz Cheever marched up to that door, jus as proud, didn't even knock, jus open the door an walks in. We was playin cross the street in a hydrant cause it was hot that day, real hot. I heard a bell tinkle and look up as she walk in. We all stop and look. Couldn't believe she jus walk in there! My Mama and the other ladies all gathered on the walk, fannin' wit them church fans, you know the ones on a stick, an we all jus watch and wait. Mama an the ladies talk a bit, but mostly was real quiet, peerin' cross that street so hard you'da thought they could see through dem walls! Was a long time afore she come back out, but she did. She look cross the street at all us and popped open her brella t'shade her head and huffed off down t'her house. I remember hearin' the door slam when she got there. She was proud, Miz Cheever was, and her bein so proud opened the way fo all us to visit Miz Iona's shop, cause after that, nobody was scared no more. Not no more."

The memory of her mother's voice trailed off to leave Soraya still standing cold and scared on the corner. She had never been in the shop. It gave her the creeps the way it sat there, untouched by what went on around it. And Iona... or Miss Iona, as she had been taught to address her elders... was creepier than the shop! But Soraya still had a feeling, and that damn dream... She had to go in there, needed to go in there, now. She raised a foot to step forward and just as the toe of her shoe broke the circle of light, she heard the door creak open and she froze. A wave of fear, strong enough to send her running if she wasn't stuck to the spot, washed over her. Soraya felt confused. She wasn't *that* scared of the old woman!

Soraya watched as the door began to slowly swing inward. She took a slow deep breath to calm herself, standing on both feet again, "This is completely stupid. I am *not* afraid of her!"

A small, dark hand followed by a tiny grey head, thrust out into the light. Soraya was suddenly fascinated by what she was seeing, her fear vanquished by curiosity. A tiny figure of a woman, bent and wrinkled even from this distance, stepped out from the doorway shading her eyes from the light. Soraya had never really seen the woman before. She just had this mental picture, drawn from all the stories, and maybe some from her dreams. *Dreams too real* she thought, and shivered again in remembrance.

"Soraya... tha'chu? C'mon in here Chile; Ah been waitin fo ya awhile nah. C'mon in," she beckoned.

Soraya was hit with another range of emotions. Curiosity, shock, fear and bewilderment rolled together in her head and her stomach. "How does she know who I am? That I'd be here?" Soraya shook herself again and began to walk, albeit slowly, towards the door of the shop. The old woman nodded her head and turned, shuffling back through the open doorway once Soraya started moving.

Soraya crossed the pool of light and taking another deep breath, plunged through the doorway of the shop. The first thing she noticed was the smells. Wonderful, spicy, soothing aromas filled the shop and she took another, involuntary, deep breath filling her lungs with the fragrance of time. She pulled the door shut behind herself and squinted into the dim light of the shop and was hit with a wave of déjà vu... except for a few minor differences, it was the shop in her dream. The main things missing, of course, were the body and the blood.

"C'mon, set over here Chile. Ah'm not one fo standin and jawin. Rather set. Dat's why d'chairs here."

Soraya rolled her eyes at Miss Iona's use of the dialect. It was worse than her mother's speech. She navigated past large pieces of furniture and boxes covered in layers of thick dust and cobwebs, all packed tightly into the tiny room. She could see that they were moving towards a fireplace set into the back wall. There was a fire burning and the old woman sat in an overstuffed chair with her stockinged feet pointed towards the flames. The room was warm but not stifling. Soraya took the old leather chair across from Iona and sat down. She thought she would have to dust it off first but surprisingly it wasn't necessary.

"Well, go head, ask me. Sumethin's got'cho mind swimmin, go head."

The invitation freely given, Soraya dove in, "Ok, First, how do you know me, I mean my name; that I was coming?"

The old woman laughed, "Hee, hee, hee, Iona knows jus bout ever'thing roun dese here parts. You been dreamin. Ah know you been dreamin. Ah been dreamin too. Knew you was comin."

Alarmed, Soraya said, "You mean you had the same dream I did?"

"No, Chile, no. Not da same dream, but dreamin jus the same. No, mah dream was tell'o you comin."

Disappointed, Soraya said, "Oh. My dream didn't have you in it. My mother said I needed to come see you though."

Iona cocked her head to the side and looked at Soraya through slanted eyes. It made Soraya uneasy, those eyes. Like the old woman could see inside her head, or her heart… or her soul.

"You was suppose t'come here dis night. You know you was suppose t'come here."

Soraya dropped her head and sighed nervously. Iona was voicing things she didn't want to admit, wasn't ready to know. "I have a… feeling I'm supposed to be here, talking with you, but I came because my mother suggested it. I really don't know what I expect you to do. Silly, really, to be bothering you so late…"

Iona's voice was strong and a bit gravelly where Soraya would have expected it to be frail and weak sounding, considering what the woman's age was supposed to be. The strength she heard was something else that made her uneasy about being in her presence.

"Might've been yo mama's idea that sparked it, but'chu here on yo own Chile."

"Okay, you're right. I knew I had to come see you. But I don't know why."

The old woman smiled, "Oh, Ah think you know why too. Might not git it, but'chu know why."

The words rushed out of Soraya's mouth, like she had no control over her own tongue, "My dreams. It was an awful dream…"

"What'chu see Chile, what'chu see in dat dream?" Iona leaned forward, all her attention focused on Soraya's face.

Soraya was so uneasy with Iona's eagerness, she involuntarily leaned back in her chair, away from Iona, and started talking, struggling to tell everything in order. She had to fight the urge to jump to the end. "The shop looked like yours, Miss Iona…"

"Jus call me Iona Chile. Ain't been no *Miz* in so long'a time, don fit me no more," she smiled, thick lips pulled back over a full set of teeth.

"Iona… the shop looked like yours, but it was a man who owned it."

"Where you was Chile?"

Soraya looked past the old woman in concentration, "I think it was Chicago." She always had good recall of the scenes in her dreams, but details, not so much. She had to concentrate to pull the details from her memory.

With a sharp intake of breath, Iona asked, "Whut his name, Chile, whut his name is?"

Soraya frowned. Names always were the hardest to remember when she had dreams like this. "Ummm, Zachary, Zacharias. Yes, it was Zacharias..."

Iona jumped up from the chair throwing her hands into the air. She walked the edges of the throw rug in quick circles adding to the trench already visible in the nap.

"Aiiiiii! Not Zacharias! He suppose to had longer den me! Aiiiiiii!"

Taken aback by the sudden outburst, Soraya just sat there for a few moments. Then, trying to get Iona's attention, "Iona! It was just a dream Iona..."

Iona stopped her frantic pacing abruptly and looked Soraya right in the eyes, "No Chile, not jus a dream. You what *Da Circle* calls a *seer* Chile. Not jus a dream. You is seein da *now*'o things."

"You can't mean that was real?" Soraya couldn't keep the panic out of her voice.

The old woman took a deep breath, calming herself and sat back down in her chair. "Ah'm gonna tell you a story. Only dis story's da truth, for da reals."

Feeling warm, Soraya realized she still has her coat on and slips out of it while Iona begins her story. She felt she was going to be here for awhile, and now the examination of her dream was going to have to wait.

"We come over here from da Mother Country. Africa. Way back afore you and mos dese here young'uns was born or thought of. Dem ships come, took mos'us wit out pe'mission, jus took us. But, some us come ourself's, me an a few others. We come to watch over. Help out, and watch over. We spread far now, was pretty close t'gether at fust. Now we's far apart, but still connected. We been watchin over ever'thing here, keepin *Us* t'gether. Keepin what we got lef from da Mother, alive an well. Makin sure it gits passed on't y'all young'uns." Iona leaned back and closed her eyes as she spoke. "Me an Zacharias, we's da oldest with Fanny Mae bein next.

Zacharias was in Chicago. Fanny Mae in Miami. All gon be scared now. Zacharias wasn't supposed to be fust. Dis ain't right. Don't know how we's gonna fix it, but we's gotta try."

Silent now, and her eyes still closed, Iona seemed to nod off. Soraya wanted to ask another question, but didn't want to wake her.

"Ain't sleep, Chile; ask away."

Soraya jumped. It was as if the old woman read her mind.

Soraya took a deep breath and started, "So, let me see if I have this straight. You and the man I dreamt of are part of a network of, what… witches?"

Iona laughed, eyes popping open abruptly, "Hee, hee, hee, oh Chile, thas a good one, witches, hee, hee, hee, witches! We's not witches, Chile; dems from that dere Urope country… witches." She stopped laughing abruptly and looked straight into Soraya's eyes again, her brow wrinkling even deeper than it already was with the intensity of her words, "We's called Kuhani, Makuhani; soothsayers in dis here tongue. We is *Da Circle*, tribal medicine. Witches learn't from *US* Chile. We was here fust. We was roun long afore dem witches."

"Sorry! I didn't know. How could I know?" Soraya was embarrassed for the whiny singsong her voice seemed to take on all by itself. It was in reaction to the tinge of anger behind Iona's words.

Iona leaned back in her chair and sighed heavily. "Zacharias was second in d'order. Ah'm fust. Should'a been me t'go fust."

Soraya heard such resignation in the old woman's voice that it renewed her fears, but for a different reason. "You keep talking about this Zacharias as if he was really dead. It was only a dream Iona."

Iona raised her head, cocking it sideways again to look at Soraya. "You suppose t'be a smart girl. Ain't you been payin 'tention? Dem's not jus dreams you have Chile! Dem's visions; real sights you is havin, not jus dreams. Zacharias dead jus sure as Ah'm settin here wit'chu."

Soraya started shaking her head no again, "That's not true! It can't be true! They're dreams, just dreams! There's no such thing as visions; and if there were, *I* wouldn't be having them. I'm nobody, nothing special; just a girl who has bad dreams!" Soraya's voice raised an octave with every denial. She was screeching by the time she finished.

"Tsk, tsk, tsk."

It sounded like somebody sucking neckbones when Iona did that, and it made Soraya wince. She hated that sound. It made her skin crawl.

"You a mess, Chile. Ain't nuthin t'be shamed of, havin visions. Means you chosen, you suppose t'be here, raght now."

Soraya didn't know whether to believe the old woman or grab her coat and run for the door. She felt like she'd been dropped into an old episode of the *Twilight Zone*. Shock seemed out of place and confusion not enough of an emotion for the rocking and reeling her head and stomach were doing. Her voice shook when she spoke, "So, let me see if I understand you. My dreams are real visions of... what might happen?"

"Hee, hee, hee, no Chile. Not what might happen, but what *IS* happenin. You is seein the *NOW* o'things."

Soraya shuddered and leaned closer to the fire, suddenly cold despite the heat in the room. "My dreams are visions."

"Das right Chile."

"What I'm seeing is really happening."

"Ummm hmmmm, Chile, das raght."

"And, Zacharias is really dead?"

"Sure as you settin here Chile. Now, we's got t'figure out what t'do bout dat."

"*We* have to figure out what to do? What about the rest of your... circle? Shouldn't you be calling on *them* to fix this problem instead of me?" she screeched.

Iona began to rock back and forth in her chair. It wasn't a rocker, so it was just her body that moved to a rhythm Soraya thought she could almost feel vibrating through the room.

"Soraya, Ah is real sorry dis here is happenin now. We should'a had nother year or two afore you come to Iona. But Chile, somethin's wrong. Real wrong. All y'all prentices bein called early, afore some is ready, like you, but time is nigh. Can't deny it, time is nigh."

Soraya watched Iona closely, fear-borne curiosity mixing in her stomach like a soured milkshake. "So, now what do we do?"

"Chile, you like dat word 'so' don'chu. Hee, hee, hee, *so*... we's gonna start trainin you now, afore somethin happins t'me. Gotta git you basics done fast."

The urgency Soraya heard in Iona's words was palpable. It scared her to think about what it meant.

Iona stood and stretched her little old body, then shuffled to the entrance of the hallway at the back of the shop. An old, threadbare curtain, patched so many times that the original threads holding the patches together were almost translucent, hung over the doorway. "Comin t'bed Chile? You be stayin here fo now on. Go head n'gitsome sleep afore mornin gits here altogether."

"Wait a minute," Soraya said as she stood up, "I didn't know staying here would be part of the plan. I have a home Iona. I don't need to crowd you." Soraya looked around the tiny shop as she spoke. This place had always given her the creeps, and now she was going to call it home? She didn't think so.

"Chile, think! If you at yo mama's house, how kin you learn what'chu need t'know? You mah 'prentice; dat means you mah shadow from now on."

"But…"

"Now there's a word I don like much, dat 'but'. Cept fo you backside, dat word shouldn't be used a'tall." Iona walked past the curtain, and Soraya heard her shuffle down the hallway. She sat back down in the old leather chair and watched the fire die to angry red embers before she finally sighed and stood to follow the old woman down the hallway to see *her room*. She didn't like it, but she could *FEEL* that Iona was right. She could just leave, of course, but then she thought of her mother and how peacefully she was sleeping when she left the house. Of necessity, this was going to be home, at least until she could figure out how to get out of this apprentice thing.

TWO

The sun was just creeping up the horizon when Soraya finally woke for the day. She woke up staring at a ceiling she didn't recognize, and she didn't remember where she was at first. Then the smell of bacon hit her nose, and she remembered that she wasn't home; she was still at Iona's in the back of the shop. She had dropped off to sleep quickly after lying down, physically exhausted from the whole ordeal. Now she tried to piece together everything she remembered from the night before, starting with what Iona said about the apparent significance of her dreams.

The bedroom was hardly bigger than a closet, the twin bed she was curled up in and a tiny dressing table with mirror and chair being the only furniture that could possibly fit into it. Soraya wondered where she'd keep all her clothes, as another waft from the kitchen made her mouth water. Her mother never cooked bacon for breakfast. She smiled as she thought about what her mother always said about pork "Pig meat's for seasonin, Soraya, not eatin. Stuff too salty fo eatin. Watch dems dat eats it. They be goin down wi'Moses sooner'n us!"

Soraya took a deep breath, savoring the smell. She didn't eat it often, but every once in awhile, a little *pig meat* was good for breakfast. She stretched and threw the blanket off to get up. Just as her feet hit the cold wood of the floor, she heard Iona call.

It's bout time you was up Chile! You got things t'do! Rise up now and come git some grits'n bacon. They's wash water in the pitcher an'a face towel's in'a bowl."

Soraya smiled "On my way!" she called. Grits; hadn't had any of those in awhile either. She quickly splashed some water into the bowl and did a quick wash up before dressing. Out of habit, Soraya checked the time as she put her watch on and was surprised to note it was only six-thirty. For getting only a few hours of sleep, it was curious that she felt totally rested. Pulling her jeans back on for the third time in twenty-four hours, she felt like she needed a real bath but knew it would have to wait until later. Soraya followed her nose to find Iona in a tiny kitchen that she hadn't even seen on passing down the hallway to her new bedroom.

"Good morning Iona."

"Mornin Chile. See here, Ah got'chu a plate ready." Using a timeworn spatula, Iona pointed to a small table and chair sitting in the corner of what had to be the smallest kitchen Soraya had ever seen. She asked, "So… what is it I have to do today?"

Iona shook her head, the gray wisps of her thinning hair that had escaped her two braids flailed in a dizzy dance around her face, "Chile, yo fust lesson is t'think! I'm not tellin you this'un. You tell me!"

Soraya took the plate Iona handed her and watched as the old woman stood, hands on her hips, tapping a foot in earnest.

"Okay, okay," she began, watching from beneath her lashes for Iona's reaction to her words. "Let's see. I guess you would expect me to collect my things to stay here, which we still need to talk about…"

"Nothin t'talk bout." Iona sniffed, "You is stayin so's you kin stop askin bout dat."

"Iona, I really don't feel it's necessary for me to live here with you to learn what I have to learn." Soraya winced at Iona's expression, ducking her head to pick up the fork lying on the table. She quickly sat down and shoveled in a mouthful of eggs and cracklin to keep from saying anything for a minute.

Iona continued to stare down at her not saying a word. Soraya could feel the intensity of her eyes without looking up to meet them. "Iona, what if I don't want to be your apprentice?" she asked after swallowing.

Iona sighed and turned that sideways, slant-eyed look on Soraya. "You is stayin Chile. You got no choice in dat. Tis portant you is here all hours cause you learnin is part of you livin. So… since you like usin dat word, you kin stop askin and worryin bout dat."

Soraya chewed in silence, staring at the plate. She couldn't decide whether to be angry or to just let it drop. She felt like she was being forced to do this, but part of her felt relieved that the decision was being made for her. This way, if it was the wrong decision, it wouldn't be her fault.

Iona started moving again, this time not looking at Soraya's face when she spoke "Chile, if'n you think you kin leave here an not come back, you go head."

Soraya thought about her dreams, and the last words her mother said before she left the house that morning. "Will the dreams ever stop if I don't do this?"

"No Soraya. Dem's part o'yo gifts. Jus cause you don want it don' mean it's gon stop."

The kitchen was filled with the sound of the bacon sizzling and the spatula scraping the skillet. Soraya stared at the table, absently stirring the grits on her plate. She sighed again, finally resigned to a fate she still wasn't happy with.

Iona paused, her expression changing, the lines in her face softening, "Nah, you ain't done Chile I'll warm it if'n it gits too cold. Keep goin."

Soraya looked up, damming up her anger and frustration "Got to say goodbye to Mama."

Iona laughed out loud, "C'mon Chile, you is stallin! Sayin g'bye to yo mama ain't ne'ssary. You ain't leavin, jus movin down da street!"

Soraya put the fork down and cleared her throat as if caught in the middle of a lie "Alright. After bringing my things here and telling Mama I'm staying here for awhile, I don't know where else I should go or what else there is for me to do." She was trying hard to keep that childish whine out of her voice.

Now Iona smiled a toothsome grin. "Good! Good! You finally got it! You got t'realize you don' know ever'thing if'n you goin t'learn anything. Fust lesson done! Hee, hee, hee!"

Soraya waited for something more as Iona turned back to her cooking. That high, squeaky laugh muffled by the bacon spitting in the frying pan. After several minutes, she picked up the fork and began eating again. Soraya was surprised to find the food still warm and while she ate, her mind raced over her agenda for the day, at least the part she knew about. She wondered just what the old witch had in store for the afternoon, again thinking about the revelations of her arrival.

With her back turned, Iona said "Ask Chile. No sense stewin bout it. Ask me."

Soraya looked up from cleaning her plate of the last mouthful, just as Iona came to the table with her own breakfast. Clearing the table of her dishes, she asked, "Last night… or this morning, you said there was a network of you, but you only named three. Is that all of you?"

Iona answered between bites "No Soraya. Dey's one of us in ever' big city. We's a circle… *The Circle*: Ah's here, Fanny Mae's in Miami-Family Shop; Zacharias, bless his soul, Chicago-Hearth Shop; Ruby Jewel in N'Olins-Beloved Shop; Willamae in Washin'ton D.C.-Love Shop; Abraham in St. Louis-Glory Shop; Lois Jean in Dallas-House Shop; Walterine in L.A.-Faith Shop; AnnaMae in Denver-Health Shop; Andrew in Birmingham-Life Shop; Athlene in Seattle-Heart Shop; and Cleasta in Atlanta-Balance Shop. Twelve us altogether, well… leven nah."

She lowered her head and finished eating. Soraya thought about this while she ran water for the dishes. Twelve. Something about that number was important, something she'd heard somewhere else. She turned around again to find Iona watching her closely. "Ok, so why am I so important? I mean, you said you need an apprentice, and I guess that's me."

"Yes, it's you Chile. Stop dancin roun the question."

She sighed, "If having an apprentice is so important, why doesn't Zacharias have one? And do the others?"

Iona stood and handed Soraya her dishes. "Well nah, Chile dat be's a question or two by the sound of'em. You is important cause you kin *see*. Now, Ah told you bout dat this mornin. Zacharias didn know dem boys was a comin fo'im. 'Sides, his prentice been chosin, jus like you was fo me. Nah, t'others? Dey's all got prentices; but, like Zacharias, they might not been innerduced yet. Dat's one o'dem things we's gon have t'find out."

"What about…"

"Nah, dat's nough fo a minit. Ahs got t'open up! You finish dem dishes den git on with dem other things you got t'do at yo mamas. We kin talk more later on."

Soraya watched Iona raise her tiny body up from the chair and shuffle out of the kitchen. She listened as her footsteps faded up the hallway. When she heard the little bell over the door tinkle as Iona opened it up, a shiver ran down her back. She took a deep breath and turned to finish the dishes, remembering a black-gloved hand holding another little bell.

Washing dishes was a mindless task, and Soraya was able to take in a little more of her surroundings while she scrubbed the plates and skillet. The kitchen was so small that the way they had eaten this morning, first one then the other, would have to be the norm. Tightly packed cabinets lined three walls and the fourth wall was almost all doorway. The gas stove was one of those tiny apartment-sized ones with four burners and an oven just big enough to fit a small turkey for Thanksgiving dinner. There was a four-paned window over the sink that looked out onto the alleyway. Iona had a small flower box on the windowsill lined with tiny plants that Soraya guessed were herbs of some kind. She'd never seen anyone grow anything but flowers in a window box, but none of these plants had buds. She smiled. Herbs growing in a window box were unusual, especially in Harlem. She wondered at the variety and was reminded that she had called Iona a witch.

There was an old copper clock shaped like a teapot hanging on the back wall where it made the dingy, yellow wallpaper less noticeable. It was sandwiched between the overhead cabinets and the top of a small refrigerator. The table and chair rounded out the furnishings, and Soraya wondered how the two of them, two grown women, would *ever* be able to live with each other in such tight quarters.

The teapot said it was pushing seven o'clock as Soraya dried her hands on a towel hanging from a magnet on the refrigerator door. She went back to her room to get her things. When she entered, she spotted her purse lying on the tiny dressing table and her coat lying across the bed. She hadn't heard the old woman come back down the hallway with them, but she hadn't been listening for her footsteps either. The bed was already made up too. Not a good sign as far as Soraya was concerned; it foreshadowed expectations from the old woman. She shook her head. How could Iona be so neat about the back rooms when the shop was such a cluttered, dusty mess?

Soraya put on her coat and walked to the front of the shop. The first stop would be her mothers' house.

"See you later, Iona."

"Don' be too long Chile. We's got lots to git done t'day."

Soraya smiled and nodded, and as she stepped across the threshold onto the street, her breath caught. Walking back into the world outside the shop felt like coming up for air when you had been under water for too long, only without the pain in your lungs. She turned to look back through the door. Iona waved her off smiling while she bent to polish something large and silver behind the dusty counter.

Soraya turned towards her mother's house and started walking. She savored the sights and sounds of Harlem waking up in the morning, noticing things she usually took for granted. She could hear the grating sound of metal on metal as the subway train dragged itself above 118th street on its way uptown. Traffic was already building on the expressway by seven-thirty and lights were flashing on in windows all up and down the street. Soraya nodded hello as the neighborhood hookers passed her returning home for the day. The rising sun was filling the sky with enough light to make the patches between the buildings a pretty blue. This was an observation Soraya doubted even the pastor of their family church would notice most mornings because the buildings were so tightly packed together and the exhaust fumes were so strong by mid-morning that most people squinted too much to see anything but where they were going.

Six blocks later, Soraya was thinking again about Iona, living with her and what she was going to tell her mother. Climbing the front steps to the old brownstone, her agitation was replaced by a total calmness. This was right and her mother would understand. She still didn't like it, but she *knew* it was right. Her feeling of certainty was as strong as the conviction she had used to resist the idea. Soraya heard footsteps inside as she placed the key in the lock and the door opened before she could reach for the handle.

"Soraya? Dat'chu?"

"Yes, Mama, I'm home."

"You OK baby? I was a bit worried when you wasn't here dis mornin'."

Soraya shut the door and dove right in to the heart of the matter. "I'm moving in with Iona, Mama. I think its best just now."

Constance looked at her funny, a haunted look in her eyes. Her voice was small and quiet when she spoke. "She claim you, didn she. I knew she would. They said you was marked. Guess I gots t'blieve em now." Suddenly, her mother flung her arms around her and squeezed tight. "No matter what Soraya, you always *MY* Chile. I love you, and I is yo Mama!"

Soraya hugged her back, "I know Mama! I love you too, always. I'll never be far away; and if you need me for anything, you just have to call, and I'll come." She blinked back tears while stroking her mother's head with a trembling hand. It was different, holding her mother. It had always been the other way around. So much was happening so fast that Soraya felt fear wrap around her spine making her legs weak. Her mother was scared of losing a daughter. Soraya didn't exactly know *what* she was afraid of, just that she was afraid.

Constance spoke through tears. "I didn know she was goin t'take my baby away, I wouldn't have sent you to her."

"Mama, she's not taking me away from you."

"Like you always say, dem's jus dreams." Constance sniffed.

Soraya took a deep breath, "Mama, you were right to send me to see Iona. My dream was really bad this time."

"I knows dat Soraya. Yo dreams is *always* bad." She pulled away and looked into Soraya's eyes as she spoke. "Why's dis one so special?"

Soraya hugged her close again. They stood that way, huddled together in the front hall for more than a few minutes before Soraya felt that she had gotten her wits about her, and then she backed away with a final squeeze. Taking her mothers hand, they started walking down the hallway together. "This dream was different. I saw a man die this time Mama and Ms. Iona says he's really dead…"

Constance stiffened and Soraya turned to face her. She knew she had said the wrong thing. Soraya watched her mother's eyes grow round with fear, and she winced at the high pitch of her voice. "Thas worser! You is gittin volved in peoples bein kilt!"

"Mama, mama, please. I'll be alright." Soraya reached for her mother, but Constance backed away.

"How kin you say it gonna be alright? Peoples dyin. You not gon be here. It ain't good, Soraya. Won't be no good come o'dis here."

Soraya tried to sound confident, "Mama, I don't like this any more than you do."

"Then why you goin?" Constance asked, defiance coloring her words.

"I'm going because I have to. If I don't go, the dreams won't go away. I can't shut them off, so I need to understand them. We both know its right

Mama. You felt it last night. That's why you sent me to Miss Iona. I knew it, and that's why I went."

They stood that way, Constance on the verge of crying again and Soraya trying to exude a confidence she wasn't really feeling. Constance drew herself up, "You gon take all yo things?" she said, turning back to walk up the hallway.

Soraya took this acceptance as a good sign. "Well, I was hoping I could leave most of it here, Mama. Miss Iona really doesn't have the room for me to move everything into her shop."

"She live there at the shop?"

"Yeah, there are rooms in the back."

They walked together down the hall towards Soraya's room. Constance stopped at a closet along the way to pull a suitcase out. As they stepped into Soraya's room her mother spoke again. "What'chu want me t'do with the rest of yo things baby?"

"Mama, that's really up to you. I can pack everything in boxes if you want, then you can store them in the shed out back and use my room for something else."

"Oh *NO* Soraya! That's *yo* room! I don' want t'do nothin with yo room!"

Soraya took the suitcase from her and tossed it onto the bed. "It's okay Mama! It's okay! You don't have to do anything with my room. Maybe I'll even be able to come and stay with you for a few days now and then. Would that be okay?" Her words had the effect she was hoping for. Her mother visibly relaxed and calmed down. Her voice was pitched at a more normal level when she spoke again.

"Oh, that be jus fine Soraya baby, that be jus fine. You come stay with yo mama fo a spell, and yo room be waitin fo you."

Soraya opened the suitcase and started pulling things off the dressing table to go in it.

"You want some coffee, honey? I got some perkin."

"Sure Mama, a cup of coffee would be great. I'm going to take a quick shower and change clothes before I finish packing."

As she watched her mother's back retreat towards the kitchen, Soraya was flooded with such a strong feeling of *right* that it almost knocked her down. She had to sit on the edge of the bed just to keep her legs from giving out beneath her. She tried to shake off the feeling and hoped with a passion that being an *apprentice* didn't mean she'd feel like that a lot.

Soraya finished her shower, dressed in a clean skirt and blouse and was about halfway finished packing when her mother reappeared with two steaming mugs and a plate of tea biscuits and homemade jam on a tray. She smiled but didn't say anything; she knew the coffee hadn't been made, she didn't smell it when she came into the house. She took a biscuit and started to nibble on it even though she wasn't hungry after having breakfast at Iona's.

"Thanks Mama." She sipped the coffee gingerly; Constance always made it too hot.

"You packin fast; don fa'get nothing you gon need."

"I won't forget anything Mama. But, if I do need something I don't take this time, it'll give me an extra reason to come and see you!"

That made Constance smile, and then she pulled a chair out of the corner and sat down as if to watch a show. "You ain't eatin much."

Soraya shrugged, "I'm really not very hungry. I ate breakfast at Miss Iona's before I left."

"Ol' woman kin cook, huh… What she fix? Got t'make sure she gonna take care o'my baby." Constance pursed her lips in scrutiny.

Soraya laughed, "She made bacon, grits and cracklin eggs, Mama."

"Lord a-mercy, she got you eatin pig meat! You be careful eatin dat mess. Maybe I better talk t'dat woman bout feedin young folk."

Still laughing, Soraya said, "Mama, I'll be alright! I won't eat like that every day, I promise. You taught me better!"

Constance settled down in the chair again, "Well, I should say you won't, I'll come fetch you meals if'n I need t."

Soraya was trying not to laugh when she said, "Mama, I tell you what, I'll stop and get some things at the grocery store before I go back."

"Dat be good. Make sure you git some oatmeal, dat's better'n dat pig meat."

"I will, Mama." Soraya paused in her folding of a pair of pants to look at her mother. "Mama?"

"Yeah baby?"

"Mama… you remember that story you told me about Miss Iona and when she came here?"

"You mean dat story bout Miz Cheever?"

"Yes, that's the one."

"Why sure I member, why you ask?"

"Well, this is 2016."

"Suga, I know what year tis."

"Yeah, but, the story you told me about Miss Cheever happened when you were a child, but…"

"Uh huh, sure was. Jus a young'un I was."

"But, if she came over on the ships, she had to be here before you were born, Mama."

"Un huh, I spect dat's true Soraya."

"So, where was she before the shop showed up? Was she here? Did she grow up here?"

Constance began rocking side to side, "I see, hmmmm, I see. You is wonderin jus where she from?"

Soraya watched in amusement. She wondered if that rocking motion helped when thinking. Both her mother and Miss Iona rocked when they were thinking. She said, "Where and when. Miss Iona was a grown woman when you were a child. She had to come here from somewhere."

"Yeah, she come from somewhere." Constance was quiet for a moment, sipping her coffee.

Soraya decided to push a little. "Let me make a guess, Mama. Miss Iona's shop wasn't always in Harlem was it? It started somewhere else first, right?"

Constance put the mug down on the chair between her legs and shook a finger at Soraya when she spoke, "Alls I know is she was there one day an afore she wasn't. You should ask *her* where she from!"

Constance picked her mug back up and took a sip, waving her hand in the familiar gesture that was her mother's *aint't nothin else t'say bout it*, adding finality to her statement. Soraya knew she wouldn't get anything more, so she changed the subject.

"Why'd you have me so late, Mama."

Constance looked askance at Soraya.

"Nah, why you ask such a question of yo mama?"

Soraya took a deep breath before answering, "Well, Mama, I don't know. Something tells me I need to know some things I've never had the… nerve to ask you before."

Constance let out a whoop and slapped her palm to her leg, "Well, you sho gotta nerve t'day huh!"

Soraya laughed too, "I guess I do at that! Will you tell me?"

Her mother carefully sat the cup down again before saying anything else. "Soraya, Baby, you was always special. I wasn't suppose t'be able t'have no chil'ren. Doctors all say I's barren." She shook her head in disappointment but continued before Soraya could say anything. "Man come along t'me late in life. I wasn't lookin fo it, jus happen. He was nice'n all, but didn' stay roun. Didn' really think he was gon stay roun anyways. But he did stay fo a little while. You come from dat little while."

Soraya watched her mother tell the story in fascination. Constance Rawlings had a warm light shining from her eyes that Soraya had never seen there before. She'd never really asked much about her father, and this was more then she expected. That he didn't stay around was typical of most black men from her experience with them. They were only just beginning to realize that their presence was important to a family.

"Why don't you have any pictures of him, Mama? I would like to have seen what he looked like."

Constance looked into Soraya's eyes, "He look like you baby, or maybe I should say you look like him. Same dark curly hair and almond shaped, light brown eyes. Spit you out like'uh seed, he did. You did take some o'my colorin though, you not quite as dark as him. Lord takes care of dem things, yes he do."

"What do you mean *The Lord takes care of those things?*"

"We's always sayin dat when a Chile born; the Lord takes care o'the details cause He know when things goin t'work out tween folks, and when it ain't."

Soraya pursed her lips in bewilderment, "I still don't get it, Mama."

Constance sighed, "Like, when a Chile's mama is white an daddy is black if'n daddy ain't gon be roun, Chile always look white stead o'black. Lord takes care."

As suddenly as it was there, the light and excitement faded from her mother's eyes. Soraya guessed that the story was at an end, at least for today.

"Thank you Mama."

"Baby, I haven't done a thing." Constance held her mug cradled in both hands as if they were cold.

Soraya dropped what she was folding and cupped her mother's hands around the mug. "Yes you have, Mama, you've given me a bit more of a foundation. I mean, you've always been this pillar I could lean on, always there. Now you've given me the cement to lock it in place."

Constance just looked at her over the rim of the coffee mug, eyes tearing up just a little. "You welcome, Soraya, you welcome."

Soraya finished packing. Her mother had pulled the only bag with wheels on it from the closet, as if she'd known it would be the right one. It could be packed to bursting and still be handled. When she finally got it closed and latched, she sat on the edge of the bed to finish her coffee. "Are you really alright with this Mama?"

"What'chu mean... you goin' t'live at Iona's?"

"Well, yes, and that I'll be her apprentice."

Constance was quiet for a moment, "Nes'sary. It's nes'sary Baby. You is right. I knows it, jus like you say."

Soraya placed the mug on the dresser, stood and walked over to her mother. "I love you Mama, just remember that. If you *ever* need me, I'll be here."

"I know Baby, I know." Her mother smiled and threw her arms around her middle, almost dropping the now empty mug.

Soraya held her for a long time before they finally parted. She picked up the suitcase and carried it to the front door. When she looked back up the hallway, her mother had both mugs in her hands and was headed toward the kitchen humming *Amazing Grace*.

Soraya didn't say goodbye when she left. It didn't seem to fit, and she didn't like saying *goodbye* to anybody, especially her mother. She looked at her watch as she stood at the top of the stairs leading to her mother's door. She expected the whole morning to be gone, but it was only eleven. Picking up the suitcase again, she carried it to the sidewalk pulling the handle out in practiced style as she put it down. She walked three steps when she remembered again that she *did* have a car. She shook her head in mild disbelief, *"How can I keep forgetting something like that!"*

She turned around and circled the brownstone using the flagstone path on the side. Her car was parked under the carport behind the old building.

Soraya stuffed the suitcase into the back seat of her little coupe, and then slid behind the wheel. The little white Honda puffed and wheezed as the engine came to life.

As she backed out of the driveway, Soraya decided that she would keep her word and stop at the grocery store before returning to Iona's shop. Besides the promise to her mother, there were just a few things that she wanted to add to the kitchen since she would be eating there. She pulled into the market's parking lot a few minutes later and checked her wallet before going in. *Hmmm, only twenty-five dollars; I do hope Iona's shop produces a little cash or we're going to be hungry!*

She wondered just how much the shop brought in on a daily basis. Remembering how crowded the shop was with stuff, she didn't have high hopes. If all the dust and clutter was evidence, somebody was going to need a second job.

Shrugging it off as a problem for later, she went into the store and bought some of the basics she noticed missing from Iona's kitchen: plain yoghurt, English muffins, lettuce and tomatoes, brown bread, honey and of course, oatmeal, were a few of the items she picked up. The list in her head was longer than her money, so she stuck with the necessities.

Iona doesn't eat very healthy for her age, Soraya mused, and something in the back of her mind questioned just what *healthy* might really be for someone of Iona's age... whatever it was. When she finally returned to the shop, she drove around the back through the alley. There was a small space between a vegetable patch she had missed seeing that morning and a wooden fence in dire need of a coat of paint. She wasn't happy about parking her little car in the dirt but decided parking on the street in front would be worse than having to give the car a bath more often.

Grabbing the suitcase in one hand and the three grocery bags in the other, she carried them all to the back door and was surprised when it wasn't locked. "Iona? Are you alright?" she called as she stepped through the door.

"Up front Chile. Put you bags up and come up here Soraya."

"Okay, be there in a minute. I've got to unload some things first."

Leaving her suitcase at the door, Soraya put the bags on the kitchen table. She closed and locked the back door before returning to the kitchen to put the groceries away. When she dropped her suitcase onto the bed, she noticed a small dresser had been added to her new bedroom during her short absence this morning and wondered how Iona ever got it into the room.

Soraya was humming the same hymn as her mother when she walked into the storefront.

"Well, you been busy!" Iona said, stepping from behind one of the dusty counters. She was holding a large, oversized, leather-bound book.

"Not really," Soraya replied. "Just doing what needed to be done."

Iona grunted with the weight of the book as she spoke, shaking her head as Soraya started toward her with her hands held out to help with it. "Could tell from dem bags you was carryin you did a bit mor'n what was on yo list."

Soraya smiled, "I stopped at the corner market for a few things after I left Mama's house. It isn't much, but I think the additions will be welcome."

Iona chuckled, "Ever little bit'l help, Chile." She finished crossing the room, shuffling under the weight of the book, and Soraya quickly made room for the thing atop one of the tables.

She squinted trying to read the cover through the layer of dust. "So, what's with the book?"

Iona smiled, carefully dusting the cover off. She turned it to reveal thick, yellowed pages covered in line upon line of the tiny, thin, handwritten script of someone using a very sharp writing instrument. "Dis here's the Hist'ry, Chile. We's all played a part in writin dis here book."

After turning a few pages, Soraya noticed that the handwriting was different on some pages. "How many people have written in it?"

"Dis here's a special book, Soraya. It writes itself. The writin's differnt cause we's all differnt."

"You mean *The Circle*?" Soraya's voice was a hushed whisper, giving respect to what Iona was saying.

"Yeah, *Da Circle*. Each us sees things, hears things. Cause we's kinnected. It's all writ in the book."

Soraya shook her head in disbelief. This was too much. "Iona, books don't write themselves…"

Smiling, Iona took her by the hand, "Here Chile, let me show you."

Iona turned to a page just past the middle of the book. Soraya was amazed. While she watched, the page began to fill with words. She grabbed the counter to steady herself from the shock of what she was seeing and what it meant. Not only was the book recording her morning's activities, but the script was in her own handwriting!

"H-h-how does it *DO* that!" she whispered.

Iona said, "Tol you. You suppose t'be here, Chile. Da spirit power knows you already."

"Power?"

"Wha'chu think, Chile? We's connected by sumpthin to make *Da Circle* strong. To *make* it a Circle. It's a real thing. You kin touch it, feel it, use it; even see it if'n you lookin fo it."

Soraya started breathing again when she realized she'd been holding her breath. "Well, I know you didn't pull it out just to show it to me. Is there something in it we need?" she sputtered.

Iona gently took the book from Soraya's hands, turning it to face her on the table. She gingerly turned the thick leaves until she was about one quarter of the way back through the pages. "Dis here, you need t'read dis here. Dis might splain some o'what we's got t'do."

Iona spun the book back around so that Soraya could read it; her dark wrinkled hands almost caressing the pages as she pointed to a certain paragraph. Soraya read aloud, feeling the passage called for such attention. "And so the twelve were chosen from the youngest that showed *talent*. They were both males and females, although more of the latter (the women always were stronger.) Their charge was simple: *KEEP US TOGETHER*; keep the fabric that binds us as a people alive, no matter what the odds or the consequences. The only rule to follow is: *Do Not Interfere*. The power of *The Circle* shall not be used to interfere in the way of things, only to protect and keep the foundation."

Soraya looked up from the words and watched Iona nod her head slowly. "These twelve... you and the others... are those twelve? That makes you over four hundred..."

"Yes Chile, we's dat same twelve young'uns they pulled from all over. Ever tribe was lookin and only dem wit real strong gifts was even measured. We was tested then; sumthin like Ah'm bout t'do wit'chu now."

Soraya just looked at the old woman, her mind reeling. She knew it was time. Knew it wouldn't be long from the moment she crossed into that pool of light early this morning. She wanted to run screaming from the shop; but as hard as she was fighting it, she knew this was why she had come. Why she had *had* to come.

Iona took the book from her, treating it as the treasure it surely was. "Dis book's always ready, Soraya. You read it any time, Chile."

"Thank you. I think I'll do that." She watched as Iona closed the book and stood, leaving it on the table.

"C'mon Chile, best git this testin over'n done wit." Iona turned towards the hallway as she spoke.

Soraya looked around the shop before moving to follow her. "Aren't we going to lock up first?"

"Lock up? What fo? Dey ain't comin here next. You my prentice. God don' grant den take it back dat quick, Chile. We's got some time afore somebody comes fo me. We's got some time."

Soraya didn't like it that the old woman was so trusting and as soon as Iona was through the curtain, she closed and locked the door anyway. Then she followed Iona back through the curtained hallway to the kitchen. Iona stopped and bent to the floor where she started rolling up the throw rug in front of the sink. As she rolled, a trap door with seams so tight water would have a hard time passing through was revealed.

Iona put the rug behind her and said, "Ah keeps my workshop downstairs. Most dese here houses don' have no cellars. Made sure mine did. All da shops got dirt under'em, stead o'cement."

The old woman heaved on a metal ring big enough for a basketball to pass through that was set into the trapdoor, and the piece of flooring rose on creaking hinges to reveal a narrow staircase leading down. "Go head, dey's nuthin down there t'git cha! Hee, hee, hee!"

Soraya moved doubtfully to the doorway and slowly started down the stairs. The first time she looked back up, Iona was staring down at her with a wide grin on her face. She looked up again just before reaching the bottom, but the old woman was climbing down herself by then.

Brushing dust and cobwebs from her skirt, Soraya asked, "Just what do I have to do in this test?"

"Don' worry, Chile, it won' hurt! Hee, hee, hee!"

A wave of apprehension washed over Soraya so strong that it surprised her in its strength. She hadn't thought about pain. "I hope you aren't kidding about that."

Iona's feet landed at the bottom of the steps in a cloud of dust and dirt. Soraya watched in the dim light that filtered down from the kitchen as Iona flicked a wrist with the quick ease of a practiced hand. The stairs rose up and the door closed at the top, momentarily leaving them in complete darkness. Or so she thought.

As her eyes slowly adjusted, Soraya heard Iona's soft footsteps as she walked past her, then a warm, yellow glow flooded the room slowly building until it was bright enough to make out everything. Tiny electric Christmas tree lights covered the ceiling in random patterns. There were dozens of them, giving the place a comfortable feeling. Soraya turned around in a circle, taking in all the details of the room. There were bottles and jars lining shelves that were strangely free of dust, considering the floor was dirt. In mild surprise, she realized that there wasn't even a single cobweb hanging in the room. An amazing contradiction to the condition of the shop above them and the stairway they'd just traversed. She caught Iona watching her.

"This is such a difference from upstairs..."

"Upstairs suppose to feel old. Down here's mah space, mah place. Feels like me."

Soraya nodded, it did feel like Iona. Like the old woman belonged here. Iona moved over to a shelf that was only half full of bottles and beckoned Soraya to join her there.

"Pull up that stool and have a seat, Chile. You gon do all the work, and might need it."

Soraya grabbed the stool and sat watching as the old woman walked to the opposite corner of the room. A small worktable was nestled there and she began pulling things from the shelves. With deft precision, the bottles and bags each gave up some of their contents into a small stone bowl Iona pulled from a tiny cupboard set into the shadows cast between the two shelves above the worktable.

"What exactly are you mixing?" Soraya asked, her curiosity getting the better part of her fear.

"It's somethin t'relax you Chile. You need t'be calm and open for dis here test. Don' know why we still have t'do dis here thing anyway. Ah knows you my prentice and so do you."

"So then… why are we doing this?"

Iona sighed, "Rules honey, rules. Jus cause we know, don' mean anyone else'll b'lieve us wit no proof."

"Okay, what do I have to do, drink it?" Soraya laughed.

"Hee, hee, hee, as matter o'fact, thas jus wha'chu gotta do! Den be's my job to watch for da sign." Iona laughed this time.

Soraya thought about what she was doing. Sitting on a stool in the cellar trusting an old woman she used to call a witch, waiting to drink some strange concoction that she really didn't know what it would do when she did. Was she nuts? Panic began to rise, and her eyes started darting around the room looking for another way out. There wasn't one. Iona was standing in front of her, watching her closely like she was waiting for something to happen, or for Soraya to say something.

Soraya took a deep breath, trying to calm herself. She started this journey just this morning and she *knew* she had to be here; but she still wanted to jump down off the stool, grab the rope dangling from the stairway and bolt. Her eyes followed the rope up to the ceiling and traced the lines made by the wood planks that were the floor above. It made her think about the blood, Zacharias' blood, slowly seeping through the cracks in the floor to dully drip into the dirt-floored room she now knew was under the floor in the room he died in. The memory made a shiver run up her spine. She sucked in another breath reluctantly taking the bowl from Iona's outstretched hands, inhaled the pungent aroma the mixture was giving off and then timidly took a sip of it. It didn't smell too bad, and after swallowing the first sip she decided it didn't taste too bad either. So she finished it quickly, just in case it was worse at the bottom.

Iona took the bowl, and Soraya adjusted herself on the stool. It was one of those fancy ones that had a back to it, and she settled into it, preparing herself for whatever would happen next. Through eyes barely open, Soraya watched as Iona nodded and began to circle the room spreading a fine white powder into the corners. Next, she placed several short, fat candles in sconces that hung from each wall; and when she turned the overhead lights off, Soraya thought she saw the candles flame up all at once. She shook her head in disbelief of what her eyes told her. Iona must have lit them when she put them into the sconces.

Watching Iona move back and forth, weaving around the room made Soraya feel sleepy. She stopped trying to follow her movements and closed her eyes. There was an immediate change in the feeling of her surroundings. It was a strong feeling that was accented by the rhythmic sound of drums that arose from around her, filling the room and beating with a pulse that rocked her soul.

Iona began to chant in a language that was foreign to Soraya, but the sound of the words stirred memories of being familiar to her ears. The drums gradually got louder, blending with the words and the sound of Iona's voice to make a throbbing, musical work. It pulled at Soraya incessantly, and her body began to sway from side to side as she moved to the beat that became part of her being.

Soraya slowly began to rise from the stool, the drums filling her to the point that they needed release; *she* needed release. She began to dance, moving to the music, her body twisting of its own volition, her feet keeping pace with the beat of the drums.

Iona sat in the chair in front of the worktable as Soraya moved about the little room, the dance pulling her into the rhythm. Soraya's feet took her from one corner to the other, spinning so that Iona might have worried for things being knocked from their shelves. But it was all expected. The old woman smiled as she crooned in her native tongue, words flowing through the drumbeats like water over smooth stones in a fast moving stream. Iona liked this part of the ritual, and watching it again brought back memories she cherished from before the passage.

Soraya was lost, moving around the room, oblivious to everything but the sound of the music and the beat of the drums. Iona tapped her left foot keeping time. She watched Soraya's body move like a thick fluid made quicksilver by each candle flicker that washed across her spinning form. As the drums reached a crescendo, Iona stopped her chanting and Soraya dropped to the dirt floor, her body heaving with the effort to drag the now dusty air into her lungs.

Iona got up and moved quickly, grabbing a tiny pouch tied around her own neck. The cord reached just long enough for the end of the bag to bury itself between her sagging breasts. Kneeling at Soraya's side, she grabbed the girl's chin in her hand and gently forced her lips apart. She sprinkled a few grains of the dust from the bag into Soraya's mouth. When she released her, Soraya's limp body lay sweating in a dusty heap.

Iona went to her table and took a rough-edged knife from a hook on the wall. Retracing her steps to where Soraya lay, she cut a small square of cloth from the cotton skirt the girl was wearing, tsk-tsking the loss of such a pretty thing. Into the scrap of cloth she cut a few strands of hair from the nape of Soraya's head. Then, using the broad edge of the knife blade, she scraped some skin from the base of Soraya's left hand. Following this, she used the tip of the blade to pierce the girls' third finger of her left hand, squeezing a few drops of blood onto the contents of the cloth.

Iona took all of this to the worktable and spread the cloth open all the while listening for Soraya's breathing to become less ragged as she slept. Satisfied that she was past the crisis point, the old woman began to hum as she made Soraya's fetish. She finished tying the cord to it, and after checking Soraya's pulse and feeling her brow to make sure the girl wasn't feverish, she tied it around Soraya's neck and climbed the steps to the shop level. Iona hummed to herself, smiling and satisfied that Soraya had passed the first test. Now she too wore a bag at her breasts.

THREE

Soraya woke to the smell of earth, burning candles and more aches and pains than she could ever remember having at one time. She lay still for a moment taking slow deep breaths through the cloth of her sleeve, trying to remember where she was and what happened. Pulling herself into a sitting position, she was surprised to find the little room had not changed, except for where she was sitting. But *she* felt different, changed somehow. She also couldn't explain her expectation that the room had changed in some way.

Soraya finally unfolded herself and stood, brushing the dirt from her skirt. Iona's voice made her jump when she spoke from the shadows in the corner where the worktable was.

"You slept long, Chile. How you feelin?" she asked while extending a small cup of water to her.

Soraya took the cup and opened her mouth to answer, but her tongue and throat were so dry she had to swallow several gulps before speaking. "I feel… tired more than anything else. A little sore too."

Iona smiled, "To be 'spected. You danced a long time, Chile."

Soraya stumbled towards the worktable. "I'm still kinda dizzy, and my head is fuzzy; but did I hear you say I danced?"

"Think Chile, you'll 'member. It sometimes takes a bit to rise up, but the memry's there."

Soraya leaned against the table rubbing her head. "I remember the drums. It was like they spoke to me. I felt them… inside like, like… Oh, it's hard to explain!"

"Hee, hee, hee, you doin all right, Chile!" Iona cackled.

Soraya looked around the room again. "How long have we been down here?"

"Only a few hours, Chile. Shop's closed, and dinner's been keepin fo a bit." Iona said.

Soraya reached to scratch an itch at her neck, and her hand touched the rawhide cord with the little bag attached to the ends.

Iona spoke before Soraya had a chance to ask any questions. "Dat is portant, Soraya."

Soraya looked at Iona and was met with an intense gaze from the old woman. She also noted that for the second time this day, Iona had used her given name, rather than the now familiar *Chile* she was becoming accustomed to hearing.

Iona continued, "The bag at the end of dat cord is both a symbol and a truth. It is a symbol of the transfer o'power. My power to you."

Soraya toyed with the little bag while she spoke, "May I make a guess?"

The old woman nodded, the ghost of a smile touching her lips.

Soraya continued, "This marks me as your apprentice; for anybody that would care to look, that is."

"Yes, yes, very good, Soraya. You learn quickly. Dat is very good. And the truth?"

Soraya grabbed the little sack and for the first time noticed the pattern of the cloth. In alarm she let it go to fall to her chest, and she grabbed up the hem of her skirt, frowning. She shot a look of contempt at Iona, but the old woman seemed to ignore it. With a groan of dismissal, she dropped the folds of material that made up the rest of the now ruined skirt and grabbed the little bag again, this time rolling it between her fingers. She could feel that there was something in the bag and that whatever it was, there was very little of it. "The truth... it's part of me, somehow."

Iona smiled wide this time, "Good Chile, very good! Tis true, it's part of you, bound up with what makes you, you. Dat bag ain't much to look at, but it be da focus fo you power."

Soraya frowned, "You mean that without this I won't be able..."

"No Chile, you missin da point here. It be a focus, jus a piece. You power inside. Nobody kin take dat from you. It *is* you."

Soraya signed heavily, the frown lines deepening as she turned to lean against the worktable, "Then I don't understand."

Iona stood up from the chair and stepped closer to Soraya, "You hear tell stories of dem witches you was talkin bout earlier needin a familiar? Or mebbe somethin bout crystals an such, how power kin be focused in'em?"

"You mean those stories are true?" Soraya asked, incredulous.

"Hee, hee, hee, well Chile, Ah ain't one t'say whether dem stories all tru o'not, but, dems dat practice what folks call magic, do use a focus fo dey power."

Soraya looked at the little bag again with more respect. "So, this is my focus... What's inside?"

Iona smiled again, "Well Chile, some o'you, some o'me, some other things…"

Soraya could tell she wasn't going to get a better answer to her question, so she tried a different angle. "Why did you use my skirt? This wasn't what I'd call a cheap piece of clothing."

Iona shrugged and turned towards the stairway, reaching for the handrail. "Had to be sumthin touchin yo skin while you danced. Yo skirt was easier than trying t'git to than yo bloomers. Blow dem candles out, Chile, and lets git some supper."

Iona was already at the stop of the stairs by the time Soraya finished putting all the candles out. She climbed the stairs without saying another word. The rumble coming from her stomach confirmed that she was starving and the fact that dinner, whatever it was, smelled delicious was making her mouth water.

Soraya closed the trap door and kicked the rug back into place. She took a deep breath and shook her head in amazement when she turned to see Iona heaping mashed sweet potatoes, dripping with butter, onto a plate already loaded with fried chicken and green beans. "Do you always cook like this Iona?"

"Like what Chile? Dis here might seem like a lot, but Ah ain't had nobody t'cook fo in a long while. Humor an old woman fo a spell, okay?"

Soraya took the plate Iona offered and had to grin herself at the old woman's smiling face. "All right, but if we keep eating like this, neither one of us will be able to fit between those counters out front!"

"Hee, hee, hee, you probly right!"

Soraya sat in the kitchen chair and began to eat. It seemed only a matter of minutes before the plate was clean, except for the bones from the chicken. She looked at Iona who was sitting in a folding chair that was now wedged in the doorway so she could use the corner of the table to hold her plate. Soraya was embarrassed that she hadn't offered to sit at the corner.

"Iona, I'm sorry, I should have brought in the other chair and let you have this one."

"And you tell me, missy, jus why is dat?"

"It's the way I was taught. Older folks should be able to rely on us younger ones." Soraya answered, standing to refill her plate.

Iona said, "Not when so many'o y'all are lookin t'rip us off!"

The sharp edge to Iona's voice sounded like a warning, so Soraya deftly changed the subject. "Ok, so tell me about this little sack around my neck." Her fingers idly fingered the bag while she ate. She knew there had to be a whopper of an explanation for the bag's existence, not to mention the loss of a good skirt... it had been one of her favorites. She watched as Iona just sat there, with her eyes closed, fork in hand. Soraya was just beginning to wonder whether the old woman had dozed off when she opened her eyes and spoke.

"You member the drums?"

Soraya blinked, "Yes, I remember drums..."

"You danced *The Awakening*, Chile. Twas nes'sary fo you t'wake up afore we b'gin any teachin."

"Miss Iona, I don't understand. I was awake... at least I was before dancing." Soraya couldn't keep the frustration from her voice.

Calmly, Iona said, "You body was awake, yes, but you mind was elsewhere."

Soraya thought about that and tried hard to remember dancing. She watched Iona finish her plate and methodically gather the dishes and go to the sink. "Iona, tell me what you did. I remember a drink, the drums, then the rest is a blur of color, sound and emotions. I can't seem to fit it all together into any kind of cohesive memory in my head."

Iona wrung out the dishrag she was using to wash the dishes. "What you drunk was a simple potion. Nothin sinister: some herbs, a root or two and a bit o'water. You was nervous and needed somethin t'relax you fo the magic t'flow."

"Magic?" Soraya couldn't keep the disbelief out of her voice.

"Don' sound so shocked, Chile. Wha'chu think we been talkin bout?"

"I…, well…"

"Yes, it's magic, Chile. Not dat storybook mess dey fill young'uns heads wit, but real magic."

"When you say *real magic*, what exactly are you talking about?" Hearing her own voice, Soraya realized she sounded petulant; like a child who heard the command when told not to do something, but was planning on doing it anyway.

"Shuga, it's all right t'be a little scared. You gon unlearn most wha'chu been taught all yo life. Understandable t'be a bit scared."

Soraya took a deep breath. "What happened downstairs… was it really magic?"

"Well, of a kind." Iona answered.

She crossed the tiny kitchen in two steps and sat back down in her chair. "All us got a kernel, buried deep inside, what kinnects us t'the mother country."

"Is that what I felt, I mean, when the drums started?"

"Umm hmmm", Iona murmured. "Dat's wha'chu felt. Dem drums strike you, in the heart o'yo African soul."

Soraya reached for the bag at her neck as Iona spoke. "Sounds like what they call a *race memory*," she mused. "What if I hadn't felt them? If the drums hadn't…"

"Now Chile, don start wishin fo what ain't! You did feel'em, and dat's dat." Iona slapped the table with finality, her hand making a wet, thwapping sound; and she moved so quickly that it startled Soraya and she jumped in her seat.

"Nah, the little sack holds the seeds of yo power. Tis a mixture of what's yours with a little bit o'what's mine to set the spark."

Staring at the bag that had once been the hem of her skirt, she rolled it between her fingers. It felt empty.

"My power…"

Iona suddenly clapped her hands together. "Come Chile, it's time fo you next less'n. You got to learn t'focus you thoughts and you vision."

"Focus. Uh, Miss Iona, you don't think it's getting a little late to be starting class"?

"Hee, hee, hee, you sho is funny, Chile. Like the time mean sumthin t'us!"

Harlem Angel

Soraya thought about it and realized that it was kind of funny. Neither of them had any place else to go. She smiled, "Okay, next lesson... focus."

Iona stood and grabbed a cup and saucer from the dish rack. She placed them in the middle of the little table and said, "Look a'here. Tell me wha'chu see?"

Soraya squared her chair so she was sitting directly in front of the cup and saucer. "It's a cup and saucer."

"Is dat all it is?" Iona asked, disdain dripping from the words.

Soraya frowned, "Yeah, that's all it is."

"What else do you see, girl. They's more there than jus a cup'n saucer."

Soraya looked at the pieces again and concentrated. "No matter what I do, or how I look at them, I still see a cup and saucer." She sighed, shaking her head.

Iona's voice held the sound of patience being held at a price. It would have made Soraya angry under other circumstances, and she was hard-pressed to ignore it even so.

"Look Chile. See dat wha'chu got here is more'n jus a cup'n saucer. You got two pieces here: one flat, one not. Both got curves..."

"I think I see what you mean. Let me try again."

"We'll see." Iona hissed between her teeth.

Soraya took a slow deep breath as Iona crossed her arms and leaned back in her chair. "The two pieces are opposites, like you just said, but they are also the same somehow."

"Go on," Iona breathed, eyes now closed.

Encouraged, Soraya continued describing the dishes, "They are both solid pieces. Even the cup, although it's shape makes two hollow places also. The colors blend, blue into white, white into gold, there's a flow."

Iona's voice was a whisper, "Ah got a pi'ture, Chile, go on."

Soraya felt beads of perspiration form on her forehead and roll down her cheeks as she stared at the dishes. She ignored the tickle.

Abruptly, Iona said, "'Nuff, Soraya. Dats nuff fo t'night." Iona touched Soraya's shoulder.

Soraya looked up to find the old woman staring at her with an intensity to match her own concentration during the exercise. "Was that okay? Did I do okay?" she felt like a child in grade school again, seeking the approval of a favorite teacher. She was also embarrassed to be squeaking like that child Iona called her.

"Chile, dis here jus da beginnin. You got a lot more t'learn afore you be ready fo battle," she said.

"Battle?" Soraya wasn't that child anymore. "What do you mean battle?"

Iona's voice was devoid of emotion when she answered, "We's preparin fo battle jus as sure as you has dem dreams o'yourn. Somebody done discover'd we's here."

Soraya nodded. She could see the wisdom in Iona's words and knew the old woman was right. But, she didn't like it. She didn't like it at all. A battle was just what it felt like it was going to be.

"'Tis gittin late, Chile. Best we turn in fo the night. T'morrow we start a full day of learnin fo you. You gonna need a clear head fo what we's got t'git through."

"Alright." Soraya stood and stretched, a yawn taking her breath away before she could finish. "Is there anything I can do to help you close up?"

"Hee, hee, hee, Chile, we's been closed up since sundown. But, den, you was a bit fuzzy bout dat time, hee, hee, hee."

Iona rose from the table, and they left the kitchen together. Soraya reached up and pulled on the light's chain. "Goodnight, Iona."

"Nite, Chile. Now, y'all call me if'n you need somethin."

Soraya smiled, "I'll be all right, but thank you."

She watched Iona close her bedroom door, which was half-way up the hall towards the front of the shop. As she walked down the hallway, Soraya could just see through the gap in the curtains that the front door was indeed shut and locked up tight. The only light burning in the front room was a small night-light shaped like a seashell and plugged into the socket next to the main counter.

After a quick stop in the bathroom to brush her teeth, Soraya checked the back door again. When she reached her room, she opened her suitcase and propped it against the back of the chair. She undressed quickly and pulled on a flannel nightgown she took from the neat stacks of clothing in the bag. It was one of the few warm pieces of sleepwear that she owned and she was glad she'd packed it. Except for the kitchen, the rooms at the back of the shop were cool compared to those up front.

Soraya crawled into bed and pulled the feather comforter that covered it, up to her chin. When she reached to turn the lamp off, she was reminded just how small the room was because she scraped her knuckles on the wall.

Soraya just lay there, listening to the sounds of Iona getting ready for bed, the street sounds retreating as folks got home and quieted down for the night. She decided to practice some of the lesson she'd been taught after dinner. Closing her eyes, she listened for every little sound she could hear. She made the extra effort to visualize a picture to match what she was hearing.

The first thing she became aware of was that the picture she drew up in her mind's eye was every bit as detailed as if she was actually looking into Iona's room. Soraya was amazed at the detail. She could hear the rustle of fabric and see clearly as Iona pulled a long white gown from a chest of drawers in the corner of the room. She heard the flicker of the candle flame before fully realizing that the short fat candle on Iona's nightstand was the only source of light in the room. Soraya watched and listened intently, waiting for something else to happen. Iona slowly turned towards the door and Soraya saw her smile.

"Go to sleep Soraya," she whispered. Ah tol you, you is gon need dis night's rest. Hee, hee, hee."

Soraya snapped her eyes open and lay there in shock. Iona had known! Did that mean that she had actually been there, in the room with the old woman? "But... that's not possible!" she whispered to herself. Soraya took a long, deep breath and exhaled slowly, calming herself, willing her heart to slow down. She rationalized, "Iona did laugh about it, and that's encouraging." Taking another deep breath, Soraya decided she would leave the questions for morning, when she could ask Iona. She closed her eyes again, but this time only to sleep.

Soraya slept soundly until about midnight. This time, the street was brightly lit with street lamps lining both sides. Soraya walked down the sidewalk, her step unsure. She knew what she was looking for... a shop. This one was called *Love*. Three more lamps and she saw it. Sitting back from the street, like Ionas', like Zacharias', dim light clawing to get through filthy windows. Her breath caught in her throat like she'd swallowed a peach pit, and she started to run. The two men she knew would be coming were already at the door.

"No! Leave her alone!" Soraya screamed, but there was no response from the men. Soraya heard them talking as she came to a stop almost between them. These were two different men than the first set.

"Why we pickin on this old woman Boogie?" the first one asked.

The second man, much heavier than the first, shrugged, "Boss say it n'sary, Foley. We even gittin extra fer doin'er."

"Mus be sumpthin special." Boogie grunted.

"Special or not, I's gots a bad feelin bout wackin a woman," Foley said.

Boogie, the fatter of the two, spoke with distaste, "Then why you take the job man?"

"Cause, I tol' you, it payin sumthin extra!" Foley's whisper was almost a yell.

"Shhhh, now, we don want t'scare the old thing afore we find'er."

Soraya was horrified. These two were dressed almost identical to the two men who killed Zacharias, right down to the gloves and weapons, but they were two different men. She went into the shop before them, looking for Willamae. Soraya knew she was in D.C. She remembered Iona's litany of circle members and it felt right. If she could only get Willamae's attention the way she had gotten Iona's earlier tonight…

"Willamae! Willamae! Oh *PLEASE* see me!" She said, yelling so loud that she thought the men might hear her too.

The fat man said, "Hurry up Foley, this place feels… I dunno, creepy!"

"Hush you face! Quit talkin like that! Don' want no haint's a comin fer us Boogie!" Foley replied with urgency.

Soraya was standing in front of Willamae. The old woman was busy cleaning the dirt off an old platter. "Oh, what am I doing wrong?" Soraya cried. "Look up!" she screamed. "Damn it old woman, *LOOK UP*!"

Her final effort did pay off, but it was still too late. Foley reached through Soraya and grabbed Willamae by the throat.

"This is too easy! Hey man, help me with'er feet," Foley said.

Soraya watched, helpless again, as they carried Willamae to the front of the shop and systematically cut her throat and beat her until her life was bleeding away through the floorboards.

"Ok, we's finished here. C'mon, let's git Boogie."

"Got'cha Foley."

This time, when Soraya woke crying, it was Iona who rocked her. She held the old woman tight around her tiny waist as Iona crooned softly into her ear, "S'all right Chile, s'all right. Iona's here, hush baby, hush."

Through heavy sobs, Soraya told her what she'd seen in her dream. "It, it, happened again," she choked, "This time it was Willamae."

Soraya felt Iona stiffen at the name, but she continued to stroke her back, "S'all right baby, jus means we gots less time than we thought. Oh Lord, time is surely short."

Soraya pushed herself away from Iona's bosom. She knew she must look terrible, eyes puffy and face tear-streaked, but she didn't think it mattered here. "Why me Iona? Why do I see these things?"

"You Mama tol you dat you was special. She was raght," Iona said, matter-of-factly.

"I don't want it!" Soraya screamed, "I don't want to be special! I didn't ask for it, and I don't want it!" She was shaking so hard that Iona wrapped her arms around her again before she spoke.

Iona's voice was quiet and steady when she spoke, "Chile, none us chooses dis. You think bout wha'chu sayin."

Soraya was now ranting, "I know what I'm saying! I mean this, Iona! *I DON'T WANT THIS… GIFT!*"

There was silence between the two women. Soraya watched Iona closely as the old woman closed her eyes. She was suddenly afraid that she had finally pushed her to some limit. Iona slowly began to sway, then to chant; barely audible at first, but her voice began building volume with each verse. Unconsciously, Soraya began to rock with her, keeping up with the rhythm of the words. Her eyes began to glaze over, and she slowly fell into a hypnotic trance.

As if looking through cheesecloth, Soraya began to *see* things. At first what she saw made no sense; but the longer she watched the scenes playing across her inner vision, the more she understood what she was *seeing*.

A tall, thick black woman, wearing rather ornate clothing spoke, "The children are ready to be tested, my Chief."

The *Chief* was a big, tall, black man who was seated in a large, elaborate chair that he dwarfed in size. "Perhaps", he said.

Soraya studied the faces of the people and their surroundings closely. She realized that she was *seeing* the past; Iona's past, to be exact. It was a time long before Soraya's birth, long before the birth of any of Iona's people on this continent. The woman, maybe she was the Chief's wife, spoke again, "This must be done quickly. These men who have come to take from our fruits will not tarry long, my Chief."

"Nor will we," said the Chief.

"Will you oversee all of the testing, my Chief?"

The big man sighed, reluctance heavy in his voice, "Yes, I will see that only the strongest are chosen to make this journey."

Soraya watched in fascination as the ceremony began. She felt honored that Iona would transfer to her the knowledge of the First Choosing. Soraya watched as the children, hundreds of small, frightened young children, each trembling but standing proudly as they waited to enter the hut, one at a time, to be tested and chosen or rejected for the journey across the water, far from their homes and families.

The Chief said, "We need twelve. Their number will spread across the new land they journey to. They will be the link."

The woman gestured to another group of older men and women to come forward. They began to weave through the children standing in line, testing, choosing, and rejecting. Those that were rejected left the line with relief painted across their faces, while those chosen reflected nothing but fear. They remained in line, waiting to enter the hut where further testing would be done.

The woman spoke again, "My Chief has done a great thing by getting such cooperation from all of the tribes."

The man leveled his gaze at her, "All of our countrymen, even those who thought they could protect themselves by joining our enemies in cooperation, have realized the truth of the matter. Our people will be alone in this new place they are being spirited away to. They will need a point of focus. They will need a way to find the connection to their home."

The woman ducked her head when she spoke her next words, "My Chief, I have need to question only one piece of your grand plan."

Soraya got a full view of the Chief's face as he turned his full attention on the woman. She was immediately drawn to his eyes. Dark and fathomless in their depth, his eyes made the smoothness of the skin on his dark-brown face seem rough. "And what might that question be, oh trusted advisor?"

"That you test and choose to send only… children, my Chief." The woman lifted her chin in pride as she finished her sentence.

"Ahhhh…," the Chief said, nodding his head as a bit of a smile touched his lips. "I wondered which of you would have the courage to challenge my choice."

"Oh, no, my Chief, no challenge is offered here, merely a request for enlightenment," the woman said, smiling and bowing her head in response.

After a short pause, the Chief answered, "I commend you for your courage and therefore answer your challenge. I choose children because our *keepers* must be strong enough to live and last through several hundred years of this captivity we send them into. It is through them that the roots will be maintained. It is through them that we will survive this journey."

"My Chief, you speak as if you see the future."

"And, indeed, is it not my duty to do just that?" his voice held a note of contempt for the questioner. She ducked her head and bowed herself away from his immediate presence as the children began to file into the room from the doorway.

They were lined up according to age, and the line extended across the Chief's reception area and out the door. The number of children had been reduced from hundreds to perhaps fifty or so. Those older men and women who had been responsible for the first culling of the group, the medicine people, were from every tribe represented by the children. They were the *official* testers and were led to seats placed on either side of the Chief's dais.

As the shuffling and noise died, the Chief spoke to the group, "Begin."

Each child was directed to walk before the Chief, and he scrutinized each of them individually. From down the line, nearly at the end of the line, there was a murmur that reached his ears. He said, "It appears that there is one of exception?"

"Defiance is more what I would call it, my Chief," the tall woman, who now stood behind the Chief, said.

The Chief narrowed his eyes and gazed along the line of remaining children to be tested. "Let me see this… Defiant One."

At a signal from the Chief's advisor, a youngster was brought before him. It was a female child of eleven years. Soraya could see from the eyes that it was Iona.

The Chief stared at her for a few minutes before speaking. "What is it that makes you act so?"

"You choose for something important here. I should be chosen." The little girl spoke loudly and with none of the fear or deference that most children show when speaking with any adult, let alone what the adults showed when speaking to their Chief.

The Chief's voice was tinged with amusement when he said, "And why are you so sure that one of the chosen should be you?"

"Because, I have already been chosen," the girl said.

The Chief stared at the child again while everyone else in the room held their breath. Such insolence would surely not be tolerated.

"Test her now," the Chief ordered.

The child tested as the strongest of the entire group. After the line of children was gone, the Chief spoke with the defiant little girl again. "You realize this means you must leave your tribe, your family, never to return here?"

"I know this, my Chief. While it is not my choice, I know this."

The Chief looked into the eyes of the eleven year old and knew it to be so. He declared, "So be it. Mark this one as leader."

The scene began to fade away and Soraya shook her head to clear it as the images faded and her bedroom came back into focus. "You show me this to make me understand my responsibility," she said, her voice full of humility.

"I show you this because you are chosen. There is no decision on your part but to accept."

Soraya was taken aback by several things all at once, the least of them being that Iona had spoken those last words with no trace of ghetto dialect. The words were as clear as if Iona had attended school with her. The second was that the visions she had just witnessed were now a part of her own memory. She could recall everything, like she had actually been there. And finally, she no longer felt that she had the right to deny her place in what Iona had termed *the coming battle*.

"Iona, I understand now... I still don't like it, but I understand." Resignation was heavy in her voice and how she felt.

"Good Chile, Am'm glad. Now you git some sleep, you gon need it. We'll talk bout Willamae in the mornin."

Soraya sighed, defeated, "You keep saying that Iona, but I don't know how much sleep I'll get after that dre... vision."

"Let it rest, Chile. Dat be d'only one for t'night. Dey's takin us out one at a time."

Soraya felt slightly guilty thinking only of herself as Iona stood to leave the room, her face full of sorrow and eyes full of tears at the loss of Willamae. The old woman squeezed Soraya's hand and shuffled back down the hallway to her room.

Soraya reached for the lamp stem and then decided to leave it on. The light from the small lamp wasn't that bright. Pulling the comforter up to her chin again, Soraya lay there, staring at the ceiling, trying not to think. "Mama was really right. I need to be here. But what do I *DO*? What *CAN* I do? All these people dying... murdered, and I haven't even the slightest idea what I'm supposed to do about it."

Soraya woke the next morning before Iona, and decided to let her sleep in. She made a pot of coffee and then went into the shop to find the History book. Sitting at the same little table in front of the hearth where she first sat with Iona, she started flipping pages. Fascinated by the scenes in the picture, Soraya used her index finger to follow the sequence of events played out across the pages.

"The way the magic works is not always predictable, nor totally controllable. You cannot expect to affect everything that can possibly occur in the world at any one given time. However, you CAN affect a specific instance concerning a specific time and place. For example, the San Francisco earthquake caused massive damage, loss of life and disruption to life in general for the populace in the state of California. But, there was a family living in the middle of the destruction's wake, whose home was only slightly damaged and no family members died during the quake while their neighbors were crushed in the debris of their crumbling homes."

The more Soraya read, the heavier her eyelids felt and the words seemed to blur of their own accord on the pages. She closed the book and sat mulling over what she'd read. Only a few minutes had passed when she heard Iona coming down the hallway, humming to herself.

"Iona, this book..."

"Ummmm hmmmm, the Histr'y. What bout it?"

"Well, maybe it's my imagination, but I think it turned its own pages..."

"Hee, hee, hee, yep, it'll do that sumtimes," she grinned.

"And, the language has changed."

"Now, wha'chu mean Chile?"

"The language, how it's written has changed. It's written in more proper English now."

"Oh, I see. Hmmm, jus one mo' sign. You da one, Chile, you s'pose t'be here."

"You're talking in riddles again Iona, please explain what you mean."

Iona sat in the other chair and Soraya watched her closely. She could tell that whatever the explanation coming, it wasn't easy for the old woman.

"Soraya, I said I knew you was comin, 'member?"

"Yes, last night, when I came to you."

"Well, the thang 'bout havin yo 'prentice show up is that you also know yo time is up, that *HE* gonna be takin ya home soon. I've known fo awhile dat you was comin."

"Yes, but what does that have to do with the book…" Soraya wasn't trying to rush her, but she'd heard most of this already.

"Gimme a chance Chile! Slow down a bit! There are signs that say when a change be comin. One is dat the hist'ry started changin. The words was movin and lookin unfamiliar. The fact that it moves fo you, that you kin read it easy, says it was makin ready fo you Chile."

"Iona, surely this has to be a slow change! You've been here so long, it can't be changing so fast!"

"Oh Chile, it s'all right! It s'pose t'be this way!"

The old woman's smile made Soraya uneasy, but is also made another question come to mind. "Iona, if you knew I was coming, what about the others?"

"Well nah, dat's a intrestin question, dat. I set up a sendin dis mo'nin, dey's all scared Soraya."

"That's as they should be Iona. We don't know who's going to be next, and our enemy strikes with no warning."

"So you sez. Ah asked who had 'prentices comin. Only two said dey knew who dey was, Abraham an Athlene. With me'n you, dat only makes three us kin make ready!"

Soraya thought for a minute and took a sip of coffee, frowning when the now cold liquid hit her tongue. She hated cold coffee, but it told her she'd been sitting up here longer than she realized. "Iona, is there some way to find out whether Willamae and Zacharias had apprentices lined up?"

Iona stood, took Soraya's cup and headed down the hallway to the kitchen. Soraya followed her, stretching as she stood up.

Iona said, "Well, lessee... might be a way at dat!"

"What do we need to do?"

"Well, fust we go t'da cellar."

Soraya helped wash and put the cups away, flipping the coffee pot to *off*. "Did you open the shop?"

"Not t'day Chile, we gots work t'do."

Soraya thought about that and realized that today was probably the first time in the *Home* shops history it was going to stay closed in the middle of the week. "Do you think that's a good idea?" she asked.

"Well, I s'pose it might make folks think a bit; but wit us in'a cellar, who gon' run it?"

"Good point."

With that, Iona flipped back the throw rug, and they went down to the workshop.

FOUR

Ray Crosser, the Executive Administrative Assistant to the President and CEO of DNAgen Biolabs, a man of slight build and questionable character, came into the room and addressed his boss, speaking quickly, "Sir, the objectives of both trials have been met."

A deep, resonant voice answered from the shadows behind a large, darkly polished wood desk, "There was no resistance?"

"No sir. Both targets were eliminated as you instructed."

"The choice of assassin was as directed?"

"Both pairs were young black men. Sheer genius it was, Sir, if I might say so, picking their own kind to do the job. It was almost too easy to recruit them."

"You paid them…"

"As you ordered sir. No ties."

"This is too easy."

Yes, it was easy… Ray started to say, then hesitated.

"We are missing something," the deep voice boomed. "This network cannot be without safeguards. They are too vulnerable."

Ray tried again, "They were pretty easy targets, but… they were old people, Mr. Kites." Ray stood with his hands stuck deep in his trouser pockets, cowering as if afraid the man sitting in the high-backed chair would stand and strike him.

"Ray, do not fear me man. Respect me, and my position," Mr. Kites admonished. Ray seemed to shrink even further into his shoes and *Mr. Kites* shrugged, giving up. "Is there anything else?" he asked.

Ray cleared his throat nervously, "Do we proceed with the third target?"

"Yes, but be cautious. The first contract was probably looked upon as a crime of opportunity. The second will surely be considered planned, or at least a suspicious coincidence. These executions must continue until the entire network is destroyed, or we are wasting our time and resources."

At this, Ray spoke with more confidence, "Since there has been no resistance, perhaps there won't ever be any."

"Don't be an idiot, Ray!" Mr. Kites snapped. "Someone has to be monitoring these people. Someone is acting as their leader for them to *BE*, to exist, for so many years, unknown and untouched."

"So, you think the targets might get harder?" Ray asked.

Kites growled, "I know they will."

After a very pregnant pause, Ray asked, "Sir, once we finish them, what will be done with that group of…"

"The coven, Ray, the coven."

"Yeah, them. What will we do with them once we finish this? The women are bad enough, but those men give me the creeps."

Mr. Kites chuckled, "Yes, their chanting can be a bit annoying, but they insist it is necessary. As for once our plans are complete, perhaps we will let them live. We might find further use for them… later."

"As you say." Ray grunted.

"Hmmm, yes, as I say."

Ray turned to leave the room. The man he'd been talking to, Shawn Kites, was so engrossed in his own thoughts that he didn't notice Ray's departure.

Shawn was worried, probably needlessly, but worried nonetheless. The first two contracts had been accomplished with the flawless precision of a surgical strike in a combat zone, but something about it bothered him. "Niggers… Dealing with Niggers always makes me feel as if I need to be extra cautious when putting my plans into action!" He pounded his fist on the polished surface of his finely carved Cherrywood desk in frustration. His own outburst made him remember that Ray Crosser had been in the room, and for the first time he noticed that the man had left.

"Good! There's no need for the subordinates to see my frustrations. Besides, Ray has enough on his mind without adding worry about *The Boss*," he thought to himself.

Shawn pushed a button on his desk and turned in his chair to stare out of the plate glass window slowly revealed in response. He watched in satisfaction as polished wood shutters folded into themselves on the ends. He wasn't sure why it made him feel good to watch it, but it did. The whole room was reflected back at him this time of night; all of the wood furnishings gave off a sort of burnished glow, as if the warmth from the fire burning in the fireplace in the corner touched everything and then radiated it back. It was his most favored time to be in the office. Midnight in Chicago was always beautiful. Shawn sighed, "The only black that is truly beautiful."

He looked past the reflection now, out into the night. "Someday very soon, this will be inherited by my loyal brethren and those whites we fight for, despite their ignorance. Someday very soon."

He leaned forward and stood placing his hands against the cool glass, gazing out over the city. His thoughts began to ramble again. "Such a beautiful night, and to think how easy it could be for us to lose it all to the Niggers while most of us are not looking."

His voice suddenly echoed, loud and rough, the words grating into the walls of the empty office. "The White Wing *MUST* triumph! It is *OUR* time!"

Shawn closed his eyes for a few moments and was quiet, slowing his breathing, calming himself, letting the darkness and silence penetrate to his soul. He opened his eyes slowly when he realized he was clenching them shut. Stars danced before his vision making the city lights seem dim in comparison. He sighed, "We must triumph this time. Their network appears weak, but I don't trust that observation. We can't trust that weakness; can't get too confident. They are sneaky, deceitful, and create sleight-of-hand by just being in the room with you. We cannot let them slip through our fingers as they have done in the past!"

There was a muffled knock at the door. Shawn turned and sat back down in the chair. "Come in," he croaked, reaching for a bottle of water.

A figure draped in the elaborate folds of a hooded dark red robe came into the room. Shawn could tell from the cut of the robe that it was one of the men, one of the *warlocks* from the coven being housed in the sub-levels of the building.

"Sir, the unit has asked that I speak with you concerning a minor issue." The man's voice was oily and seemed to slide across the room leaving a filmy residue hanging in the air.

"Yes, yes. Don't be so formal. What is your name?"

"I am called Eric, sir."

"Eric. Good, and please stop calling me *sir*. Mr. Kites will do fine."

"Excuse me... Mr. Kites, we have an issue that must be addressed as soon as possible."

"Fine Eric. What can I do for you and your people?"

Eric twitched a bit in his robe before speaking again. "Mr. Kites, we are in need of some relief. Our coven is not large, and the task you have set for us is both time consuming and physically draining."

"I realize this is a big undertaking, but I was assured by your High Priestess that you would be up to the task."

Eric's eyebrows rose in alarm, "Make no mistake, Mr. Kites. We are certainly up to the task, but you give no time for replenishment. What we are doing requires a great deal of power and energy, energy that must be replaced."

Shawn was quiet for a moment, thinking. "Tell me," he leaned forward on the desktop, hands steepled in front of his chin, "What happens if your people don't get enough rest. Is there a... breaking point?" Shawn watched Eric flinch again, and this time the recovery was not as swift.

"If someone channels the powers we are working with, without taking an appropriate rest, they could burn themselves out."

"Burn themselves out? What are you talking about? Are you saying they'll burst into flame, some kind of spontaneous combustion thing?"

"No, no, you misunderstand."

Shawn was annoyed at the tone of Eric's voice; it was that of a schoolteacher reviewing a simple lesson. He didn't like it.

"Mr. Kites, when one of our... people, works too long and too hard with a weave of power such as we are using, or a spell, as you might call it, there is great probability that they will use up their power and burn their reservoir up. Such a loss would leave them unable to function normally."

Shawn sat up straight. "You mean it is possible to drain your powers to a level so low that..."

"The vessel doesn't fill again. Yes. This is what we call *burning out*."

"Ahh, I see... So, what is the nature of your request?" Shawn's smile felt almost predatory, but it was enough. Eric visibly relaxed, making Shawn smile even more wickedly behind his again steepled fingers.

"We wish to engage the services of another coven, a sister group, if you will."

"And, what exactly will you expect them to do for you, and better yet, for me?"

"They will be our relief. There are certain times, like at the present, when the full power of the weave is not necessary."

"Umm hmm, I see," Shawn said. "And this other coven would be the maintenance crew, so-to-speak, keeping the web intact while your people rest. Hmmmm."

Eric was talking faster in his excitement, "It will soon become a necessity, Mr. Kites."

"When can they be here?"

Eric was so excited now that he was animated, "We could have them arrive before sunrise tomorrow morning!"

"So be it. But Eric…"

The man froze where he stood. Having started for the door as soon as the OK had been spoken, he had his back to Shawn, and Shawn felt he needed to snug the noose a little. "They must remain here, under the same rules, payment and agreements as your people. Make that clear. I'll have Ray draw up the appropriate documents and send them down after the morning staff meeting tomorrow."

"Yes sir… err, Mr. Kites, and thank you, sir."

The door closed with a sharp click as Eric almost ran from the room. Shawn leaned forward over the desktop, this time he folded his hands under his nose. "This was certainly unplanned. The liability grows with each passing day as we move deeper into this labyrinth," he hissed a long sigh. "Again my vision is changed by someone from the outside."

He tapped a button on the phone console, "Ray, are you still around?" At such a late hour, and having dismissed the man earlier, Shawn was surprised when a voice floated back over the speaker.

"Yes sir, I'm here."

"Come into my office Ray."

"Right away, sir."

The door opened almost immediately, and Ray walked into the office.

"What are you still doing here, Ray? I thought you went home."

"I saw the witch dude come up from the basement as I was leaving and thought I'd stick around for a bit, boss. Thought you might need something."

"Ray, your thoughtfulness and anticipation is duly noted, but you should have gone home. I need your eyes sharp and your wits about you when dealing with these people."

"Yes, sir. I'll see you in the morning then."

"One thing before you do go, Ray…"

Ray smiled, rising to his toes and rocking back on his heels in what Shawn felt was an annoying habit the man performed when he was right about something.

"Yes, Sir?"

"On your way out, notify security of some new arrivals for the offices in the sub-basement. They'll need an escort to make sure they get where they're going."

"Got it boss. See you in the morning."

"In the morning, Ray."

In the bowels of concrete below downtown Chicago, in a room guarded and warded with arcane symbols and glowing figures drawn on the walls, a circle had been formed. It was a circle borne of flesh, but filled with the power of darkness. Eric stood amidst the circle, a woman clad in the same dark red robes stood with him.

"We will be strengthened, my sister, by the coming of Oak Vein Coven."

"Ahhhh, but the power of White Oak Coven will also be diluted by the invitation to serve together."

"It is necessary," Eric replied.

"Yes, I can see that, but I still feel unease at trusting this Kites to fulfill his end of this bargain."

Eric turned towards the woman and held her hands in his "Calm yourself, Madeline. The man doesn't know what he's dealing with here. As long as he doesn't know exactly what he's got living in his basement, the longer we can use him for the means to our goal."

"I do hope you have this right, Eric. A mistake at this juncture could cost us the lives of the entire coven. Not to mention Oak Vein's members. I really don't want that on my conscience."

"I know, I know, Madeline. We'll just have to continue being careful, if for no other reason than because we are not at home here."

"And, *THAT* is reason enough!" Madeline replied.

"Agreed," Eric said.

"So, when do the others arrive?"

"I made the call before returning to our dungeon here. They should begin arriving by daybreak."

"You are really certain that Kites hasn't got a clue as to why our cooperation has been so easy to gain?"

"Madeline, that idiot is so full of racial hatred, he doesn't think straight on a good day. No, he doesn't know; and if he did, or even if he figures it out, it will be too late for him to stop our plans because we'll be too deep into his own."

"We play a dangerous game here, Eric. The power we block is old, ancient maybe. If we siphon it off too fast, or in pieces too big for the group to handle at one time, we'll burn out both covens in a single flash."

"It is worth the risk, Madeline. With this power harnessed, White Oak Coven will be the most powerful coven in the northern hemisphere. The next Sabbathian Samhain will see our rule!"

"Come Eric, we must return to The Working to lend our strength."

The two walked, arms linked, down a dimly lit hallway where the sound of chanting voices grew with each step. As they left the small antechamber where they had been talking, the door leading to the elevator lobby quietly shut with the slightest whisper of a click.

Ray moved like a shadow, hugging the walls and hoping the two people he'd been eavesdropping on wouldn't hear the elevator bell. "Hurry up elevator, hurry up!" he whispered. "Hmmmm, should I tell Mr. Kites or keep this to myself? Hmmmmm. These witches, nasty people, I don't like'em one bit. But, Mr. Kites wants'em here, fool that he is."

He darted his eyes over his shoulder, cowering as if afraid someone might have overheard his thoughts. The man jumped when the elevator finally made its arrival known. "Sheesh, Ray ol' man, you're as jumpy as a cat cornered by a hungry dog!" he scolded himself.

HARLEM ANGEL

Ray made his decision as he boarded the elevator. "This one I'll keep in the pocket. Never know when you might need an Ace."

The elevator door opened with a hiss, and Ray stuck his head out looking up and down the hallway before stepping out. He didn't want to run into Kites before he'd had time to journal his new secrets. Somehow, writing them down made it easier to pretend they didn't exist when talking to Shawn, at least not in his head. He was humming again as he approached the guard station in the main lobby.

"Hey Joe, quiet tonight?" he asked.

Joe looked up from a nudie magazine to answer. Ray never could figure the appeal of those things; not when the real deal only cost a few dollars more.

Joe said, "Yep, quiet. Any final words from the boss?"

Ray snapped back from where his thoughts were going, "As a matter of fact, he said to let you guys know that another group of people for that big project going on in the sub-basement would be arriving in the morning. Would you leave Kelso a note to get'em all checked in and ID'd before they head down? They'll be here early."

"No problem, Ray. How many this time?"

"Not exactly sure. Maybe a dozen of'em and they should all arrive together."

"You got it, Ray. Have a good night."

"You too, Joe. Hope it stays quiet."

Shawn Kites watched the street below. Ray's head seemed to bob from streetlight to streetlight as he walked to the subway station. *Ray is a good soldier in my army. He carries out orders and doesn't ask questions. Invaluable. I'll have to reward him well one day.*

Shawn took one more look across the city, sighed and turned away from the window. Unlike his employees, he was already home. He flipped the light switches off in the reception area as he walked through on his way to the private elevator in the corner of his office. It only went up from this, the twentieth floor, and it needed a key to make it run. Ray was the only other person who had one, and his was for emergencies and admitting the maid who came once a week to clean the place.

The lights came up as the elevator doors opened into a large coatroom.

He'd made the penthouse his refuge. Unless Ray brought someone up, even if a person somehow made it alone to the coatroom, to get beyond the ornate French doors into the apartment required that either he be home to answer the door, or be with you to open it himself. He'd had a retina scanner installed when the suite was completed.

As he moved through the rooms, the lights came on and softly lit the interior of the apartment. He stripped and showered, taking his time to let the hot water soak into his muscles, trying to relax. Still wet, Shawn removed his blue contact lenses and stared at the brown eyes looking back at him in the mirror. He hated his eyes. They were the only part of his body he really hated. "Brown when they should've been blue!" he hissed to the empty room. He examined his reflection. His skin was flawless as usual, darker than most white men. He made regular visits to a tanning booth in the company fitness center in the basement, and he felt it was time for another visit, even though it really wasn't necessary. "But, it *IS* necessary, for appearances sake." He turned to admire his own profile. Shawn was a very muscular, six feet two inches tall. His dark blond curly hair was cropped short so it looked as if he had it permed. Satisfied with his reflection, he put on pajama bottoms and went to bed. He slept fitfully, his dreams full of burning churches and screaming voices.

Shawn woke as dawn was breaking, still hot and sweaty from his dreams. Sometimes he wondered if the dreams were in some way repayment for his choosing to help burn those churches. The White Wing was responsible for at least 23 of the 34 or so burnt back in the late nineties. As a youngster, Shawn himself had taken part in more than a dozen. Those years had been filled with such minor distractions. It was only since the genetic discoveries his small bioengineering company stumbled upon in 2003 that he had been able to raise himself to the luxuries he enjoyed today. The treatment for Spina Bifida would make his fortune. And isolating the genetic string that directly resulted in skin color would eventually alter the way every child was conceived. It had already yielded several new patents on skin care products, and his scientists had a long list of other possibilities for its use.

The phone rang, interrupting his daydreaming. It was his mother, which meant something was wrong. She never *bothered* him unless it was something she felt was important.

"Hello Mother," he said, swinging his feet to the thick carpeting.

"Hi Shawn. A package came for you yesterday. I didn't want to bug you, but I thought it might be important. The return address says it's from your father."

He could tell from her voice that she'd been crying over that man again. His father. The biggest thorn in his existence was also the reason he did exist. "You can open it if you want Mother. There might be a note in it for you." He doubted it, but then, he doubted everything that had to do with his father. There was a pause, and then he heard paper tearing.

She sighed, "Nothing for me, but there is another small box inside and a card marked for you, personal and confidential."

"Ok, Mom. I'll try to make it by today or tomorrow to pick it up. Is there anything I can bring you when I come?"

"No, Sweetheart. Just seeing you for a few minutes will be enough. Call when you're on your way?"

She sounded pitiful. Another reason to hate the man he called *Father*. "I will, and I promise it won't be long."

"Ok, see you later, Son. I love you."

"You too, Mom. Goodbye."

Shawn hung up the phone and shook his head in continued bewilderment. He would never understand why his mother hadn't married and provided herself with some companionship. There were plenty of men who had been interested, but she never made the effort to give them any chance. His father had ruined her by his leaving. The thought provided more fuel and ferver to his hatred. When he was successful with his plans, no other black men would be around to procreate and then leave their white girlfriends to fend for themselves when they were done with them. When he was finished, there would be no other black men. He idly wondered what the man could have sent him. Considering he'd never heard from him, even after Shawn tracked him down and tried to contact him. And he was glad there wasn't a note for his mother in the box. She didn't need any help building up false hopes around the man. She had a closet full of those already.

Shawn showered again before dressing and scribbled instructions for the maid to change the sheets again. Ray would see her in and out after he arrived this morning. Despite the call from his mother, Shawn was unusually chipper, and was whistling when he stepped off the elevator onto the 29th floor where his office was. He was hoping the rest of the day went as well as his morning had started, even though his dreams had made his night restless. After checking the foreign markets, he sent an email to Ray with some follow-up instructions for the new coven and then decided to hit the fitness center for a workout before the business of the day intruded on his mood. Grabbing his workout bag, he took the elevator to the basement.

Ray watched from the security station as the new coven members began to arrive. They were being allowed to take elevators to the basement in groups of four. He'd only had five hours of sleep, and Shawn Kites didn't tell him he *had* to be here for this arrival, but he thought it was a good idea anyway.

"Hey Joe, you keepin' tabs on these people? How many names?"

"Yessir Mr. Crosser. Loggin'em in before they get into the 'vators."

"Good. The report to Mr. Kites should be complete then?"

"Yessir."

Ray loved talking to Joe. It was the only chance he got for someone to call him *sir*, and it felt good. Most of the time he felt small and inadequate, especially around Kites. The man had a way of making you feel that way even when he was trying to be nice! *Oh well*, he shrugged, *it's a good job, working for DNAgen Biolabs, even if it means kissing up to Kites. The man can't help it if having money makes him a hard-ass. I might be one too if I had his money!"*

The last of the witches boarded the elevator, and Ray watched until the doors closed and it started down. "Joe, shoot me a copy of the log for Mr. Kites."

"Sure thing sir."

"You ain't usually here by six, Mr. Crosser. These folks gonna be a problem?" Joe asked.

"Naaah, just a precaution Joe. They're only temporaries, and we got a lot of'em workin' here right now. Just keepin' tabs on all the extras."

"Nothin' I need to pass on to the other guards?"

"Only that the rules for this bunch are the same as for the last. Nobody in or out without checkin' past me,[' and no unmonitored calls."

"Got it sir."

"Good. You can reach me on the radio if there's trouble Joe."

"Yes sir, Mr. Crosser."

Ray squared his shoulders as he got on the elevator himself. Talking to Joe made him feel important for a change. He watched the little lights in the display over the door light each number as the car passed the floors. The closer he got to the penthouse, the more he seemed to shrink in stature. If anyone had been riding in the elevator with him when he got in on the first floor, they would have thought he was going to be sick.

Should I tell Kites about them witches talkin' last night or not? Com'on Ray, you decided this last night. Yeah, but what if he finds out what they said and that I didn't tell 'im what I heard? Oh, Ray, you idiot, how's he gonna know you were there unless you tell 'im!

He felt a little better after arguing with himself, and by the time the car reached the penthouse, all but the fear of being around Kites had disappeared. *The man pays good, but some of what he wants me to do is scary stuff. I mean, I think about killin' them old black folks who ain't done nothin' to nobody as far as I can see, and I wonder why? What's the point?* he sighed as he walked down the hall to his office.

Ray's office was a tiny closet-sized space on the back side of Kites office. He knew it wasn't much, but it *was* on the penthouse floor. Unlocking the door, Ray looked over his shoulder in practiced caution before entering and closing the door behind him. He sat down at his old IBM Selectric and started the report Kites would want when he came down at nine. He liked using the typewriter rather than the computer. No instant copies of anything to worry about.

"Arrival Report: Total new temps, twenty-four. The Group make-up is: fourteen women and ten men. Desk guards will report as previously instructed." Ray finished the report with his signature then flipped on the portable air-cleaner and lit a cigarette. He took a long drag on the thing as he propped his feet up on his desk and leaned back blowing smoke rings, watching them rise to the ceiling in swirls and then enlarge as they travelled toward the florescent lights and then back down the wall into the air cleaner.

Kites just has to have a good reason for the targets being so old, even if I can't imagine what it could be. I still get a bad feelin' about this, like what we're doin' is really wrong. He watched as another smoke ring slowly disappeared into the haze that now filled his office. The air cleaner never could keep up.

He's gonna ask about the next one, if the hit's ready. I can't decide whether to do Miami or swing over and do L.A., let the East side rest a bit. Ray leaned forward to stub out the butt when he noticed the call light blinking on his phone.

"Shit, Kites is in early!"

He stood and mechanically smoothed the wrinkles from his jacket with one hand while running the other through his thinning hair. Moving for the door, he reached for the receiver and the report he just typed in a single fluid movement.

"Be right there Mr. Kites."

He didn't bother waiting to hear what the man wanted; he knew his presence would be the request. Ray Crosser didn't ask many questions of his boss. After thirteen years of what some would call public servitude, Ray knew the answers before the questions were ever asked.

He entered Shawn's office without knocking because he knew he was expected. "Here's the report on the new arrivals Mr. Kites. Joe's keepin' his eye on'em."

"Thank you Ray. I appreciate your dedication to duty."

Shawn didn't look at the report and barely raised his head when Ray spoke. Sometimes Ray wondered whether he really knew he was ever there or just expected him to be and so treated the situation as such.

"Which one is our next target?" Shawn said.

Ray cringed; he hated it when the man met his expectations so closely. "Either Miami or L.A." "Hmmmm; why such a wide range between the choices?"

"Well, I figured that since the last two were so close together, we might want to try something farther away, throw anybody lookin' a crook in the pattern. On the other hand, Miami is close enough to mark the results quicker."

Hmmmm. You make a good point regarding L.A. I like your thinking Ray."

Shawn turned his back to Ray and looked out the window dismissing Ray as usual. No word, just that unnerving habit he had of forgetting he was in the room.

Ray left to give the orders for L.A. He hoped it was as easy finding the right takers for the job there as it had been here in Chicago. Even the one in D.C. hadn't been too difficult. L.A., however, might be a different story. They were more organized in L.A. He thought about that kid killed by the security guard for wearing a hoodie or that videotaped police brutality incident that caused the last big riots in L.A. And let's not forget the general feelings of racial unrest after that football players' murder trial several years back.

"This one might not be so easy Mr. Kites. Hope you're ready for any backlash this job might cause," Ray said to himself as he thought back to the first two targets and wondered again at the ease of the executions and lack of community awareness. If these people are so important, that can't last. "Somebody's gonna get wise to what we're doin'."

When he entered his tiny office this time, Ray locked the door behind himself. He reached inside the left hand desk drawer and pulled a cheap cell phone from a plastic pouch as he sat down.

Staring at the dial pad for a moment, he couldn't decide which of his contacts to call. Recruiting was always pretty easy because of the dollars offered; but for these objectives, the payoff was a depletion of the ranks. He needed good, reliable hitters that were also expendable. Ray also realized that while it was easy to recruit blacks to do the jobs in Chicago and D.C., L.A. would be different. The choice of hitters was limited for this kind of job in L.A. unless he went with the gang faction.

"Well, that's not a bad idea! They're always lookin' to off a rival. Let's see if I can pull this off."

He dialed then leaned back putting his feet up on his desk again. "Hey Juwan, this is Ray, in Chicago."

"Hey Ray, how's it hangin' man?"

"Hangin' low dude, busy but quiet here. You?"

"Busy here too, man, real busy. Movin' much green my man."

"Business is good then?"

"Yeah man, couldn't ask for better. Them makin' marijuana legal makes it easy to move it, man!" Juwan laughed, "So, what's with the call, man? Can I do sumthin' for you?"

"Well, as a matter of fact, I got some business comin' your way, Juwan. Wanna know can you handle cutting some power out there for me?"

"Hmmm, well, might be able to oblige you Ray, but that depends on whose power and how much the collection will be."

"Collection's in the neighborhood of ten. The mark's in a shop down Watt's way."

"Whoa man, dangerous for a dude down there. Can we pad the collection any?"

Ray smiled; the bait had set the hook good and deep. "Might be able to up that a bit, maybe a dozen. Think you might have a couple of takers?"

"Got two in mind. When you need this cage rattled?"

"Tonight Juwan; by midnight your time."

"Any specifics requested?"

"It'd be real nice if the hitters match and can be spent."

"So, setup fee only huh, and the mark?"

"Woman owns the *Peace* shop. You know it?"

"Yeah Man, I know it. Man, that's an old woman. Why..."

"Hey Juwan! No questions man! You know the drill!"

"Hey, sorry man, no problem, sorry!"

"Can you do it?"

"Yeah man, on-time delivery."

"On-time delivery."

Satisfied, Ray hung up the phone and sighed. Only twelve thousand dollars and the hit complete by midnight. Kites would be impressed. Or at least Ray hoped he would. He folded the little phone and put it back in the drawer. Now that the hit was ordered, he had to get those witches to focus on L.A. Ray wasn't sure he understood exactly what they were doing, only that Kites was certain it made the hits easier.

"Awww hell, whatever it takes!"

FIVE

On a whim, Shawn skipped the first basement level and went to the sub-basement where White Oak, and now Oak Vein, Covens were doing their work. It was already after six, and Eric had promised a dawn arrival. He was surprised that he hadn't run into any of the new people in the elevator, even though Ray did tell him they had all arrived. Curious, he left his bag on the elevator and cautiously walked down the corridor to the suite of rooms they occupied. He thought it was odd that he didn't hear any chanting, but he did notice that the hair on the back of his neck and arms stood on end as he drew closer to the door of the suite. As he reached for the doorknob, the door suddenly opened with a *whoosh* that confirmed the negative pressure of the building. "Hello Shawn," a sultry female voice floated out of the seemingly faceless hood in the gray robe that stood in the doorway. A pair of exquisitely manicured hands thrust from the billowing sleeves and the woman removed her hood revealing flaming red hair pulled neatly into a set of diamond encrusted ebony combs. She smiled at him, but it was deceiving. Her green eyes did not reflect the emotion she was trying to exude.

"Hello," he said as he reached to shake her hand, "a pleasure to finally meet you, High Priestess."

"Oh, please, call me Madeline. Eric has told me so much about you; I feel we've known each other for years. Come, have some coffee?" she gestured to a small table and chairs set into the corner of the tiny reception area. "Thank you, Madeline, but I was just headed for the gym and decided to drop in and see how things were going. Your backup coven has arrived?"

"So nice of you to inquire, Shawn; we are quite comfortable down here and yes, Oak Vein Coven arrived almost an hour ago. We have already initiated them into the *working* and White Oak is now taking a much needed rest."

Realizing that he was deftly being led back toward the elevators, Shawn asked, "How long does it take your... *working* to reach full power?"

"There are a couple of factors that do make some difference, like target distance and the time differential, but it usually takes between 30 and 45 minutes to reach full striking power."

"I see... would it be possible for someone to observe the procedure?"

Seeming surprised by his level of interest, Madeline answered, "Because of the level of confidentiality surrounding this project, I imagine that you are asking for yourself?"

"Yes."

"Shawn, I have no problem with your observation of the *working*, as long as you realize that there won't be anyone free to explain what's happening..."

"Oh, I wouldn't dream of becoming a burden to you, especially during such an important part of this project. Thank you so much, Madeline, for taking this time away from your rest to speak with me. I'm not sure I will be available for the next target, but thank you for permission to observe. I will take you up on it in the near future."

"Please come back whenever it is convenient, Shawn. Have a good day."

"And you, Madeline." Shawn shook her hand again and got back onto the elevator. This time, he did go to the gym to workout.

Shawn had just started the cool down of his run on the treadmill when Ray came into the room. "Hey Ray, how are the troops looking this morning?"

"Hi Shawn, and the *troops* are faring well this morning. I left the arrival report on your desk when we spoke earlier."

"Any trouble reported from the guards?"

"None reported, sir. And, I've taken care of the other matter too."

"Other matter? Oh, yes, we'll speak of that later. Thank you Ray, you are so dependable. I don't know how I would get everything done without you around."

"Thank you, sir. Is there anything else this morning?"

"When will the next team be ready? I plan to observe our witches when we go for the next target."

HARLEM ANGEL

"I've ordered the team, the entry point will be tonight."

"Hmmmm, good. Please let me know the moment they report on location."

Ray shrugged, "And, for my two-cents, I don't think we're going to have *ANY* trouble. They're asleep-at-the-wheel, sir."

Shawn held up one finger while toweling off the sweat from his face and neck. "Never underestimate an adversary, Ray. If we expect it to remain easy, that's when they'll wake up and throw sand in our faces. And, I don't want *any* mistakes."

"Yes sir."

"Go ahead and head on up to the office, Ray. I'll be up after I shower. Is there anything pressing on the calendar today?"

"No sir, not really. You've got a couple of meetings; one with the scientists from the bio-lab, and one with one of the vendors, but that's it."

"Good," Shawn said, turning his back on Ray and heading for the showers. "I'm going to run to my mother's before the meeting Ray; she called this morning and says I got a package. I need to get it now so I can keep my mind clear for this evening's target practice."

"Right sir, I'll call a car for you and then see you upstairs when you return." Ray turned and went to set up the conference room for the two meetings and confirm the L.A. contract with the *go* signal.

Shawn showered and changed into a suit so he would be ready for the meetings when he returned. When he got to his mothers' house, he was still agitated at having to make the trip. "I'll just be a few minutes, so please wait," he told the driver.

I would rather have had Ray pick this thing up, but I'm curious because that man sent it, he thought as he climbed the stairs to his mother's room.

"Hello Mother," he said, trying hard to keep the disdain out of his voice. He reached across the bed and grabbed her hand. "I'm sorry, but I don't have much time. I've got two meetings that I need to be back for very soon. Where is this package?"

Chrystal Kites smiled when Shawn touched her hand, "I'm so glad you were able to get away and come to get it Shawn. I haven't heard from your father in decades, so it must be important," her voice was filled with obvious joy.

Shawn tried hard not to sneer, "I'm sure it really has no bearing on anything to do with us Mother. It's been so long, and he's not been part of our lives; what could he possibly have to offer us at this juncture!"

She sighed, "That may be true sweetheart, but he knew where to find us. That means he's been keeping tabs on us, at least."

Shawn counted to ten; he just didn't understand how his mother could still have any positive feelings for this man. Shaking his head he asked, "Where's the package Mother?"

"It's here," and she reached to the shelf below the bedside table to pull out the small cardboard box and hand it to Shawn.

He took the box from her and stood, "Thank you Mother, I'll open it later. I've really got to go."

Chrystal watched him in silence for a few seconds before she said, "I hope it is as special as I think it is, baby. Please open it soon. I love you Shawn…" her voice trailed off as tears welled up in her eyes.

Shawn kissed her on the forehead, "Goodbye mother. If there's anything you need, just give Ray a call, and he'll be sure you get it."

He was down the steps and back in the car as if his feet were on fire. "Back to the office, please." He sat there staring at the box. He was almost afraid to open it. He shook it, and other than a slight shift in weight, he couldn't tell whether there was anything substantial in the box. "Well, it'll keep until later." He spent the rest of the trip trying not to be angry at having to leave his office to pick it up.

Eric watched as Madeline gave instructions to the newly arrived Oak Vein Coven members. "Kites is running the show here. We are working for him with the knowledge that what we accomplish will help us in our own endeavors. What he doesn't know won't hurt us." There was a wave of laughter at her words.

She continued after a brief pause, "The weave is strong and has to be maintained on a constant basis. We channel the focus depending on instructions from Ray Crosser. Ray is Kites' lackey and is clueless as to what is going on here. They've been delivering one location every other day, so we expect the third one any time now."

"What exactly is the weave?"

"Good question! It's a combination of Earth, Air and Fire. Its purpose is to counter the existing power now over the target cities listed on the chart on the wall. The power we've been hired to counter is old, old. Eric feels our own sources have roots in this flow."

"How much danger will be encountered?"

"Kris, anytime you counter another power source there is a danger of burn out, as you know. The biggest danger with this one is that the source is unknown. We've figured out how to counter it, but it's not active. That may be why it's been so easy to weave around it."

"Have there been any signs that someone might be looking at what we're doing?"

Eric stepped in, "Not at this time. So far, there's been no resistance. However, we don't expect this ease to last. On the contrary, that's why we called for your help."

Madeline nodded, "Yes. When this network of users awakens from their sleep, they will be a formidable force, and we must be ready if we are to triumph in the upcoming battle and absorb their power base as our own."

"What makes you two so sure of their strength if you've met no resistance so far?"

Eric smiled, "Come brother, and taste of this new power source!"

Eric turned as the group began to rise as one, and they followed him down the hallway to the room where their circle was now etched into the concrete beneath the tile that covered the floor. He was pleased with their reaction. He had no doubt that they could feel the flows being woven around the ball of power that hovered at the center of the circle.

It was a roiling ball of angry colors. A cloudy sphere that sent sparks into the air charging it with electricity every time one of the coven members passed a point of the star engraved in the circle.

"Come, taste its sweetness, its difference, from the power we are accustomed to."

Eric took the hand of the man who had spoken of his doubt and led him to the circle's edge. Those maintaining the circle made space for him as he joined them in their circuit. The others watched as first surprise and then pleasure crossed his face. After two passes, one of those who had been making the circuit, dropped from the circle to bring the number back to thirteen again. The young woman dipped her head towards Eric before leaving the room. She looked tired, her face drained of color, but no one seemed to notice this. Enthralled with the sight of the circle and the feel of the power as it pulsed through the room, they were oblivious to such a small detail.

"You will all get a chance to taste of this, in turn. Please, return to the first room and we ask that you draw lots for the order in which you will take up your place in the circle. The next change-over should be in two hours."

As they filed from the room, Madeline slipped past them and whispered to Eric, "Ray's waiting outside."

Eric frowned, "Be sure they choose their order and get the next ones in here at the stroke of seven. Our members are tired and we need to get them all relieved as soon as possible."

"Do we have to wait the whole two hours?"

"This first time yes. After they've all been initiated, we'll be able to change-over faster and more than two at a time. We can't risk losing our hold by changing too many at once when we're adding new people."

"Ok, I'll see to it."

"I'll take care of Ray. He's probably brought our next target."

Eric followed Madeline out of the room and pulled the doors shut behind them. Ray was hovering close enough to see inside when they were opened, and Eric figured he'd probably seen enough.

"Hello Mr. Crosser, can I help you?"

"Yeah. Eric ain't it?"

Eric nodded.

"Yeah, I've got the next target city. It's L.A."

"That one's a tall order. There's a lot of underlying emanation from that city."

"Will there be a problem with it?" Ray asked, frowning.

Eric pursed his lips in amusement. These people had no idea what they were dealing with. "No, it will not be a problem, Mr. Crosser, just a need for caution."

"OK then," Ray said.

Eric said, "The peak hour will be the same only Pacific time."

"I'll let Mr. Kites know."

Ray continued to stand there, looking like he was trying to see past Eric and through the closed doors into the working room. "Is there something else I can help you with Mr. Crosser?"

"No, no, nothing else. Just wanted to take a peek…"

"I'm afraid that wouldn't be such a good idea Mr. Crosser. It might interrupt what we're doing here and cause a problem in L.A."

Eric was pleased with himself at Ray's reaction.

"Oh, no! It's OK, I don't want to cause any trouble!"

"Thank you Mr. Crosser."

"Hey, no problem."

Eric watched the man go back up the hallway and waited until the elevator doors closed before following Madeline to help with the newcomers.

Dude gives me the creeps and it should be the other way around! He either doesn't understand who and what we are, or he's too stupid to care. He was still shaking his head in disgust when he joined Madeline and the new recruits.

"… The reason we have to wait two hours before each shift change is to give you newbies time to acclimate once you join the circle. If we change too fast, you won't be able to understand the flows and hold them when there isn't a member of White Oak in the circle."

"You speak as if we don't have a clue as to how a work in progress is held," one of the younger men said with anger clearly coloring his words.

Eric stepped in, "No, no, no, we mean nothing of the sort. In fact, the mere proof of our confidence in you is the invitation for you to join us!"

"Then why all the secrecy and pretense?" A young blond woman seated in the back row stood as she spoke.

"The secrecy is necessary. We are working for someone else here. He doesn't know all of our plans, nor does he understand exactly what we do here. Likewise, we must assume that we are not getting the whole picture from him."

"Ahhhh, I see. Caution is the better part of valor in this case."

"Exactly!"

Eric made a mental note to find out the young lady's name when the orientation was completed. She was sharp."

Madeline continued where she left off before all the questions. "As Eric mentioned earlier, the flows we are using are Earth, Air and Fire. What we're binding with this is not completely known to us. There are elements flowing through the power current that none of us recognize."

"Has anyone tried to examine the strands separately?" This question came from the skeptic sitting in front. Eric made a note to find out his name too. He was a little too vocal about his distrust.

Madeline answered, "We've had people studying the thing since we caught it. Any insight you could lend would help and surely be appreciated."

The young woman asked, "Is the power flow primarily water? I note that element is missing from the weave."

Madeline nodded towards Eric, and he answered, "Water has proven to feed the source rather than helping to bend it, so we've eliminated it from the weave." He watched their responses as his answer was accepted by the questioning woman and the angry young man.

Madeline paused for a moment then asked, "Are there any further questions?" She looked around the room and made eye contact with the two questioners. "Good. You'll find your rooms down the hall and to the left. You can relax until you're needed. Someone will come and get you when it's time. Anyone anxious to help with the project is welcome to join our researchers in the observation room to the right of the circle chamber. There is food available in the kitchen at the end of the hallway where your rooms are. Please help yourself to whatever you need. Thank you all for joining us, I hope it will prove to be as rewarding an experience for you as we expect it to be."

Eric said, "Madeline, Ray brought the next target."

"You look worried. Where is it?"

"L.A."

"Hmmmm, a real hot spot. Did you tell him?"

"I told him, but I don't think he got the picture. We're going to need this one stronger than the last two were combined."

"So, what do you think? Should we continue pulling White Oak out of the circle or slow the change-over down until L.A.'s done?"

"I know our people are tired, but we can't afford to miss a step at this point in the game. Let the weaker ones out, but replace them with Oak Vein's strongest. Those two headstrong ones will be good and strong; we can use their obstinance. Start building them to the peak level and call me in about six hours."

Harlem Angel

"Is this one set for the same time?"

"Yeah, midnight; but Pacific time. Gives us an extra three hours in the pocket."

"Well, I hope we don't need it. I'll inform the replacements personally. Get some rest Eric, we're going to need you for this one."

Ray arrived back at the penthouse floor satisfied that he could relax for the rest of the day. The hit was set, and the witches had their orders. It had been a fruitful morning and he had a little kick to his step when he got off the elevator.

"Ray, Mr. Kites wants to see you."

"OK Vicki. Thanks."

Ray stopped and took a deep breath before entering Shawn's office. It wasn't often that he had anyone relay a message to him, least of all Vicki. She was Shawn's administrative assistant. She always acts like she has more authority than she does. While efficient at her work, she rarely spoke to Ray. And Ray didn't have much more respect for her than she did for him. After all, she was just a secretary with a fancy title.

"You wanted to see me Mr. Kites?"

The chair spun around from the window so fast it startled Ray.

"Ray... I didn't expect Vicki to find you so quickly. Everything going smoothly?"

"Yes Sir. The new ones are here and have been instructed as to what's going on. Here's the log sheet."

Shawn took the piece of paper Ray handed him, barely glancing at it before speaking again. "Ray, I wanted to know whether L.A. was set to go yet?"

"Yes sir, it's been arranged."

Ray's confidence slid to the floor as he heard Shawn sigh.

"Well, can't be helped I guess."

"Sir?"

"Nothing to be done about it Ray, we'll have to go with what we've got."

Ray's voice raised an octave when he repeated himself, "Sir?"

"Oh, sorry Ray. If you hadn't ordered the target yet I was going to change it to Miami."

"Why sir? Is there a problem with L.A.? I can cancel the order if we need to, there's still time…"

"No, no Ray, it's ok. Probably just my nerves having all these witches in the building has got me on edge."

"Yeah, I understand that, sir. I feel it too."

"Well, can't be helped. Carry on Ray. Let me know what happens, especially if there's any trouble."

"Sure thing, Mr. Kites."

When Ray left Shawn's office, he felt the hair on the back of his neck rise and reached up with his hand to rub it. "Sure hope there's no trouble Mr. Kites. I don't wanna deal with any trouble like what happens in L.A. anyway," he mumbled to himself. He got back to his own office and had to fight the urge to call Juwan and make sure there wasn't any trouble. After sitting and staring at the phone for half-an-hour, he finally got up to wander the halls for awhile. "If anything happens, Juwan'll call."

He slid past Vicki hoping he'd reach the elevator before she looked up. Once in the safety of the little metal box, he sighed and wondered again at exactly what a pack of witches were doing in the basement of DNAgen Biolabs Corporate Headquarters. And what was so special about that room at the end of the hallway where all the noise was coming from?

He'd made the decision to find out before he even realized the elevator was headed to the sub-basement again. Determination took the place of his fear. "There's something going on in that room and I'm gonna find out what it is."

SIX

The balance of the day went without further difficulties. Shawn was eager, almost excited, at the promise of the third assassination's success. He could almost FEEL the coven's power beginning to build. It was nearing six-thirty p.m. and all the employees but the swing shift in manufacturing, were gone home. He'd invited Ray to dinner and was watching the city lights come on when the man came into his office.

"Beautiful evening, sir."

"Yes, it is, Ray. Thank you for joining me for dinner."

"My pleasure, sir."

"You know, Ray, you are not my servant, but my assistant. The title of *sir* is *REALLY* not necessary."

"I know, you've told me that before, sir; but I am more comfortable calling you *sir*, rather than Shawn. I mean no disrespect… sir, but I will do my best, sir."

Shawn sighed, "As you will then. I'll give up trying to change that."

"Thank you, sir."

There was a quiet knock at the door, and Ray got up to let the caterers in to set the table.

"I hope you enjoy my dinner choice, Ray. Does steak and lobster suit you?" Shawn asked.

Ray nodded yes. Shawn could see that his dinner choice met with approval.

He circled the desk and, pushing the access panel that revealed a wet bar in the corner, he asked, "Drink?"

"Any J.D. in there?"

"Jack Daniels it is. On the rocks?"

"Please."

Shawn hummed a tune while he poured. The ice popped adding a beat to the melody. He handed the drink to Ray.

"Thank you, sir. Do you need me to stick around tonight, after dinner?"

Shawn sipped his drink. "Might be a good idea, Ray. I'm not exactly sure what I'm in for when I intrude on our... *visitors* in the sub-basement."

"You think there'll be trouble?"

"Perhaps. I've just got a feeling..."

"Hey, don't sweat it, sir. I'll be right here."

"Thank you, Ray. I really appreciate what you do for me."

"No problem, sir."

There was another knock at the door.

"Ahhhh, that'll be dinner." Shawn said.

This time the caterer entered without Ray having to open the door. A black man dressed in a white uniform, pushed a cart into the room.

"Do you wish me to serve, sir?" the man asked.

Shawn thought about it, "No, that's not necessary tonight."

"When should I return for the cart?"

"We should be finished by eight."

"Very good, sir." And the man left.

Ray pushed the cart closer to the small round table that took up the corner opposite from the wet bar. Shawn stood to join him, stopping at the bar first to refresh his drink.

"Can I tighten up your drink, Ray?"

"Sure, thanks."

Shawn grabbed Ray's glass off the desk and proceeded to make both of them new drinks. He then joined Ray at the table. The utensils clanged against each other as they served themselves, and Ray asked, "So, you really believe in all this hocus-pocus stuff the witches claim to be real?"

"Well, it's like this Ray, whether or not I believe it, before we engaged their help, we couldn't get anybody near these people to take them out." He let out a heavy sigh as he prepared to dig into steaming plates of lobster, steak, baked potatoes and some kind of vegetable mix. They ate in relative silence. This dinner, a monthly ritual Shawn relished, gave him the opportunity to observe Ray outside of the normal daily routine. Oblivious to the absurdity of his logic, Shawn watched Ray closely while they ate.

Seeing Ray fidget under his gaze matched the succulence of the lobster on his fork. He bit and chewed the morsel, swallowing deliberately and said, "So, tell me Ray, what *IS* your personal opinion of the grand scheme we are perpetuating?"

"Sir?..." Ray reacted with surprise at the question.

Shawn smiled, "Surely you have a personal opinion of the orders you carry out? Not that there's any problem, I'd just like to know exactly where you stand, on a personal level."

He waited, chewing and sipping in quiet repose. Ray seemed disconcerted. He wiped his chin and took a large gulp of Jack Daniels before answering the question.

"Well, Sir... I do have an opinion."

"Everyone has an opinion, Ray. It's what that opinion is and where it puts you that matters." Shawn smiled and leaned back in his chair, idly sipping his drink, all his attention now focused on Ray.

Ray shuddered, looking him right in the eyes when he spoke again, "I don't argue with the economics of what DNAgen is doing; there is definitely a market for the drugs we are producing."

"But..." Shawn prompted.

"But, because we target a... certain population over another, I think we'll have problems... Sir."

"So, you disagree with our marketing strategy... Do you have an alternative you feel will be more... palatable to our critical public?"

Ray looked up quickly, and Shawn smiled, congratulating himself for surprising the man again. He wasn't able to surprise Ray very often. The man could do a *Radar O'Reilly* on him because he'd been his assistant for so long. So, twice in one day was a delicious coup.

Ray dropped his fork, wiped his mouth and reached for his drink again, as if the deliberateness of his movements would help him to regain his composure. Shawn waited patiently for his answer, already finished with his own meal.

Ray cleared his throat, "Sir, I fully support the grand plan, which is to reduce and eventually end the mixing of our race." He paused to take another swallow, "I do, however, believe that we may have some trouble executing our plan if those who don't agree get wind of it."

Shawn sighed happily, "So glad you understand the magnitude of what we're doing here, Ray."

Ray smiled back and said, "Sir, you chose well those who are close to you."

"So it seems…"

They were interrupted by a knock on the door, and their server came in to retrieve the remains of their dinner. "Will there be anything else, Sir?"

Shawn absently dismissed him with a wave, and then watched with chagrin as Ray slipped the man a ten dollar bill when he left. He was glaring at Ray when he turned around.

"Always helps to add a little grease to the wheels," Ray said, "Keeps service in top form."

"Ahhh, but isn't it a shame it has to be bought?" Shawn said, stating the obvious.

Ray shrugged, "A small expenditure to assure that no one spits in your food."

Shawn nodded in thoughtful agreement but still felt put out at having the gesture made on his behalf. He stood and walked back to the window and its view.

Joining him, Ray asked, "When are you expected down below?"

"There was no specific time attached to the invitation, but I am keenly interested in watching them work. I think I'll go down around eleven, just before they reach the peak in their power." He grinned, "The *witching hour*, you might say!"

Shaking his head, Ray asked, "Is there anything you need me to do before then?"

"No Ray, you've got the next couple of hours free. I do want you around when I'm down there, though. Just in case."

"No problem, Sir. I've got a couple of things to take care of, but I'll be back before you head down."

"Thank you Ray."

Shawn didn't turn around when Ray left. He drained the last of his drink and decided to change into something more comfortable for the evening's activities.

He traversed the floor in silence, looking around the data pool as if he expected to find someone working here at this hour. The place still had a *hum* to it, like it was alive of its own volition and didn't need his employees to be productive.

On the elevator ride up to his apartment, Shawn wondered briefly what was so important that Ray had to leave so quickly after dinner, *not that he had any real reason for staying*. He changed into a set of lightweight sweats, fixed himself another drink and scanned the news channels for something interesting to kill the time. He still had a couple of hours before he really needed to head downstairs. The television wasn't offering anything of significance, so Shawn decided to do some Internet surfing. "I wonder just how much information I can find on our basement guests. Hmmm, witches, Wicca, warlocks… that should bring up something…" He studied the computer screen and took notes filling the whole two hours before realizing he'd thoroughly blown through the time. Checking his watch, he stood and stretched, yawning.

"I wonder if Ray is back yet." He switched off the computer and lights and went down to the main lobby first. Ray came in the side door as he stepped off the elevator.

"Hi Ray, you get everything taken care of?"

"Yes sir, and I didn't thank you for dinner.

it was delicious, thank you."

"Alright!" Shawn clapped his hands together, rubbing vigorously, "On with the show! I haven't been this excited since we discovered Melacrit!" With that, Shawn turned back to the elevators and went to the sub-basement.

Madeline was waiting for him when the doors opened. "Good evening, Shawn. "Raymond told us you would be down this evening, but I wasn't sure you'd really come."

"Evening Madeline. Good ol' Ray, always takes care of the details. Of course I wouldn't miss this opportunity. My schedule may not permit it later."

"Of course."

Shawn stepped off the elevator and inhaled sharply, hissing under his breath. Ray hung back, trying to disappear.

Madeline smiled, "Oh! You can feel the power!"

"Is *THAT* what it is? Sorry, I wasn't ready for that."

"Well, there isn't any reason you should have been ready for it. Most mortals are oblivious to the flows."

"Mortals?"

Her laugh was a twitter, "Sorry, my turn to apologize; our word for you common folk who don't have the power."

They walked together down the hallway to the room where the work was going on.

"I see," Shawn replied and then he stopped in front of the door to the suite and grabbed for the wall, slumping forward.

"Are you alright? Perhaps you should sit for a few minutes."

"No…" He shook his head and took a deep breath, "I'm alright. Just not used to what I'm feeling." He stood up straight and steadied himself. "Shall we go in?" he said, looking Madeline in the eyes.

She had a little frown on her face and uncertainty in her eyes, but she nodded yes.

"We'll need to be as quiet as possible," she whispered as she reached for the doorknob.

"May I ask questions?" Shawn said, blinking rapidly to adjust his eyes to the lower lighting.

"If you must. But try to hold them until after the peak."

Madeline led him through the next doorway into the conference room for the suite of offices they occupied. Shawn barely recognized it from the last time he'd been in it. The walls were draped with soft folds of black silk. Instead of lights, what illumination there was came from dozens of candles placed in sconces, safely distanced from the now very flammable walls. The floor was adorned with a five-pointed star within a circle. There was a person standing at each star point, arms outstretched, and faces hidden deep within the hoods of their robes. Around the circle, holding hands and chanting something barely audible, were at least twenty others. They seemed oblivious to the presence of the observers.

From the corner of his eye, Shawn saw Madeline gesture for him to join her on the other side of the room. He looked back over his shoulder, then back at her. *When did she cross the room?* Slowly, he made his way to her, stopping twice to regain his balance. What is wrong with me!" he whispered to himself.

Madeline urged him to sit in a chair that he hadn't seen behind her. She whispered, "Are you OK? You look a little pale."

"I'm OK, a little dizzy that's all."

He sat in the chair and she moved to stand near him. Shawn watched in awe as a small sphere of yellow appeared at the center of the five-pointed star. He was barely aware that Madeline began to sway to the chant. He was even more unaware that he was swaying himself.

The outer circle of witches began to move counter-clockwise, and with their movement, a drumbeat began, echoing eerily from the corner of the room opposite Shawn and Madeline. He saw a gray-robed figure slumped over a small drum. The figure's hands were only visible when raised to strike the surface. Shadows flickered wildly as those in the circle began to gesticulate, like a gigantic snake going through convulsions as it held its own tail in its mouth.

The room was heady with the pungent scent of something burning, which added to the feeling that *something* was about to happen.

Shawn's body moved to the beat of the drum, and he was on his feet, eyes closed, moving with the rhythm of the music that was the chant.

Madeline was suddenly aware of her guest's total involvement and signaled to another disciple who was shadowed in the hallway. Eric was the one who approached her, dodging Shawn's now sinuously revolving body.

She whispered, "He's awakening! We need a vessel!"

Eric whispered back, "Did you know he was a latent?!?"

"Of course not!" she snapped. "If I'd bothered to check when he was here earlier today, we would've been ready. So… hurry up, gather the tools, they've almost reached the peak!"

Eric almost ran from the room, returning quickly with the scissors, string and a bedroll, which he spread on the floor behind the chair that Shawn had been sitting in. Once everything was in place, Madeline removed the chair and stationed Eric on the other side of Shawn's spinning body.

She quickly blessed herself and the utensils, then prepared to move in as the chanting and drums reached their crescendo. Shawn was totally oblivious to what was happening around him. As the chanting ritual plateaued and held, he collapsed into Eric's arms. Eric maneuvered him onto the bedroll, and then Madeline moved in quickly with the scissors and a sterile lancet. In ritualistic order, she clipped a lock of his hair, pricked the middle finger of his left hand squeezing several drops of blood into a waiting bowl. She also clipped a small square of material from his pants at the cuff. Without hesitation, she pulled a small pouch from around her waist and took a pinch of whatever was inside to add to the bowl. Using a pestle, she ground the contents into a paste, which she first smeared on Shawn's forehead and wrists before spreading the balance on the piece of cloth cut from his sweat pants. She then tied the piece of cloth into a small pouch, which she then tied to his left wrist.

As she stood from her work, Madeline and Eric turned as one toward each other, the room literally humming with the strength of the power flow. A wave of power, emanating from the center of the five–pointed star, swept through the room and everyone in it. Drawing an involuntary deep breath, Madeline met Eric's gaze again as the power wave residue subsided. She bent again to Shawn's brow. "He'll sleep for at least a couple of hours", she said.

"He can't stay so close to the working being just awakened", Eric whispered back. "They'll hold that level for several hours until Ray gives the all clear."

"Yes, we'll need to get Shawn out of the proximity or we'll burn him out." She frowned, "Check his pants for a key. Maybe we can get him back to his office."

Eric bent to her orders. "There's only a cell phone…" He handed it to Madeline.

Pursing her lips in thought, she tapped the screen. There was already a number on it. "Seems he may have anticipated needing help. More proof of his latent talents." She pressed send and wasn't the least surprised at the voice on the other end.

"Yes sir? Trouble?"

Madeline answered, "Ray, it's Madeline. We've had a little… event down here. I believe Mr. Kites should be taken home."

"I'll be right down."

Ray had been sitting at the guard station watching TV when Madeline called. "Wonder what the idiot's done this time", he grumbled under his breath as he raced for the elevator. When the doors opened to the sub-basement, Eric was waiting for him.

"Where is Mr. Kites?"

Eric quickly, silently, ushered him down the hall in response. What he saw stopped him cold. His was voice full of alarm when he said, "What happened?!?!"

Madeline's voice was warm and soothing, "It's alright, Ray. Mr. Kites just had an… unexpected response to being near the power flows."

Ray crossed the room and was kneeling at Shawn's head in seconds.

"He's just sleeping", she said.

Ray stood slowly, "Explain to me exactly what happened."

Madeline looked at him hard. "When we reached the peak, he passed out. We made him as comfortable as possible until we were able to call you.

Ray looked at Shawn again and noticed the smile on his lips for the first time.

"What are the smudges on his forehead and wrists?"

"Nothing harmful. They can be washed off later. I will need to speak with him as soon as he wakes; is there somewhere I can wait?" Madeline asked.

Ray looked at Eric who shrugged. Ray asked "Why is it you need to be near when he wakes?"

"He will have many questions, and I have the answers." Her eyes were penetrating. They dared him to question her further.

Ray shrugged, "I'll show you where you can wait." He bent to pick Shawn up from the bedroll on the floor. Eric was immediately on the other side, throwing Shawn's arm around his neck and grabbing his waist. Together they stumbled and half-dragged him to the elevator, Madeline close behind them. When the elevator doors opened, she got in first and held the doors open for them. They rode to the penthouse in silence. Once they finally arrived up the second elevator, in Shawn's suite, Eric helped Ray get him to his bed. They laid him across it and quietly left the room. Then Eric bowed and left.

Madeline stood in the center of the living room, arms folded, eyes on Ray.

"Must you be here?" he asked her, his voice cracking with barely bridled anger.

She blinked, took a deep breath and visibly relaxed as she said, "Ray, I wouldn't ask to be here if it wasn't highly necessary. You don't have to stay, but that's up to you." She walked to the sofa and sat down.

Ray looked around, spotted the TV's remote and grabbed it, handing it to her as he spoke. "I'll be downstairs. Ring me on his cell when he begins to awaken."

"Certainly", she said, pointing the remote and turning on the TV. Ray dimmed the lights as he left, shaking his head.

Madeline turned the sound down low and got up to look around. She was amazed at how little furniture was in the apartment, or how very little there was of anything that would give away any of Shawn's personality. The walls were bare, the tables spotless. No pictures, no knick knacks, no mail lying around. The whole place was cold. There was no emotion at all attached to any of it. She peeked into the bedroom at Shawn and listened. His breathing was strong, slow and steady. She knew his dreams would be vivid, sharp and extremely important when he woke. She sat in front of the TV again, not really paying attention to the program or the silly commercials that were meant to entertain as well as sell their wares. Idly, she speculated on just what Shawn's newly awakened power would mean to his plans for the coven. Oh, she knew he still needed them but, once he learned what his strengths were, how much would he interfere where he'd only been a spectator before? And, how would his magic manifest? She knew he was strong… *VERY* strong. But what was his power base? She still couldn't believe that she missed the spark when they first met, and the dizziness when he came to the basement tonight. He should have rocked her off her feet, especially when they shook hands!

The sound of the bed creaking as he moved broke her reverie. She dialed the number on the cell phone again to summon Ray. Noting the time at three am, she mentally patted herself on the back. "Two hours exactly!"

When Ray stepped off the elevator, Shawn was just sitting up. He shook his head as if trying to clear it from something that had covered him. He took some deep breaths trying to fathom just what had happened to him. Glancing at the alarm clock, he was momentarily stunned by what it said. It had only been eleven o'clock when he'd descended to the sub-basement. It was now just after three am. Shawn swung his legs over the side of bed and grabbed his head against the wave of dizziness that swept over him. His nerves felt raw, like he'd been sleeping next to a jackhammer. Suddenly, he *felt* another presence in his home. Focusing on the feeling, he knew that Ray was one of the people. The other he wasn't certain of, but he knew it was a woman. Shaking his head again, he stood and walked unsteadily to the bathroom. As he splashed water on his face and looked into the mirror, he could hear Ray's voice, "So, he's awake?"

The woman's voice answered, "I think so. I heard the bed creak and thought I'd better call you."

Ray crossed the room putting his ear to the bedroom door, "I hear water running. He'll be out soon, no doubt. Thank you for calling, Madeline. I wasn't sure you would."

"You said it was a good idea for you to be here, so I called." She answered with a shrug. They sat in relative silence, the TV buzzing in the background, waiting for Shawn to emerge.

Bewildered and full of questions, Shawn washed the smear of whatever it was off his forehead and wrists, stripped his soggy clothes off noting two things almost at once: his sweats had a small, neatly cut square hole in them that definitely wasn't there before, and there was a small pouch, made of what looked like the piece missing from his sweats, tied around his wrist. He fingered the pouch and suddenly stopped sort of ripping it from his body.

Shawn listened to the conversation while changing. Still a bit confused and giving Madeline some credit, he did indeed have lots of questions to ask. Shawn opened the bedroom door and the light from the living room, although muted, hit him in the face like a camera flash. He held onto the doorknob to help keep him steady and blinked rapidly to keep from tearing up before entering and traversing the room. He didn't meet their gazes or speak until he was seated on the opposite end of the sofa from Madeline. Ray was seated in the only other chair in the room. Grabbing the remote and hitting the mute button, Shawn leveled a gaze at Madeline. "I remember the beginning, or when I first arrived in the chamber where your coven is working. They were chanting and it felt like the air in the room was charged."

"Go on," she said, staring at him.

Nervously, Shawn rubbed his hands on his thighs and glanced sideways at Ray whose expression was blank, unreadable. "I could feel the power they were using. There was a cadence, a beat to it that seemed to engulf me. I remember the sound of the chant and bright flashes of colored light, and then... nothing. At least for a time."

"Must've been the point where you passed out," Ray interjected.

Shawn looked at Ray and then Madeline. His voice very quiet, he said, "Ray, I think I'll be fine. You can go now. I know you haven't slept, and I won't expect to see you until sometime this afternoon. Thank you."

"Thank you, Sir." Ray stood and looked at them both before leaving.

Shawn watched as Ray left then turned back to Madeline. "What exactly happened to me Madeline?"

"The close proximity of the power flows we were working triggered a response in you."

"Come now, I'm not so naïve that I don't know that!" Shawn snapped. "What did it trigger and how?"

Nervously clearing her throat, Madeline said, "Your proximity to the power triggered an awakening of latent power in you Shawn."

"So, does that mean I'm one of you?"

"No, not exactly. Yours is a different power base, probably akin to that which we are blocking."

He was quiet, digesting the information. "Please explain."

"Near as I can figure, the power in you lay dormant until we touched it last night. I don't know your strength or your affinity as yet, but what you have is very potent."

"I want to know two more things tonight before you go. Was it necessary to ruin a perfectly good pair of sweats and," he fingered the little pouch, "What *is* this?" He watched Madeline closely for her response.

"It contains a mixture of many things: a lock of your hair, a few drops of your blood, a few grains of magic's foundation."

Shawn frowned, "Magic's foundation? Explain please."

Madeline's face was void of expression as she said, "You are a Warlock; a man who possesses magic. And a very strong latent. I didn't feel the spark when we met."

"So, what I felt, the buzzing, the... power..."

"You felt the weave."

"The weave?"

"What the disciples were doing. The music, chanting..."

"Gesticulating?"

"Yes, I suppose an observer might call it that."

"Don't be defensive. Continue."

"The Power of Magic courses over the earth much like our air flows. There are rivers of such powers, their sources distinct to users. Each person who is attuned to the rivers can see them, can feel them. And can use them; if they know how."

Shawn was quiet for a moment. "These rivers — anyone *attuned* can use them?"

"Some are stronger than others and some require more expertise to work with them, but yes, essentially."

"What is the purpose of the *weave* your people work?"

"Each river of power has a specific origin: Earth, Fire, Water, Air. Some are older than others, and therefore stronger. We determine the origin of the power we wish to block and use it's opposite to block the river. To dam it up."

"This weaving... it is difficult to maintain?"

"We fight against nature to block a flow. Any blockage is temporary. How long is determined by the strength of the weavers."

Shawn exhaled slowly, didn't realize he was holding his breath. "What happened to me?"

"Your close proximity to the weave triggered what was a potential for controlling the power. Your body became a resonant chamber where the seed of your personal power base, your magic, quickened and blossomed. The resonation awakened your magic."

"You said that you didn't *feel* me when we first met. What did you mean by that?"

"Someone who is as strong as your power seems to be should have triggered a resonance in me."

"But it didn't?"

"No."

"And just what does that mean?"

"It means that your power base is probably more closely related to the flow we are blocking, rather than the weave we used to block it."

Shawn stared at the picture on the television screen, but he wasn't looking at it. His fingers idly played with the small bag on his wrist. "Tell me, Madeline, does the fact that *magic's seed* came from the pouch around your neck have any significance?" he said, turning to stare in her eyes.

Madeline shifted, visibly nervous under Shawn's penetrating gaze. "Well…" she hesitated, "Yes. It means that I am your teacher, by default."

"Yes, but can you adequately instruct outside of your own flow attachment?"

"The fundamentals are the same: How to use your power, how to gather it's strength, how to focus and direct your…"

"Yes? My what?" Shawn felt, instinctively, that her next revelation would be a key to this whole thing.

"Your desire, your will, your influence, upon it."

Shawn almost saw the illumination from the light he felt go on in his head. He was right, it was a key. Quite possibly *THE* key. "So, tell me, Madeline," his smile was almost wicked; "How much training is required before I can fly solo?"

Madeline breathed a heavy sigh, "Shawn, your progress is measured by how fast you learn and how well you listen."

"There are laws, of course, but you didn't answer my question." Shawn was enjoying this game, now. It had been a long time since anyone had presented such a riveting challenge to his intelligence.

"The fastest apprentice known was casting on his own in six months."

"Ahhhh, finally, a measure. And the slowest?"

"No one has ever stopped."

"Explain that please?" he said frowning again.

"Once you begin a witches' quest, the journey is only interrupted by periods of rest."

"Hmmmm," Shawn smirked, "Litany."

He continued to stare, this time at Madeline. He watched in satisfaction as she spluttered over her next words.

"Well, um, n-no one I know has ever ended their training, short of death. The nature of magic is such that a witch is always learning something new." She ended her sentence, palms up, almost in a gesture of surrender.

Shawn was getting angry. His question still not been answered to his satisfaction. He thought for a moment, breathing deeply before he spoke again, rephrasing the question; "Madeline, how long has your oldest known disciple been studying? And at what age did he or she sever the tie with their teacher?" He could almost see her mind working.

She spoke with renewed confidence in her voice, "I know of a coven with an Elder who is approaching his 91st birthday this year. Most disciples, as you called them, never really sever the tie with their teacher because it is not physically possible. However, most are able to strike out in their own direction within the first year."

"Any prodigies?"

She frowned.

"Have there ever been any disciples who were able to make that break early?"

"None that I know of, but I suppose there's always a first time," she smiled wryly. Madeline looked around the room as if searching for something and Shawn suddenly realized his debriefing was over. But, he wasn't done yet.

"Does the fact that you are my teacher have any bearing on how fast I will be able to advance?"

She turned to stare back at him, eyes wide. "No, you will only be limited by your own strengths and weaknesses."

He stood abruptly and reached for her hand, "Thank you for taking time away from your work to inform me of the change I've experienced. I will be available after three pm today. Will you be able to rearrange your schedule to begin my training?"

She extended her hand as she stood. "Three o'clock will work fine."

"Good! See you then. Ray will see you up this afternoon. Sleep well." He quickly shuffled her out the door.

Shawn sighed and shook his head as he crossed the room pausing only long enough to turn the TV and lamp off. He went straight to the computer in the den he called his office. After booting it up, he did his first of eight searches. The first was on witches. He was astounded at the number of references. *Millions... Amazing, who ever would have guessed.* He printed off several pages, and then his next search was Wicca, then Magic, Spells, Casting, Power flows, and Magic Apprenticeship. By nine am he had a stack of reading eight inches high. He pushed away from the desk and stretched. *Nine a.m.* He'd been sitting in one place for five hours, and his body was rebelling from the neglect. He checked his schedule and added his appointment with Madeline; he knew Ray would take care of moving the others. "I better call Ray and make sure there aren't any problems this morning."

He called the security station in the lobby.

"DNAgen…"

"Hey Ray, all quiet?

"Normal quiet, Shawn… Sir… You OK?"

"Yeah, tired – going to catch a few hours sleep, then I'll be down."

"No problem."

Shawn hung up the phone and stretched again. He strode to the bathroom to shower, humming. He lay across the bed. Instinct… was that what it was? Or intuition… He knew he needed to sleep. The stack of printouts would wait. He wanted to be sharp at three. "A couple of hours should recharge my batteries." He was out before his head hit the pillow.

Ray had stuck around after Shawn dismissed him. He knew something was different about the man.

The assassination had been successful, but there had been a witness. From the report, the men had just completed the mission when a woman walked in on them. They freaked out so badly that neither of them had been able to give a clear description of her. The only thing they both agreed on was that she was pretty. He waited an hour, and then turned in, locking the door to the lounge. He was awakened an hour later by building security. "Sir, you asked to be awakened when the elevator left the penthouse?"

"Yes, thank you Rodney." Ray looked at his watch marking the time-three-thirty. "Guess he didn't have as many questions as I do about this crap!" He pulled his jacket over his shoulder and went back to sleep. By seven, he was awake as usual, and after a trip to the men's room to wash his face and brush his teeth, he donned his jacked after a good shake and went to the lobby security station.

"Mornin' Rod, quiet all night?" Ray winced as the man sucked his teeth before he spoke.

"Thsssst, yes sir. Last elevator moved 'bout three-thirty am. Nothin' til the troops started arrivin' at seven."

"Good. Nothing from the boss yet?"

He asked the question knowing what the answer would be, but asked it anyway.

"No sir. Nothin' yet."

"Thanks Rod. You can split early. I'll man the station until Joe comes in."

"Thank you sir, appreciate it."

"No problem."

Ray settled himself behind the computer surveillance screens. The report on the third mission was going to piss Shawn off, and he was deciding just when to tell him. Oh, there was no question he'd report the problem, just when. *Boy, last night was weird.* "The boss was out cold. Like somebody popped him one upside the head," he snickered. "I've got to keep my eyes and ears open today. Something important happened last night."

Employees began arriving in two's and three's. Joe showed up at ten and Ray turned the station over to him. He took the call from Shawn at nine, and then after going to his own office, Ray pulled the day's calendar and moved two of Shawn's appointments to late morning and early afternoon. The man would be down by eleven; he was *never* any later. Ever. He noted that the calendar had a new entry; "M @ three."

"Now, just who do you suppose that is…" Shaking his head, Ray closed the calendar. The appointment showed that Shawn was serious about what had happened. Ray wondered when the other shoe would drop. He wondered how his news about the third target could be used to his advantage to gain some info about what happened to Shawn last night. He yawned, "Well, we'll see what happens." He made his way to the smoking terrace before returning to his office to await Shawn's arrival.

Madeline spent most of the morning pacing the small room she was using as sleeping quarters. The relief crew was keeping the flows in check, and the members of her coven were sleeping like she should have been. Even Eric was asleep when she returned from the penthouse. He'd left her tea in the microwave, and she smiled at his thoughtfulness. After heating the tea, she stuck her head into the weave room. Satisfied at the resonant power level, she continued to her sleeping room where she began pacing. Sipping the hot tea gingerly, she wrapped herself in a blanket and paced, reflecting on the evenings' events. "You scare me Shawn Kites. I've never seen anyone so strong and so determined." She sipped her tea again. "How do I teach such arrogance?" She sighed as the voice of her Master echoed in her mind, *"Arrogance is simply a mechanism used by people of low self-esteem to falsely present an inner strength they don't possess."*

Shaking her head, Madeline said aloud "Yes, that may be true, but those people *present* and are *perceived* to be strong by others. This gives them their power." She placed her almost empty mug on the floor in the corner by the bed and pulled her blanket tighter as if against a cold wind; she knew it was a strange gesture in the small warm room. "We didn't talk enough tonight. I have no foundation to begin his instruction." She crossed the tiny room to rummage through her duffel bag. She was looking for something very small and specific. "Ahhhh, I knew I'd brought it!" Her fingers closed around a palm-sized, cold blue and white stone; her power focus. Going back to sit on the bed, she tucked her feet under the blanket and pulled it tight, rubbing the smooth stone to make it warm before its use. "I wonder what he'll choose for his focus point. There was certainly nothing in his home that could be used…" Madeline pictured Shawn's living room. Wrongly named in his case, because there was nothing reflecting life in the whole room. "It probably means he's dead inside. But of consequence or choice; hmmmm, I wonder." She decided, right then, that she needed to do some detective work. "DNAgen… just what does this company of his do? Or make? I've got to get an answer to that question before he gets here this afternoon." She sighed and put the lights out, lying down. "He doesn't have a girlfriend… perhaps he's gay? Either way, I can take advantage of it!"

SEVEN

Soraya's head was spinning. She'd been studying hard with Iona for so many hours straight, that it felt like days. She'd been pushing herself, motivated by the fear that if she didn't hurry, her dreams would drive her crazy being unable to effect change in them. And watching people die was more painful than if she herself was the victim. She knew, or thought she knew, that they only had a matter of days to make a difference. If the circle was completely decimated, they were doomed to total failure. And no matter how strong Iona said she was, she knew that if the Circle was gone, she had little or no chance of putting it all back together. The others needed their apprentices, and the two mentors that were already dead were a hole in the fabric that even her newly awakened magic could sense. Soraya rubbed her eyes yawning. They felt like they were full of sand.

"You is awful tired Chile, you still want t'work?" Iona smiled, rocking herself in the old rocking chair in front of the fireplace.

They had moved from the cellar to the shop a couple of hours ago. They were spending a lot of time there in front of the fireplace, exercising Soraya's magic, or so Iona called it. To Soraya, it was mental gymnastics and games. She sighed aloud, "I guess once more through the maze won't kill me."

Iona just laughed and rocked faster. Soraya was sitting cross-legged on the floor. She closed her eyes and focused on the sound of the flames flickering in the fireplace. "I see the flames," she said. Her voice sounded far away compared to the sound of the flames. "I feel their heat."

"Nah, Chile, put dem out," Iona whispered.

Soraya's concentration was solid. The flames were making her face sweat. She wanted them out. Abruptly, she decided on water as her medium. It started as a sprinkle. Then, using the steam as reinforcement, the trickle became a downpour and the flames went out. She opened her eyes to see Iona nodding, a big smile on her face.

"You see Chile, I tol' you. Like to like!"

"I think I understand. I created the flames, so the water to put them out had to come from the same place."

Iona was nodding again, leaning forward in her chair expectantly.

Soraya returned the smile. "I did it Iona, I put the flames out!"

Iona leaned back, still grinning, "You is progressin' well Chile. But, thas'nough for t'day."

Soraya sighed, stretching her arms over her head. "There's just one more thing I want to do before we quit for the day."

"Whas' dat Chile?"

"Iona, how do you all keep in touch with each other?"

"You mean me an t'others? Well, by phone mos'ly."

"Was it always that way? I mean, you've all been here a long time, and telephones weren't always around. How did you do it before?"

"Hmmm, come t'think, we used to send leas' once a week."

"Send… What exactly does that mean? How did you do it, and why did you stop?"

"Chile, you always so fulla questions! Hmmmm, lemme see. I guess we jus got tired Chile. The phone seem so much easier. Didn' take near so much strength or pow'r to dial up. Hee, hee, hee!"

Soraya shook her head, "You know, I think that was your mistake. Can I make a guess?"

"Go head, Chile."

"Once you all started calling instead of *sending*, your contacts with each other got farther and farther apart. Probably only hear from each other, what, once every three months or so right now, right?"

Iona squinted at her, "Das'bout right. But surely you don't think that jus cause we don't talk so much…"

"You're out of touch, Iona. None of you knows what's going on with the others. We have to fix that. That's a big problem, made even bigger with the gaps left by the deaths of Zacharias and Willamae."

Iona poured water for them both and sat in one of the chairs. "Lord, I jus don't know. Settin' up the strength to do a proper sendin ain't gon be easy. We's all kinda on in years nah..."

"I know Iona, but that's why it's all the more important to get those links reestablished."

Soraya took a long swallow from her cup and watched Iona for a few minutes. The woman somehow looked older this evening.

"How much money do you have stashed Iona?"

"Now Chile, don't go lookin' f'buried treasure! Ain't nothin' to call riches roun here!"

Soraya suppressed a giggle, "No, no, you misunderstand what I'm trying to do. I'm not looking for your nest egg; I just need to know what we've got to work with here. I have a few ideas about how to get the Circle reconnected. But before I spring them on you, I need to know what our resources are." She took a deep breath before plunging ahead, "Iona, I want to get us a computer, and I want to put one in each of the other shops too."

"We don't need any of *dem* dang thangs!"

Iona's response was vehement, and Soraya thought, pretty typical of people in their elder years. "Bear with me for a minute, please?"

Iona's face stayed in the frown that appeared with the mention of a computer, but she stopped talking. Soraya hoped she was listening too, "A computer is a good idea, Iona. If we get one, and we place one in each of the other shops, it will be a much easier way to help get the communication between us reestablished. It is a quick way that uses little personal energy to get us all talking again. This way a *sending*... which apparently takes quite a bit of personal power, right?"

Iona nodded yes.

"Can be given the time we need to get it reestablished. But, in the meantime, we can all be aware of what the status of each shop is right now, in real time."

"How 'dis gon work? All t'others are in the same boat's me, tired. I got you Soraya, what bout t'others?"

Soraya took another deep breath; this was the other big request she'd come up with. "Well, they're going to have to call in their apprentices... Now."

Iona stared at Soraya, lips pursed and brow furrowed, "That be sumthin' we kin do fer the ones still here," she said, her voice trailing off.

"What about Zacharias' and Willamaes? Can we get to theirs?"

"Thas whut I was jus thinkin' bout…"

"I want to contact the rest of The Circle. They need to call their apprentices now. If we lose another one before they make the call…" her voice trailed off full of foreboding.

Iona sucked her teeth, looking thoughtful. "Hmmm, I think you is right, Chile. An it'll give'em some warnin on whas't come."

"So, what do we have to do?" Soraya asked, surprised at the surge of energy she felt with the anticipation.

"Well Chile, we's gon do a sendin!"

"We can just do this? No warning to the others that it's coming, no prearranged time?" Soraya asked. She was concerned that if it took so much power, it might fail if nobody knew it was coming.

Iona stood and went to one of the dusty shelves in the shop room. She pulled a big box from the back after clearing some smaller items out of the way. Soraya rose from her place on the floor. "Let me help."

They carried the box to the floor in front of the fireplace where Soraya had been sitting. She sat cross-legged beside it while Iona wiggled back into the rocker's feather cushion that she rested on, looking every bit of an old mother hen.

"What'chu starin at Chile?"

Iona caught her zoning out. "Sorry," she shook her head to clear it, "Nothing. Just fixating, I guess I am tired."

Iona laughed, "Hee, hee, hee, Chile, you is a wonda! You is one stubbern Chile, hee, hee, hee."

Soraya smiled, "So, tell me about the box?"

Iona laughed again, "Hee, hee, hee, you is one stubbern Chile!" Sucking her teeth again, Iona reached for the lid of the box.

Soraya was proud of her self-control. She hadn't winced either time.

"'Dis here box is much too dusty. Give witness t' how lil it bin used," she shook her head, this time tsk, tsking the shame of its neglect.

"What does it do, or what's in it?"

Iona's voice was hushed, "Dese be yours soon. Tahm you seen'em enyways." She lifted the lid, and Soraya looked inside.

Curious, Soraya reached for a fat yellow candle that was sitting atop another, smaller chest. "This feels different than the other candles."

Harlem Angel

Iona's cackle was beginning to grate, "Hee, hee, hee, thas good Chile. Tis different. Made o'pure beeswax. Bes kinda candle, beeswax."

Soraya frowned, "Why is beeswax so special?"

"Beeswax burns clean, Chile. No drippin' & runnin like mos candles, an no smoke. An it don need no perfume in it. Tis nat'rally sweet smellin, like da' honey it used t'hold," she pursed her lips, nodding.

Soraya put the candle on the floor and went back to the box. It looked like there were only two items left in it. The other, chest like, smaller box. It was cold, dark and smooth to the touch. "What's this made of Iona? It looks a little like lead, but it's awfully dark and much lighter than lead would be." Soraya had worked with lead in a jewelry class she took in college, but this was different. It weighed at least half of what even a thinly walled lead box would. She handed it to Iona's outstretched hands.

"'Dis a special box, Soraya."

Soraya listened closely. It wasn't lost on her that Iona called her by her given name rather than the now familiar *Chile*. She only did that when the next words were going to be *very* important.

"'Dis box is pr'tected. Cain't be opened by just ennyone. Mos cain't even see it raght."

Soraya frowned, "What do you mean, most people can't see it?"

Iona sucked her teeth, "You ain't lis'nen, Gurl. Focus on what I'm sayin. 'Dis here box is pr'tected. Dem's dat kin see it know what its fo, or are learnin what it's fo."

"Like me."

"Lahk you, Chile."

Soraya put the small box aside and reached into the larger one again. Her hand touched what she thought was the bottom of the box, at first. It was soft, like felt, but there were folds where her fingers expected to touch the hard bottom of the box. "What's this?" she said lifting a dark colored cloth folded many times. She wasn't sure of its color because it appeared to change from black to dark blue or purple while she was looking at it, and she was also wrong about it being made of felt. "It feels so nice and smooth but it's heavy. I thought it was felt, but I've never seen felt like this!" She was running her hands through the folds imagining what it would feel like against her body. "I would love to have a dress made of this!"

97

Soraya looked up to find Iona staring at her. Any hint of her former rocking or playfulness, was gone.

"Dat be a small piece'o a much larger piece'o heavy silk. Dat silk special. It be older'n me, hee, hee, hee, and dat be pretty old!"

Soraya smiled at Iona's laughter. She began to unfold the piece of silk as she said, "I'm sure there's a story to go with it," her voice trailed off as she spread the piece on the floor. There were patterns woven into and through a twelve pointed star wrought of golden threads. At the tip of each point were symbols. Soraya frowned as she recognized a little similarity of one to the sign on the lintel above the door to the shop, but they were each very different from anything she'd ever seen before.

"Iona…"

"Hush Chile, hush. Nah, lis'en here. Dis silk is from da Mutha Lan' and dem gol' threads too. Each symbol rep'sent da family and da tribe o'each one'o us in da Circle."

She paused in her narrative, and Soraya jumped at the chance to ask, "This piece… each of you have one like it?"

Iona nodded, "Like it, but not like it. Dey is a little differnce in each one."

Soraya looked closely at the patterns in each star point. "They look like they're moving."

"Hee, hee, hee, dey all move in sum' way, but dey's each differnt."

Soraya squinted, trying to make the tiny figures more recognizable. "This one looks like its part of two animals, but I'm not sure which ones."

Iona just sucked her teeth in answer, so Soraya bent to give the patterns more scrutiny. As she watched, mesmerized, the little figures began to move. They each had their own peculiar motions that would execute, end and repeat over and over again. When she finally shook her head and looked up again, Iona was nodding her head.

"Each one is a rep'sentation o'a special trait from da ancestral spirit dat watches o'er da tribe'o each us."

"Like a protective foundation?"

"Yes, Chile, dat's it. Pr'tection and connection. Nah, spread da cloth out and grab dat lil' box agin."

Soraya reached for the little chest and opened it. Inside the six by ten inch box were twelve small trinkets, delicately carved figures that vaguely matched the embroidered patterns on the cloth, with the addition of another tiny picture sketched into the bottom of each one, like a signature stamp. They were each sitting in their own, silk-lined compartment, some shiny, some dull. They were each made of a different substance and were about one inch in height.

Iona smiled, "Dis here rep'sent each us."

"What are they made of?"

"Dey each made'o sum'in differnt. Take dat one..." she pointed to a shiny gold figure. "Dis here rep'sent me; tis made'o gold cause my people were miners-had da stuff all over da place. Dat white one dere made'o ivory and dat other little less white, be made'o bone."

"So each one has a direct connection to each of your homes."

"Das right, Chile. Nah, place each figure below da symbol dat matches."

"What about the designs sketched into the bottom?"

"Hee, hee, hee, nah dat is the sign fo each'o da shops!"

Soraya turned the little gold figure over and saw that the sketch looked like a hut or little house. "The *Home Shop*, I get it!"

Soraya delicately placed each tiny work of art below its embroidered picture. Then she looked into the chest again.

"Dey is a small pocket in the lid. You'll fin'a small key in it. Da key fit into dat hole in'a bottom."

Soraya peered into the chest, found the key then felt around in the bottom for the hole. She put the key in the hole and turned it. There was an audible click and a small panel popped out of the bottom of the box. She opened the little door and warily reached inside until her fingers touched something smooth and round. There was barely enough room for her to get two fingers into the little compartment, but she managed to grab whatever it was and pulled it into the light. With her eyes trying to pop their sockets, she looked at Iona for explanation. Iona's face was serious, her eyes intent on Soraya's face.

"Dat be da key. 'Tis round cause round is continuous, don have no beginnin', don have no end."

"Like a Circle," Soraya nodded.

"Nah, you watch close, Chile. I be da sender dis tahm, but den it be up to you!"

Soraya handed the disc, which was the size of her palm and was made of what looked like flawless crystal, or maybe glass, to Iona. It was smooth, no facets, and cool to the touch. Could have been a diamond, but she didn't think so. She felt it would more likely be made of some type of crystal, maybe quartz. "What's it made of?"

"Why, dis be a diamon, Chile. Pure, from da earth, caint be broke. Tis'da focus fo da Power we gon use to make dis call!"

"Oh! I thought it was a quartz crystal."

Iona smiled, "Chile, wha'chu think a diamon be but a crystal?

Soraya shook her head at her stupidity; of course a diamond was a crystal! She had more questions, and was actually shocked that it actually was a diamond. She'd *never* seen one that size. But she decided that her questions could wait until after they made the call. She watched as Iona gingerly placed the disc upon a tiny tripod she'd put at the center of the star.

"So, how do we start?"

Iona slipped out of the chair to the floor like oil being poured, to sit across from Soraya. "Wit yo'hep, we kin make dis call. Two us be dead. You bein here will hep make da Circle kinnect."

"But, I only make it eleven. That still leaves a hole."

"Yes, Chile, but you is young n'strong and you learnin' fast. You push hard wit'us hep'in and we'll pull least one'o dem 'prentices, if not both."

Soraya shook her head, "I hope you're right."

Iona reached forward and grabbed Soraya's hands, "*You* is all we got, Chile! I mus be raght!" She squeezed before she let go, and Soraya was reminded of how strong the old woman really was, despite how frail she looked.

Soraya found a small box of matches and started to light the candle which she had placed off to the side of the cloth.

Iona shoo her head. "Place d'candle in'a center. Nah, light d'candle how we bin practicin as we b'gin."

Soraya blinked, dropped the matches and concentrated on the flame that would light the candle.

Once the flame popped into being and the candle wick began to fizzle, Iona said, "Peat afta me nah Chile: "*We reach across through time and space to make the circle that links our race. We serve to answer, we serve to keep, the souls of black folk, the Shepherd's sheep. I call the Circle, I forge the link, from heart to heart and mind to mind, I call the Circle, we all must meet.'"*

Soraya's voice seemed to echo as the last words in the summoning verse left her lips. The room felt cold and still. Then she felt a gradual warming roll over her like a warm ocean wave. She closed her eyes and time and space snapped around her. She saw the candle flame burning at the center of the pattern. Iona was there, sitting behind and to the right of her so that their symbol, the one for the *Home* shop, was between them. She could feel the magic of the place in her vision, and as she looked to each of the symbols, another person would materialize – except for two. She wanted to turn and ask Iona if they could hold the Circle with two points missing.

As if in answer to her unspoken question and speaking aloud, Iona's voice filled the air, "Dey spirits not quite gone yet, but soon. We's gon call dey prentices t'night too."

Once the places were filled, Soraya gave her full attention to The Circle. Iona spoke so they could all hear her.

"Hello, my bretheren. S'been much too long since we've spoken and nah we's in danger. You see two us missin. Dis why we call. An dis here is Soraya, my prentice. It'b her wish't 'dress you." Iona signaled her quietly and Soraya took up the narrative.

"Hello. This is all new to me but it was important we speak tonight. Zacharias and Willamae are dead. The Circle is being targeted. You must all call your apprentices – tonight is not too soon. Be wary. Keep your Wards up. The enemy is unknown, but won't stay that way if we are diligent in our watch." She finished almost panting.

Iona spoke again, "We mus' end dis call wit a secon one to reach Zacharias and Willamae's 'prentices. If we kin git'em tonight, it will hep keep us connected. Soraya be watchin, but she cain't work jus yet. She only come t'me since two days hence, but she doin' well and learnin fas."

Soraya bowed her head in deference to Iona who continued, *"We is da Circle dat binds our race. We call all prentices from dis, our space. A special call, for Zacharias and Willamae, hold to the Circle til yo prentices in place."*

Then, in total unison, eleven voices said, *"We serve to answer, we serve to keep, the souls of black folk, The Sheherd's sheep."*

Slowly, each of the other members nodded their heads and dissolved out of being, leaving Soraya and Iona alone again. Soraya opened her eyes to meet Iona's heavy gaze.

"Chile, I hope das nough," Iona shook her head as she spoke.

"Iona, it has to be enough. It's all we've got." Soraya put the candle out, and Iona helped her pack the silk and other items back into the chest.

"Chile, you keep it in yo room. They's things of magic and need t'be roun yo aura."

Soraya stood, picked up the chest and yawned largely. "I think I'll skip any dinner tonight. I'm beat!"

Iona laughed "Hee, hee, hee, Chile you is sump'in else! I'll fix you a lil snack. Cain't recharge wit no fuel!"

She knew there was no arguing with her from the look on her face. Soraya carried the chest to her room trying to figure out exactly where she was going to squeeze it in. She entered her room and turned the light on. Surprised, she quickly shoved the chest into the corner behind the wash table. "I don't remember that corner being bare this morning." She said as she splashed some water into the bowl from the pitcher that seemed always full. After washing up and dressing for bed, she shuffled into the kitchen where Iona was coaxing some mouth-watering smells from a skillet on the stove.

"I thought you were making a snack!" she said through another yawn.

"Tis'a snack Chile. Won't set heavy and will still nourish da body." Iona answered as she filled a plate.

Soraya took the plate and sat at the table. She didn't even recognize what it was and was too tired to ask. Instead, she just started shoveling. "It's very good," she mumbled through a mouthful.

"Jus a lil fish-n-rice, da hominy is fo flavor. Don need nuthin heavy when you gon sleep on it," she smiled.

Soraya finished her plate with another yawn and asked a question. "Iona, why were there no questions?"

"Hrumph… what dey gon say, Chile? We was callin dem, don nun'us call if'n it ain't po'ent." Iona started eating and didn't look up from her plate until it was empty. "What, Chile? You got a'nutha question hangin, I kin tell," she handed her plate to Soraya, and Soraya took both plates to the sink to wash them.

"How can we just expect the apprentices to just show up?"

Iona cackled, "We call'd em, Chile! Creates a pull. Dey'll wander by da empty shops, and da door'll open fo'em."

Soraya turned from the sink to stare, "You mean they'll just come?!? I wouldn't just walk into an empty shop-especially one with yellow police tape on the door and blood on the floor!"

"Blood be gon by da tahm dey gits dere. Police tape don stop nobody," Iona said with a sniff.

Soraya's next question was interrupted by a yawn.

"Tahm you git't bed, Chile. Tmorrow's anutha day, an we still gotta git through da naht!"

Soraya finished washing the dishes and headed for bed, "Night, Iona," she kissed the old woman and gave her a hug.

Iona whispered, "Jus call if ya need me, Chile."

Soraya nodded and went to bed. She was exhausted and hoped her dreams would be quiet.

Of course, they weren't. Quiet, that is. Her eyes had barely closed when she was plunged into chaos. Confused by all the noise, it took her a few minutes to get her bearings. Once the fog of confusion cleared, she knew immediately where she was. It was Zacharias' shop. Almost as she'd last seen it the night he died. She was standing in the doorway again in almost the same place she'd stood that night. She reached up and touched the bell and jumped when it tinkled to her touch. Staring at her hands, she took a step forward and touched the desk. Instead of passing through it, her hand felt hard, well-oiled wood. It was cool and smooth under her fingertips. Suddenly realizing where she was standing, Soraya looked down expecting blood but saw only dry wooden slats. "Amazing. That old woman is always right," she whispered.

She heard something fall down the hallway and froze. Trying not to panic, she moved quickly behind the counter and ducked out of sight. The floor slats creaked slightly, and she knew that whoever was there was walking up the hallway toward her. Soraya never wanted to be invisible as badly as right then. The footsteps stopped just inside the room. She rose up just enough to see over the counter and had to cover her mouth with her hand. Standing in the doorway was a young man. Mid-to late twenties, blond curly hair spiked straight on top. As he stood there, his silhouette facing her, she realized he was as ethereal as she was. *"Who is he? Why is he here! What is he looking for?"* And then she felt a strong tug pulling her West, away from Chicago.

In the blink of an eye, she was now in another shop. She felt a breeze and saw palm trees ruffle through the window. "We're not in Kansas anymore," she said under her breath. She heard a heavy grunt and fear raced down her back. Tip-toeing through the room, she started down the hallway. Then she could hear the dull thud of something heavy hitting a body, the sound of which she was by now far too familiar with, and she knew she was too late again. When she stepped into the kitchen, two men looked up from a bloody, indiscernible heap on the floor.

"Who the fuck are you!" one man said to her.

"Hey man, we'd better blow this place!" the other stated.

"She seen us!" the first one said, both of them speaking as if she wasn't there, when they could both obviously see her.

"We's ain't gittin paid fer two bodies," the second man said.

Realizing they were too confused to think straight, Soraya picked up the first thing she could get her hands on and threw it at them. The sound of the vase breaking was louder than she expected, and the two men jumped up and ran out the back door of the shop. Soraya's eyes watered real tears. She could feel them now, even here. Distraught at yet another failure, she opened her mouth and shivered at the ghostly wail that came out. Abruptly, she was pulled back into the real world by Iona's strong hands on her shaking her by the shoulders. Soraya woke with tears streaming down her face, and for a brief moment she didn't know why she was crying. The memory of her vision, or visitation, came rushing back to her conscious thought making the tears flow faster. But this time, while still emotionally upset, she was also pissed.

"Soraya calm down. Don't do this t'yo sef! You cain't spect to know what to do raght nah. You is jus startin, Chile!"

"Iona, you don't understand. There was another one! I think it was in Los Angeles or Miami. There were palm trees outside the shop!"

The old woman held her tight as ragged sobs escaped uncontrollably from Soraya's lips. "It makes me feel so helpless! Watching as these old people, *OUR* people, are... sliced and mashed like, like potatoes! Iona, this has to stop! There has to be something we can do to strengthen the wards around The Circle!"

HARLEM ANGEL

"S'all right, Chile, s'all right! Today we make a plan. You gon learn t'git roun on the plain. Dey won't git the next one us so easy. You'll see."

Soraya tried hard to stop crying. She took a deep breath, mulling over Iona's words and gently pushed away from Iona, "You know, it was different this time. I wasn't just a... a ghost... You... you can teach me to do that? To be *real* when I'm there?" she stammered.

"Iona brushed soggy curls from across Soraya's forehead. "Teach you t'do what, Chile?"

"You said I was going to learn to get around on the plain. You mean where I am when I see these things, right?"

Iona smiled and nodded, "You heard right, Chile. You gonna learn dat t'day an lots more if'n I has enythin t'do wit it! We's stronger t'day den we was b'fo you come t'me."

Soraya stood and began pacing the tiny room, "There was something different this time. Before I was pulled to the shop in LA, or Miami, I was back in Zacharias' shop, and there was someone else there."

Iona rose and grabbed Soraya by the hands, "What'chu mean, Chile? Who else was dere?"

Taking a slow deep breath, Soraya made a great effort to calm down so she could remember the details. "I felt him first, I knew someone else was in the shop. When I heard his..."

Iona interrupted, "Why you say *he,* Chile?" and she drew her back to the bed to sit down.

"It felt like a male. I'm not exactly sure why, but I knew it was a man."

"Go head."

"I heard his footsteps, in the kitchen maybe, and when I touched the bell over the door, my hand didn't pass through it this time. It tinkled, so he knew I was there."

"Did he see you? Did you git a good look at'im?"

"No, he didn't see me, and I only saw him by his profile. I was so afraid of being seen that I hid behind the counter; and just before I was pulled again, I saw him in profile. Then I was in the *Faith* shop... is that one in Miami or L.A.?"

"Dat's L.A., Chile, Walterine's shop. But go on..."

"Iona, if I hadn't made that first stop in Chicago, Walterine would still be alive!"

Iona patted Soraya's hands, "S'all right, Chile. One thing you'll learn is err'thing happin's fo'a reason. Dis man mus'b portent. We's got't think bout dis here." She pressed her lips together in thought.

Soraya straightened, "Could he have been Zacharias' apprentice?"

Iona sucked her teeth, "Hmmm, don think so, Chile. Dat'b awful fast work fo a callin't yield fruit already."

"Then who could he be?" Soraya stood and started pacing again, "Oh, there's something I forgot! He was on the plain with me."

"What'chu sayin, Chile?"

"He was ethereal, like me. He wasn't really *there*."

Iona sat straight up, "Dunno bout dis, Chile. We's got t'think bout dis…" her voice trailed off into a big yawn.

Soraya responded by giving the old woman a hug, "Well, there's nothing more we can do right now. How about we tackle this first thing in the morning, OK?"

"Yes Chile, das a good idea. We's both in need o'some sleep. An maybe dis tahm dere won't be no dreams." Iona stood and shuffled out of the room mumbling, "Poor Walterine. Hope she call her prentice. Poor Walterine…"

Soraya put out the candle that Iona lit when she came in, and then she crawled back under the blankets and just lay there. She was still a little wired and let her mind wander back over the scene comparing it to the first two murder scenes. *"If I can sift through my emotions and examine the detail, I might discover something I missed…"*

Using some of the exercises Iona taught her, she re-created Zacharias' shop in her mind. She tried to look at what happened from a third-party perspective. When she fell asleep this time, it was a deep sleep. She dreamt she was in Zacharias' shop again, but unlike her cognitive dreams, she knew that she had created this one; the edges were sharper. She knew that this time she wasn't *in* the shop but was in a *picture* of the shop. It gave her just the advantage she needed to do some detective work. By the time the suns rays peeked through the New York skyline, she had learned a great deal.

EIGHT

Madeline sat slowly sipping her morning tea. She was trying to plan for contingencies. *This man will be dangerous for someone. I need to make sure that none of my coven ends up as one of his targets.* She had gone to sleep thinking about this and woke up with it still spinning through her thoughts. *His dreams will be important. I must get him to reveal his dreams…*

Shawn descended from his penthouse at eleven am sharp and found Ray sitting at his desk as if waiting for him. "Good morning Ray. Sorry I'm late!"

"No problem, Boss."

Shawn winced. He hated when Ray called him that more than he hated his customary *Sir*, but he skipped his usual litany. "How many appointments had to be moved?"

"Just two, Sir: Dr. Boucher and his team will see you at eleven-thirty, and the gentleman from the Tribune is now scheduled for twelve-thirty."

"Boucher. What does he want this time? The man whines more than a just whelped puppy," Shawn growled.

"I believe the FDA has given approval to the Bifadene. He wants to know how to proceed with production."

Shawn stopped in front of Ray's desk turning slowly to face him. Breathlessly he asked, "They've approved it? So fast?"

"Yes, Sir. Dr. Boucher will fill you in."

Shawn laughed aloud, "Amazing! Just when I think that only greedy idiots work there." He shook his head and laughed louder. "So, nothing until 11:30 eleven-thirty?"

"Those two and you have an appointment at three."

"Ahhhh, yes. That would be a private appointment." Shawn sighed and walked past Ray into his office with a smile on his face.

"Ray…" the man was in his shadow quickly. He liked that about Ray. "Sir?"

"Ray, tell me about mission three. Was it successful last night?"

"Yes Sir, the mission was completed. But… we had a witness."

"A *WITNESS*?!" Shawn spun around to face Ray.

"Yes, Sir."

"And how is that possible, Ray? The shops are always empty at that hour."

"Sir, they said no one came through the doors, Sir. Whoever she was, they don't know where she came from."

"She? They actually saw this person?"

"They saw a woman who moved like she was a ghost."

Shawn was silent. He turned and walked to his desk and sat down, gaze intent on nothing. He was remembering his dream, or what he thought was a dream. He remembered a claustrophobic little shop where he'd felt as if someone was watching when there was no one there. He was remembering what he thought was a woman's fleeting figure fade away in the blink of an eye from behind the dusty counter. He sighed, "But the mission successful?"

"Yes Sir. The target was dispensed."

"Good. Three down, nine to go."

Shawn noted Ray's visible response. The man actually seemed to fear his reaction to bad news. It was an effort not to laugh in his face for such a ridiculous fear. After all, why would he blame Ray for the problem? It wasn't as if the man had been present and able to affect the outcome! He shook his head in bewilderment. For as long as Ray had been working for him, he still failed to understand what exactly motivated him to continue to keep him in his employ. Not that he thought he could ever replace his loyalty. He just didn't see what Ray got out of the whole deal, other than a generous salary. He shrugged off the questions and focused on his day's calendar.

"Ray, when will the Miami team be ready?"

Ray answered matter-of-factly, "The team will be set in a day or so. Intelligence has this one as a bit more of a challenge."

"Oh?" Shawn said, eyebrows rising in question, "More of a challenge than L.A. was?"

"It's the location of the shop, Sir. Unlike the other three, this one is located in the center of a bustling community with lots of night life."

Dismissing Ray's reason for caution he said, "Well, I know you'll handle it, Ray, like you always do. Just let me know when we're set, and tell our guests in the basement that they can rest for a couple of days."

"Yes sir," Ray left the room, Shawn barely acknowledging his leaving. His mind was preoccupied with what Ray said. He knew Ray would figure it out but it still disturbed him that he was worried about it. So the Miami target wouldn't be as easy as the first three. Shawn was still surprised that Miami would be more difficult than L.A. had been. Even with the Ghost Lady there, they still got the job done. Even Washington D.C. wasn't difficult; and considering the President himself is Black, he reasoned, it shouldn't have been so easy, but it was.

Shawn knew that the Miami neighborhood where the shop was located was in a racially mixed area with Blacks, Mexicans, and Haitians liberally spread throughout. The Black population was the minority here; and unlike the other three neighborhoods, the assassin team would need to be different. There was also another issue to consider; the mix of volatile magic and what it might cause.

The effort that White Oak Coven was going to make to isolate, contain and nullify the Earth magic that the old shopkeeper used was going to be difficult because of the Voodoo and other powers that would surely be around and near this shop in particular. Shawn smiled as he thought about watching the coven work the weave in order to handle the issues. He was eager to see what extra precautions White Oak would have to make in order to control the power flows as well as they had in Chicago, D.C. and LA.

Shawn sat behind his desk and glanced at the stack of paper he'd created earlier and sighed. He wasn't ready to dive into it yet. He needed to think. Spinning the chair around, he looked out over the city, his city. "At my grasp you are Chicago, at my grasp. My city. Everything is falling into place as if I were GOD and ordered it so!"

Anyone seeing his face would swear he just had an orgasm and was now basking in the afterglow. "My kingdom doth bear fruit!" he shouted to no one. "Bifadene will hit the market and launch the ship. Melacrit will fuel it into every harbor from the depths of the vessel. The world won't know what hit it until it's too late!" he gloated. Laughing, he spun back around to his desk and grabbed the first printout from the top of the stack; '*Voodoo: A Historic Journey*' was the title of the first one. Shawn began to read, voraciously devouring every word, every explanation, every idea that anyone had regarding magic, power and witchcraft.

"They are all related, merely a difference in application and belief. I wonder what White Oak Coven preaches," he said aloud. So engrossed in is reading, Shawn jumped when Ray's voice came through the intercom.

"Sir, your first meeting group will arrive in five."

"Thank you, Ray," he clicked the computer comatose and stacked the papers he'd read neatly on the edge of his desk on the right; the unfinished pile in the center. Shawn poured himself a glass of water, swallowing half the glass as he punched the intercom button. "I'll see Boucher now."

Ray stuck his head through the doorway, motioning toward the door to the conference room. "Sir, the doctors are here to see you. I've escorted them into the conference room."

"Thank you, Ray."

Shawn stood and walked to the conference room door. *So, Dr. Boucher brought his team. Such enthusiasm is impressive.* He scanned the conference room where three men in lab coats waited at the large walnut table that took up most of the space in the room. These were the men in charge of the gene experimentation project and the latest reports held the promise of Shawn's procreation. He had vowed to never have children unless there was some viable way of assuring that they would be born white and with no visible trace of the Black blood that tainted his own veins. He wanted his progeny to have no chance of the taint arising to nastily surprise them later either, like other white people with questionable heritage had suffered through the last two centuries.

Shawn walked to the head of the table and sat down, giving the men a chance to settle down and relax before he started drilling them with questions. Ray handed him a packet of documents and then sat off to the side of the conference table with a laptop to record the meeting notes.

"Good morning, Gentlemen. I am truly excited by the progress we are making on our genome project. I want to assure you that while some of our research may be considered controversial, once we reveal it to the world at-large, people will flock to support us."

The three researchers were all nodding when he finished. Just the response he was looking for. "Mr. Boucher, your report please?"

The short, bespectacled dark-haired man in a white lab coat nervously cleared his throat as he stood to speak. "Mr. Kites, the FDA is expected to give their approval for our final Melacrit study by the end of next week, before they break for the holidays."

Shawn was taken by surprise. Ray said it was the Bifadene that had met with FDA approval. He hadn't expected the Melacrit to begin moving through the approval process so soon! "They're approving the Melacrit study? Your last report indicated some delay with the initial test results. What changed since your last report?"

Dr. Boucher cleared his throat again nervously, "Well, Mr. Kites, it appears that while the proposed test population is a very narrow group, the FDA now understands the necessity of this choice. Also, our control group was also defined necessarily small. These are the reasons that study approval was taking longer than we anticipated. But, they've approved it, and we will be able to begin the final human trials right after the New Year."

Shawn was jotting down his own notes in the margins of the report document when Boucher finished. He looked to the next man, Dr. Pelier, for his report.

"Mr. Kites, the preliminary trial study results are on page four of the document you have in front of you. Of the twenty-five live births, there were no visual signs of Negroid pigmentation."

"And the DNA tests?"

"Sir, the initial blood work is negative for the race tracers. The full DNA results will be available by the end of the month."

"All twenty-five babies are truly white?"

"So far, Mr. Kites. The gene isolation appears to be complete. There is no sign of it in their blood, and their gene sequencing is expected to follow suit."

Shawn stared at the man, silently praying that their enthusiasm was not ill formed or premature. "But will it carry forth? Can you assure me that it won't recur in later generations?"

"Sir, I believe we can confidently report that none of these children will have dark skinned offspring themselves. There is no reason to assume that the eradication is not permanent."

"Excellent! What about side effects? Anything of consequence, Mr. Rogette?"

The third scientist looked at Shawn through large, wire- rimmed glasses and coughed, "Mr. Kites, the side effects appear to be minimal. We had twelve young women disqualified because the fathers of their babies were of color. Their initial chromosome mapping showed the gene in latency rather than non-existent. We felt that the Melacrit dosage we are administering is as high as we dared but not high enough to battle the influence of the gene from both parents."

"The other fathers were pure of race?" Shawn asked.

"Most certainly, Mr. Kites. They passed the preliminary chromosome tests, and the follow-up DNA tests were also negative."

"Alright. I am pleased with our progress! Would you elaborate on the side-effects, please?"

Dr. Boucher answered, "Unfortunately, the side-effects are the reason we feel we've taken the dosage as high as we dared. They range from mild stomach discomfort and headache to violent seizures and skin burning and peeling once it begins to leave the system through their pores."

Shawn's eyes narrowed, and he knew he was clenching his jaw, but he couldn't control the urge that made him want to hit something any other way.

The man hastily continued, avoiding Shawn's gaze. "These more aggressive effects only occurred when the dosage of the drug exceeded 180 mg twice a day. We have determined that the threshold dose is 40mg twice a day with the maximum of 120mg twice a day only being necessary in the more severe cases."

Shawn drew a deep breath and exhaled slowly, "Tell me, what exactly constitutes a *severe case?*"

Dr. Pelier and Dr. Boucher both looked at Dr. Rogette, "A woman who *IS* Black but has some White ancestry is a severe case, sir. The drug must overcome the dominant pigmentation gene rather than the recessive gene, as when the mother is White with Black ancestry."

The room was silent for a few minutes while Shawn mulled this over.

The men were beginning to fidget when he finally decided to speak. "These results, in essence, mean that we have the possibility of eradicating the *Black* race completely, given enough passage of time."

The men looked at each other, eyes wide in the realization of just how their research could be used as the ultimate, genocidal weapon. Dr. Rogette answered, "Yes sir, Mr. Kites, given enough passage of time."

Shawn put his pen down and faced the three men changing the subject. "I am pleased with this report, gentlemen. However, I understood that we were to discuss the Bifadene today. What is our progress on this drug?"

Dr. Boucher replied, "Oh, sir, the Bifadene was approved by the FDA. We will have the paperwork on the licenses and patents by next week!"

"Good work, gentlemen! A doubly positive report from you today! Please prepare the documentation on the Melacrit parameters and requirements for the final human trial study for my review, along with the proposed timeline and your plans for identification of the pool of volunteers. Also, get me the distribution schedule and the appropriate expected drop-ship dates for the doctor samples and the drug suppliers samples for the Bifadene on my desk by Friday please."

Ray closed the laptop and rose from his seat in the corner. "Gentlemen, I believe we are at the conclusion of this meeting."

All three of the doctors murmured their agreement and began to gather up their papers. Ray escorted them from the room and shut the door behind them.

Shawn sat alone listening to the echo of his excitement as it reverberated in his head.

Ray slipped back into the conference room and Shawn watched him hesitate before he walked to the corner to retrieve the laptop. He said, "Ray, do we believe everything they said?"

Ray stopped dead in his tracks and slowly turned to face him. "I believe they were sincere, Sir."

"No, no, no, Raymond! That's not what I'm asking!" He frowned. "Why do I not hear any fire in their voices, Ray? With all this positive, where was their passion?"

He studied Ray through narrowed eyes as the man struggled to come up with an answer. Then, a shadow fell over his face as he said "Perhaps they fear you, sir."

Shawn didn't say anything, at first. He wasn't... angry, just perturbed. Ray didn't get it. "Ray, fear is a strong catalyst. If these scientists fear me enough to produce the results I want, then fear me they must."

Ray sat heavily in a chair as Shawn continued.

"You must grasp the vision, Raymond. See through their fear to their diligence. They do their best work so that they can one day go home and never return to grace the halls of DNAgen Biolabs ever again!"

Ray shrugged, "So, fear works."

"Fear, my dear Ray, is the tree that bears the fruit we eat!" He banged his fist on the table as he spoke.

"These scientists can't wait to finish their work here and get on to their next discovery. If we motivate them to reach that goal by scaring the shit out of them, then we both win!"

"We get what we want..." Ray spoke in a whisper.

"Melacrit!!!" Shawn shouted, his face red and his voice full of vehemence.

"So, we get Melacrit, and they get... what?" Confusion clouded his features.

This upset Shawn. "Ray! They get *PAID*! They get recognition! They get the undying gratitude of *EVERY* White man in the world who wants to guarantee that *OUR* race remains *THE* dominant race of mankind!"

Shawn was standing now, arms spread wide to encompass the world in his idyllic vision.

Ray looked at his hands and said, "What if *THEY* don't share your vision, Shawn? What would you say to them to calm their fears that Melacrit will be used as a genocidal weapon?"

"Melacrit as a weapon?" Shawn asked innocently. "What would make them jump to that conclusion, a weapon?"

"Sir, may I speak freely?

Shawn nodded and sat back down heavily.

"Your scientists have been talking, and I've even heard rumblings in the data pool and operations about what your plans for Melacrit could be. The employees of color in the plant even consider the choices for your test and control group subjects suspect. Your prejudice is *VERY* well known, sir."

Shawn replied wryly, "If the N... Blacks and Mexicans who work for me don't like my politics, let'em go work somewhere else! They're lucky that there are laws that require me to hire them or they would have no jobs here!" he spat.

His voice rasped as his anger grew. "Ray, whether or not my employees *like* me is of no consequence whatsoever. Melacrit will be manufactured. In fact, before those scientists are released, I also intend for them to develop a second formula that can safely be taken by men to suppress the passing of the gene through sperm. That way there won't be a need to increase the dosage for women beyond the established safe levels. Then we can fight the spread of color on two fronts!"

Ray shifted in his seat. "Sir…" he cleared his throat and started again. "Sir, your employees don't complain. DNAgen Biolabs is by far one of the *BEST* employers in the State of Illinois. But, they know what your pet project is, and they know the potential of Melacrit."

"And…?"

"And it is a hot topic of conversation."

Shawn stood and paced. "Hmmmmm. A hot topic of conversation?"

Ray stood and grabbed the laptop. "Yes sir. There is speculation on exactly what your plans are for the drug."

"And just where does their speculation lead?"

"To the obvious reduction in the birth of children of color. And a few more imaginative people wonder that some of the other projects they're working on don't get your attention like Melacrit does."

"The other projects are not as important to me, or The White Wing, who is funding the Melacrit project."

"Yes, but your plans to distribute Melacrit for free, while the other drugs under project all have a distribution charge attached to them, lend to the debate."

Shawn stopped pacing and looked at Ray. "Your points are noted, Ray. I will consider what you have brought to my attention."

Ray nodded and left the room. Shawn let him leave without another word and continued to pace around the table mumbling to himself. *So… the worker bees are curious about my plans.* "What would they do if they knew?" The more he thought about what Ray said, the more his anger threatened to boil over. "How dare *they* pass judgment on my work? I hadn't thought of using Melacrit as an actual weapon. What a delightful idea! Certainly not my intention, but Melacrit as a weapon has a potential for my constituents that I'll need to explore."

Shawn rounded the end of the table again and stopped in front of the door. Shaking his head vigorously, he straightened his shoulder and left the room, his thoughts racing. *Whatever they think is of no consequence. They can't stop our progress, and they will have no bearing on production or distribution. Their speculation is a problem for another day.*

He took a deep breath, and deliberately placing one foot in front of the other, Shawn calmly walked down the hallway to his office, nodding to Vicki, the young woman in charge of the data pool as he passed her. Once in his office, he called Ray on the intercom. "Ray, would you please bring the notes from this mornings' meeting as soon as the pool has them ready?"

"Yes, sir."

NINE

By the time Ray showed up with the notes from the meeting, Shawn was much calmer and chided himself for letting Ray's information on employee gossip get to him. He spent the balance of the afternoon reviewing the manufacturing timetable and reaffirming his own self-worth by his company's progress.

"Come in, Ray. I've been doing some brainstorming. Hear me out." He waited until Ray was seated and looked comfortable.

"We know that genetic manipulation is just this side of illegal; but while others are so pre-occupied with the elaborate intricacies of cloning, *we* are concentrating on changing the obvious." He watched Ray closely to gauge his reaction.

"The fact is that gene manipulation has grown exponentially in the world of agriculture, and human manipulation is only a breath away. The possibilities of Melacrit need to be masked behind the other, more socially acceptable genetic achievements of DNAgen, like the discovery of the genetic anomaly that causes Spina Bifida. The Bifadene, our subsequent treatment drug, has completed the drug trials, right?"

"Yes, and the FDA has just approved it."

"Yes! That's what I mean, Ray. We should step up the distribution timeline and get the marketing engine underway so we can divert some of the heat from Melacrit." Shawn sat smugly behind his desk with his arms folded. He was proud of his mental reconciliation of Melacrit's positive aspects and eager to hear his assistant's response.

"So, what do you think?" He watched Ray closely, waiting for his answer.

"Well, Sir, you have given this problem another angle of attack. If we can get Bifadene to market before Melacrit has actually completed the final drug trials, it should do just what you want."

"Thank you for your insightful information gathering, Ray. I don't know what I'd do without your down-to-earth viewpoint. You keep me from forgetting about the *little people*," he smiled.

"Your welcome, sir." Ray said as he handed Shawn the report.

Ray left Shawn's office, and knowing he had a few minutes before his next appointment would arrive, Shawn took the opportunity to stretch and rub his eyes before he sat behind his desk again. "This is going to be a very long day!" he said smiling to himself. The intercom chimed. "Yes?"

"Sir, the reporter from the Tribune is here."

"Send him in, Ray."

The door opened and Ray ushered a tall, young black man with a press pass ID prominently secured to his jacket lapel, into the room.

"Thank you, Ray. Mr...?" Shawn said as he stood and extended his hand in greeting.

"Jenkins. DeShaun Jenkins, nice to meet you, Mr. Kites!" DeShaun said with a wide smile.

They shook hands smoothly, "Please call me DeShaun."

"DeShaun, please have a seat," Shawn said as he gestured to one of the chairs in front of his desk and sat down himself. DeShaun extended his business card as he sat in the chair. Shawn took the card, glancing at it briefly before laying it aside on the desk pad.

"What can I do for you, Mr... DeShaun?"

"Sir, it has come to our attention that your company is on the verge of a great announcement. We at the Chicago Tribune want to be the ones to help you get there."

"And why should I partner with the Tribune for my announcement rather than any other media outlet?" Shawn wasn't going to make it easy for him.

"The Tribune can offer a vast spectrum of media opportunity! The possibilities include the all social media, television, podcasts, and, of course, the paper. But we also have the international conduits through our partnerships that can provide DNAgen Biolabs with the most diverse and cost-effective advertising associations your dollars can buy on both foreign and domestic fronts!"

Shawn was amused. The man was almost panting, and out of breath trying to get his whole pitch into just as few sentences as possible. Swallowing the laugh that was trying to escape his lips, he said, "Ahhh, yes. But the points you make can be supported by the other news agencies in the city as well as the Tribune. How is the Tribune any different than USA Today, the Herald or the Sun?"

The young man appeared to falter in his pitch. Shawn steepled his fingers and leveled his gaze at DeShaun.

"Mr. Kites," he cleared his throat, trying to shake his nervousness. "Mr. Kites, I cannot speak to what the other news agencies in our fair city can offer you, but I *know* what the Chicago Tribune can do for you."

Impressed with DeShaun's candid truth about what he knows, he gained a small measure of respect in Shawn's eyes. However, Shawn could not forgive the man's color. "DeShaun, while I have not made any determination as to who will cover the story of our successes here at DNAgen, the Tribune will be a possible vehicle. However, I am not ready to commit to an exclusive with any one group."

DeShaun's face fell visibly. "Sir, may I at least get a commitment from you to call us first? This way we can offer you our best and you can use it as a measure of what the others will offer."

Shawn was quiet for a moment. He suddenly realized that he could not hold the race of the man sent by the Tribune against them. It was likely that in today's world of Black Presidents and such, every one of the media outlets would be crawling with them. He gave in, a little. "Alright, DeShaun, I will give the Tribune the first crack at filling our needs when the time comes."

DeShaun's face immediately brightened, and he smiled widely, showing perfectly whitened teeth behind his thick Negroid lips. He stood, extending his hand. "Thank you, Sir. Thank you! I have every confidence that The Chicago Tribune will be able to meet or exceed all of DNAgen's needs for getting the word out!"

Shawn walked the man to the door, letting him pump his arm once again before finally closing the door behind him. "Geez! I don't know if that was more painful because he's a reporter or because he's black!" he grumbled and shook his head as he walked back to his desk and sat down grabbing the hand sanitizer. "Why must I always cater to the sensitivities of others? What about *MY* sensitivities!" he said aloud as there was a knock and the door to his office opened again.

"Because you are a shrewd enough businessman to know that those sensitivities represent your market for our products," Ray answered.

"Yes, of course you're right, Ray. Thank you for that timely reminder," he sneered.

"Your welcome, Sir."

"Ray, tell me, what is your opinion of the people we have working in the basement?"

Ray seemed to hesitate before answering, "They're creepy! I know that isn't a very definitive answer, but it's what I feel, Shawn."

Taking note of Ray's use of his name, Shawn continued his query. "Creepy. Well, that is an expression of how they make you feel, but what of the people themselves?"

The man's face wrinkled up in a frown of frustration. "They seem competent in what they do, and what they do appears to help us get the job done. But I don't like them or their presence here."

"Hmmmmm. So, what is your feeling or opinion about their craft and what they're doing to further our efforts to reduce the.... competition?"

Silence met the question as Ray appeared to struggle with his answer. "If your asking whether I think whatever they're doing is necessary, I would have to say no, Sir."

"No?"

Ray quickly crossed the span of the room to come before Shawn's desk, "Sir, what we're doing..." and here he lowered his voice to a whisper, "What we're doing is murdering a bunch of old nig... black people who don't appear to have the strength, let alone the resources, to fight back! I don't understand why we need them dead or the witches to kill'em."

Shawn spun the chair around to face the window so that Ray wouldn't see the anger his response produced. How could he be so shortsighted after everything they'd witnessed, "Ray, do you remember when we participated in the Resurgence and helped burn all those black churches in the '90's?" He spun back around to face Ray.

Ray stammered, "Uh, yeah, I remember..."

"The goals of The White Wing were simple then: *Disrupt their foundations, cause despair, turn their focus toward preservation rather than progress."*

"Well, yeah, I remember..."

"During all that activity, The White Wing discovered a power source."

"Power source?"

"Yes, Ray. The White Wing found that there is a small group of shamanistic..."

"Preachers?"

"Well, that's not quite the word I was looking for, but it'll do. The White Wing found a small group of shamanistic preachers that are providing an extremely strong foundation of ritual, belief and spiritual power that is woven throughout the black race."

"And this, power source..."

"It's what has held all the blacks together over the centuries. And it's what strengthened them after we destroyed the churches!"

"So burning down the churches only pissed'em off."

"Precisely. We thought we were attacking their foundations, when we were merely burning buildings in effigy."

"So, why the witches?"

"The White Wing found that the power source was something intangible. We couldn't burn it because we couldn't see it, touch it."

"Ahhh, I understand. But, how did The White Wing figure out you needed witches?"

"The White Wing didn't figure it out. I did."

The smugness in Shawn's voice startled Ray, "You did, Sir? How did you..."

"How did I get it? Probably has something to do with what happened to me last night. But, suffice it to say that I had a gut feeling that what we were coming up against was much more of a spiritual than solid barrier to our goal."

"Spiritual?"

"Yeah, it was like the enemy was shielded, protected in some way from what we were trying to accomplish."

"And that's why the witches?"

"Yes Ray, that's why the witches. We needed another Power to block theirs."

"So that's what all the chanting and candles are for?"

"They're just part of the ritual. I'm not sure of what they're exact purpose is."

"So, Shawn, what exactly happened to you last night?" Ray was cautious, but eager to hear this answer. It was rare that Shawn was ever so talkative.

Shawn stared blankly, his mind racing. Dare he share the experience of last night with Ray? Ray Crosser, his right-hand man when it came to everything business at DNAgen. And yet he felt hesitation in sharing the experience, where before last night there would have been none.

"Well Ray, I'm not exactly sure what happened. Somehow I was affected by what the coven was doing last night. More than that I really can't explain." He finished, watching Ray closely, hoping that the vague explanation would be enough to satisfy him.

Undeterred, Ray sat in the chair in front of Shawn's desk and asked, "Affected... how?"

Shawn took a deep breath, "Besides knocking me out cold, I don't know what happened," he tried to sound matter-of-fact. He had the distinct feeling that he needed to keep the details to himself, at least for the moment.

They sat in silence for a moment, which was apparently too much for Ray. "Will your three o'clock be here in your office or down in the sub-basement?"

Shawn relaxed. It worked! "You know, I'm not certain but probably downstairs."

"Is there anything you'd like prepared for your meeting?"

"Oh, no, I don't think we'll need anything, but thank you Ray."

"No problem, Si... Shawn." Ray stood, and looking one last time into Shawn's eyes, he turned and left the room.

Shawn watched in silence as Ray left, then pulled the stack of printouts from the corner of his desk and started reading again. "Wicca-The Religious Practice of Witchcraft," he read aloud. "Humph," he snorted, "They have no idea what it is!"

He read until two, making notes in the margins and highlighting things he felt important with an orange marker. Pushing himself away from his desk, he looked at his progress with the stack. *Well, at least I put a dent in it,* he thought stretching. *I wonder if I need to bring anything when I meet with Madeline.* Deciding quickly, he left his office and went back upstairs to his apartment. "I'll grab something to eat, change and then head down to the sub-basement."

After he splashed some water on his face and changed into a new pair of sweats, grabbing something to eat proved to be more of a challenge than anything else after perusing his refrigerator. "Not much here, old chap! Guess we'll have to make a stop at the cafeteria first."

The cafeteria was on the basement level above the sub-basement, where the gym was located. There was a late lunch crowd still milling around when he stepped off the elevator.

A tall man turned towards him as the door closed. "Hello Mr. Kites!"

"Hello… Rogers, isn't it?"

"Yes, Sir!" the man beamed. It was all Shawn could do not to laugh in his face at the obvious impression he'd made by remembering the man's name. "Fruitful day?"

"Oh, yes sir! We've completed the auto-ship program for the Bifadene. We'll be able to fill the orders as they're received!" Rogers smile was contagious in its generosity.

"Excellent, Rogers. Excellent! I couldn't ask for a better team of programmers than you've put together."

"Thank you, sir, Thank you!"

"You have a good evening now." Shawn smiled again as he shook the man's hand.

"Oh, you too, Sir!"

Shawn stood and watched Rogers as he headed to the elevator. *He'll go home tonight in such good spirits that his wife'll be wondering what REALLY happened at work today!* He was just turning back towards the food lines when the sound of Ray's voice behind him made him jump.

"Ray! Didn't know you were back there," he said turning around again.

"Don't worry, Sir. Just covering your back."

"Did I need it with Rogers?" Shawn frowned.

"Probably not, but that's my job."

"How much of the conversation did you hear?" Shawn asked as they walked towards the grill.

"Oh, I got the gist of it."

"Do you really think what I said to him will mean so much?"

"Much and more, Sir. The *CEO* spoke to him, by name, and commended him on how he does his job?! He'll be flyin' for a week... Sir."

"A week?" Shawn was incredulous.

Ray shrugged, "And that's a conservative prediction."

"Conservative huh?"

"Yep. Once his colleagues hear about it, he'll eat lunch for free for another week. After that, while they try to figure out why you spoke to him, he'll be wined and dined so they can try to figure out how they can repeat whatever he did in the hopes of your speaking with them some day."

Shawn shook his head in bewilderment, "People are so strange."

"And that's putting it mildly, Sir."

Shawn stood silently watching the exodus of employees out of the cafeteria for a few minutes, then he glanced at his watch. "Guess I burned up the time to eat something," he sighed.

They walked back to the elevator and stopped in the lobby. Shawn could see Rogers standing outside, surrounded by a group of men listening as he gesticulated with obvious excitement.

Ray had a smile on his face, and Shawn could tell he was pleased with himself. *Just amazing how little it takes to motivate the average employee.* Shaking his head again, he turned towards the elevators with Ray in tow behind him.

"So, you haven't had dinner, Sir?"

"What's that Ray? Oh, dinner? No, haven't eaten all day, and that's where I was headed when Mr. Rogers intercepted me in the cafeteria." He pressed the call button.

"Would you like me to have something sent down?"

"Sure Ray, sure. Your choice; and send enough for Madeline too, just in case she's hungry."

"Right Sir. I'll have something sent down around five?"

"Ok, five will be fine. Thank you, Ray. Again you prove just how invaluable you are."

"It's my job, Sir; and you're welcome."

They rode the elevator down together, and Shawn got off in the sub-basement and watched as the doors closed and Ray went back up to the cafeteria. Shawn's thoughts shifted to the questions chasing themselves around in his head. The afternoon had flown by and he was eager to meet with Madeline, excited to begin his apprenticeship.

The *ding* of the car arriving to the floor above broke his reverie, and he turned to find Madeline waiting patiently a few feet away.

"I knew you would be on time," she smiled.

"Of course!"

She turned and started walking up the hallway, and he followed her lead. "Where will we be... studying?"

"I chose one of the small rooms off the back corridor. We won't be disturbed, and it's far enough away from the distraction of the Working to enable your concentration.

"Wonderful! What will we begin with today?"

"Where everyone begins, Shawn. At the beginning." She smiled again. Shawn noted how genuine it was; even her eyes smiled at him.

The room was indeed small, really no more than a storage closet that had been made more useful as a sleeping room. It had pillows strewn about and lit candles provided the light from the corner light fixtures; bulbs had been replaced with fat columns of yellow wax.

"First," she said as she closed the door behind them, "a few rules of nature." She sat on one of the larger pillows and it almost seemed to engulf her as she relaxed into it.

"Rules?" he said, looking around like he wasn't sure where to sit.

"Take a seat anywhere, Shawn," she said, gesturing to the other pillows in the room.

In answer, Shawn kicked a couple of pillows together then planted himself among them, and then he repeated, "Rules?"

"Yes, rules, just a few in the name of safety. I ask that you trust that I will not direct you into anything that would physically harm you, that you will follow my instructions without question, and that you will hold your questions until the exercise is over. Is that acceptable?"

Shawn frowned but answered, "While I'm not thrilled at your rules, I will abide by them."

"Good!" and she clapped her hands with enthusiasm.

"And so we begin?" he asked.

"Yes," she pulled a small table with a candle on it from the side of the room and sat it between them. "First, breathe deeply, in and out, to calm yourself. I can feel your excitement and eagerness, but so much emotion will block your connection to your center."

Following her instructions, Shawn closed his eyes and took a few deep, cleansing breaths. Madeline's voice interrupted his wandering thoughts.

"Begin with the candle's flame." Shawn opened his eyes.

"No, see it in your mind's eye. Use your knowledge of it to *see* it."

He closed his eyes again, anger beginning to rise in his impatience.

"I know you want to go faster, Shawn," her voice was soothing, almost a caress to his ire. "Control is this first lesson. You are *very* strong, Shawn. If you are not careful, and don't learn how to control and manipulate your power, you will burn yourself out with your first casting, no matter how simple the task."

Reluctantly heeding her warning, Shawn fought to bury his frustration and tried to concentrate on the candle, its soft, fragrant wax and the flickering, hot flame that danced at the end of the wick. It filled his mind. He could hear the flame when it flickered with the movement of air from their breathing.

"Now… the candle is lit. Put it out." Madeline calmly demanded.

Shawn's brow furrowed as he frowned in concentration. He tried to remember, tried to feel what the candle flame was. *Fire, flame is hot, will burn… everything.*

"Every force, every form of energy has an opposite," she spoke as if she could hear him thinking.

Opposite: fire, water! And with that thought, almost the mental equivalent of a yell, water splashed them both as the candle flame was drowned in about a cupful of water that suddenly appeared then fell to the floor. Shawn's eyes popped open in disbelief, and wiping his face he spluttered, "What happened?"

Madeline reached in her bag and pulled a small towel out, which she handed to him after wiping her own face. Still using her teaching voice, she answered his question with another question, "What happened, Shawn?"

"Did I do that?"

"Did you do what?"

"Put the candle out!"

"I think you did a bit more than just put the candle out."

"All right, I drowned it and gave us both a bath in the process. But what *did* I do? How did I do that?"

"Let's examine what happened. Starting at the beginning – what did you do?"

"OK, first I pictured the candle: its wax, its scent, the texture."

"Go on," she encouraged, nodding.

"I saw the flame, felt the heat of the fire. I thought about opposites. Fire's opposite is water… Then we got wet!"

"When you thought of fire's opposite… when you thought of water – what did you feel?"

Shawn was quiet for a minute thinking hard, trying to recapture exactly what he'd felt at the moment just before the water splashed them. "I felt a surge of… electricity? Like a big static charge built up and discharged all at once."

"Very good analogy! Now this time, light the candle, but try not to set us on fire in the process," she smiled.

Shawn smiled back, closing his eyes to concentrate. *Light the candle.* "Fire," he said aloud not realizing he was actually talking out loud. He pictured the candle. *Everything exists, it's just a matter of when.* When nothing happened, he went back to the point where the flame was extinguished. *There! The energy of the flame… grab it, hold it together, touch it to the wick.* "Ahhhhhh, the flame!" he finished aloud opening his eyes. To his utter surprise, the candle was lit! The flame was again flickering in the breeze made by his breathing.

"Very good, Shawn."

He looked up quickly, startled to hear another voice. He'd forgotten his teacher was even there.

"That's enough for the first lesson," Madeline said.

He nodded in agreement, wiping his forehead with his arm.

"One more thing, Shawn…"

He looked at Madeline, and their eyes locked.

"Remember your dreams, Shawn. Your dreams are important."

She broke the connection and stood up. Shawn followed her example, stretching, and they left through the now open door. This time she didn't walk him to the elevator.

As he turned toward the elevator, he noticed a cart with covered dishes sitting on it and remembered that Ray had said he would send dinner down. He turned back in the direction Madeline had gone, only to see the hem of her robe as she turned the corner. He thought about going after her and offering dinner but decided instead to take the cart with him to his suite.

The elevator arrived without his calling. Briefly, he wondered at that, but only for a second or two.

TEN

Soraya was busy writing in her journal. She decided that her dreams needed to be documented so she didn't have to rely on her memory. *That man with the curly blonde hair is important. I don't know why, but he is the key to something... and he looks so familiar!* She shook her head in frustration.

"What chu frettin bout, Chile? Yo brow is so wrinkled you face look ol'as mine! Hee, hee, hee…"

Soraya deliberately relaxed her face muscles and managed a smile. "I'm just concentrating on the dream I had last night."

"Sumthin bout dis'un differnt?"

"Yeah, there was that man in it, that… I don't know. His being there bothers me."

"Hmmm, could be sumbody po'tent. Could jus be yo magination gittin curred way."

"Well, I suppose that's possible, but I think it's the former. His being there means something, Iona."

"Tsk, tsk… What'chu think it mean?" Iona pulled the chair from the kitchen and wiggled it into Soraya's room and sat.

"I don't know, but he didn't feel… right. Like at one time, he would maybe have been *the* person we're looking for to apprentice Zacharias, but something's changed in him."

"Whut his color, Chile?"

"His color? He is very light skinned, but he is black."

"Hee, hee, hee, no Chile, not *dat* color! Whut his area color?"

"Oh! You mean his aura? Lord I didn't even *think* about that!"

"It's dere, Chile, in yo memry. Whut his color?" Iona persistently asked again.

Soraya closed her eyes and concentrated on her first glimpse of the man and realized that he did have a color around him! Her answer to Iona's question held the shock and surprise that she could actually see what Iona was asking of her. "His color is brown, Iona, with tiny flecks of bright yellow swirling through it and a few flecks of white at the edges," she gasped, not realizing she hadn't been breathing again.

Iona was quiet, eyes closed and rocking when Soraya opened her eyes and looked at her. "What does it mean?"

The old woman gripped the arm of the chair so tightly that Soraya leaned forward thinking she was about to fall out.

Iona waived her off, "I's awright, Chile, but dis here man's a problem. Dat yellow an' white mean he *was* Zacharias' prentice, but he ain't no more. Dat brown is troublesome. Dis here man is our enemy. Might be d'one been doin da killin'."

"How could he possibly be both Zacharias' killer *and* his apprentice?"

"Well, nah, let's think dis through. Every person is fected by where dey growed up an who da people is round'em. Chil'ren always come into da worl inn'cent, but once here, if dey ain't no proper ptection, evil kin taka hold in no time a'tall. Dis man's path was altered. Somewhere, sumbody didn't pratect'im right. He's not quite evil yet, but dat brown is eatin' up what white n yellow was dere. Evil be winnin'dat battle."

Listening to Iona, Soraya knew she had it right. The brown in the man's aura was a roiling mass of angry energy, and it was feeding on something deep within him. "Iona, how do we fight this man?"

"Well Chile, likely he not workin lone. We know he ain't doin his own dirt when it comes t'da killin. Ah magine he'll come to us'n we jus gotta be ready!"

Soraya's heart fell. *We just gotta be ready* was a lot less than she wanted to hear.

Iona stood and grabbed the back of the chair to pull it back into the kitchen. "How bout some meal fo breakfast?"

"Sure," Soraya replied as she closed her journal and followed Iona into the kitchen, "Oatmeal would be nice this morning."

"Ever once in awhile you gotta eat some meal. Keeps ya regler. Hee, hee, hee!"

Soraya laughed with her. "What's our lesson plan today?"

"Well, Chile, time tstretch you a bit. Git you started on buildin you arsenal."

"Arsenal? As in weapons?"

"Chile, dat man ain't lone, an he ain't playin fair, neither. We's got t'be ready when he come fo us, an our weapons better be sharp!"

"Weapons... like guns and knives?" Soraya shivered at the thought of pointing a gun at another person, let alone pulling the trigger.

"Nah, Chile. By nah you should know Ah ain't talkin bout no guns! Weapons we got nat'ral weapons... fo o'em. Jus got t'learn ye how t'use'em." Iona poured oatmeal into two bowls and sat across from Soraya adding butter and sugar to hers.

"Four weapons? Not guns or knives?"

"C'mon, Chile, think! You kin git dis without my hep!"

Soraya frowned as she stirred sugar into her oatmeal. She thought hard about what Iona would consider a weapon that they already had.

"Chile, you is thinkin way too narra... think bigger!"

The silence between them was deafening. It was obvious that Iona wasn't going to give in and tell her the answer. She closed her eyes and used free association. *Weapons, not manmade, natural, rocks – still too concrete, natural, naturally occurring, made up of what elements... elements...* "Elements!" she shouted, "You mean the elements! Four weapons: Earth, Wind, Fire, and Water!"

"Very good, Chile! Fo a minute dere, Ah thought Ah wus gon hafta tell you!"

Soraya beamed at the praise. She asked, "So, how do we use the elements as weapons?"

"Well, Chile, fust we take'em one atta time! Den we see which one is you finity."

"You have a test for that?"

"Course, Chile! But, fust we's just gon play wit'em all."

They did the dishes together and then went down to the workroom. The table in the center of the room had several bottles and bowls on it, some filled with who-knows-what and some filled with very recognizable items, like the bottle filled with water.

"You member yo fust work wit fire an water? Today we start wit da water. Sit Chile, we's gon'be here awhile!"

Soraya pulled a stool over to the table and sat in front of all the bottles and bowls. She didn't know what to expect, and her curiosity was winning over her fears.

"Ok, Chile, look at da water." Iona pulled a small wooden box out of the shadows in the corner and sat across from Soraya.

Soraya took a deep breath and focused on the bottle of water, "Water is wet, and you can see through it when it's clean…"

"Dat las part ain't quite right."

Soraya frowned, "What do you mean? You *can* see through water when it's clean."

"Tsk, tsk, Chile. Water don always be clean where y'kin see through it! Don gotta be clean to be clear, n'don gotta be clear t'be clean!"

"Oh!" Soraya said, startled, "I've never thought about it that way, you're right!" She took another deep breath and started again, "Water is wet, can be clear or murky, clean or dirty…"

"Dat's better, Chile."

"Water is heavy. Can be held by anything more solid and more dense than itself. It nourishes and nurtures but can also kill. It is the elemental opposite to fire."

"Nah, Chile, you got whut it is, let's try *where* it is…"

"Water is part of most things living. When near flame, it will sizzle and pop. When there is more of one than the other a battle is won."

"Good! Good, Soraya! Nah, Chile, you got the 'standin of it; douse da flame."

Soraya blinked, then focused on the candle flame hard. At first, nothing happened, so she tried a different angle. "Water. Water is everywhere, even in air, draw it up and drop it there!" There was an audible *pop* and the candle flame sputtered; and then a gush of water materialized and splashed on the table, putting the candle out and soaking Soraya, Iona and the dirt floor under the table.

"Hee, hee, hee, well, you shore put it out! Hee, hee, hee!"

Soraya was surprised and a little embarrassed by the overkill. "My goodness! I didn't expect so much! Since this fire was so much smaller than the last, I thought the amount of water would also be less."

"S'all right, Chile" Iona laughed, "Whas portant is, did ya *feel* where it came from? Did ya pay tention to yo'sef when da water splashed da table? Kin y'do it agin?"

Soraya breathed a small sigh of relief. She thought Iona would point out what she'd done wrong. Instead, she just continued with the lesson. "Let me see... I pictured water in my mind and recited a sort of rhyme..." she concentrated on what she'd done, trying to relive the actions and feelings. "I was breathing faster. My hands, the palms of my hands were itching, and then the water appeared and put the candle out," she said with a deep breath. She began to scratch her hands as she opened her eyes and was surprised to see another douse of water headed for the tabletop, "Oh, NO!" she shouted, and the water evaporated before splashing the table. Soraya looked at Iona to see her nodding her head.

"Very good, Chile! Nah, les see if'n you kin re-light da candle," she laughed again, "wi'out burnin us up please!"

Soraya looked at the candle, water still dripping from it and thought, *First I've gotta get rid of the water.* She concentrated on the small puddle around the wick. *The air is dry. Should be able to evaporate it.* Her brows furrowed with the effort. *This is harder than bringing the water!* It seemed to take forever for the water to disappear from around the wick. Then she turned her attention to the wick itself. "Ok. Once dry, I've got to apply the fire," she said aloud to Iona's nod. "If water is in the air, so is fire." Focusing on the candlewick she jumped when it sputtered.

Iona said, "You headed in da right drection, Chile. Don give up nah!"

Soraya narrowed her field of vision so that only the candlewick was there. "Fire is heat, hot, burning hot flame..." The wick sputtered again until a tiny blue flicker attached itself blooming into a full, yellow flame. Her shoulders slumped, weary from the energy spent to relight the candle.

Iona's face was serious, but beaming, "Nah dis'll git easier more ya practice. All's elements kin be convinced t'do yo biddin, jus takes practice."

Soraya asked, "What do you mean by 'convinced'?"

"Well Chile, here's whut tis. Take da earth, it's alive. So is d'rest o' da elements, Soraya. Dey like da blood, an other fluids o'da body. Water, fire, wind, earth: dey all d'pend on each other an dey all fected by each other. Dey appear, dispear, an behave accordin t'dey own rules. When we go t'work wit'em, dey kin be convinced t'do our biddin… or not. Da ones dat seem t'be easier t'work wit are da ones dat hold ffinity wit'chu. Da ones dat are harder, don. Tis up t'you t'figger out jus which ones like you an which ones don."

"What are their rules? How do we figure out which ones like me?"

"Hee, hee, hee, Chile, we will! Jus gon take some patience an practice t'figger it out! An mos dere rules ya already know!"

Soraya frowned, "You mean like water is wet, fire is hot…"

"Yep, yep, you got it, Chile! Tol you y'already know mos dem rules, Hee, hee, hee! Nah, you bin playin wit fire n'water; whut bout t'others?"

Soraya was quiet trying to find the words for response. The old woman just sat looking at her with an expectancy that made her even more nervous. She closed her eyes to concentrate. *Convince the elements to work for me…* Suddenly, like the proverbial light bulb popping up over her head, she got it, "Breathe deep. Breathe as the wind blows, hot as fire burns, so dry thirst builds, quenched by waters, cold and wet, devoured by the earth beneath my feet…" Soraya opened her eyes to see Iona's face wet from the tears flowing freely down her face.

She reached across the table and touched her hand, "Iona, why do you cry? Did I mess up? Did I miss something?"

"Oh Chile, I's awright. It jus move me t'see you bgin to blossom in you power. Minds me of m'younger days, afor I came here."

As Soraya opened her mouth to ask another question, Iona said, "Don' worry Chile. We'll have 'nough tahm f' you t' hear ma stories! Dis here is yo time! Start agin…"

Feeling a hundred questions running into the wall that Iona had just placed in her mind with her words, Soraya suppressed the urge to ask them and concentrated on the task at hand. She hoped she really would have the chance to hear Iona's stories, but she had a nagging feeling that she wouldn't. She spent hours practicing her pull on the elements. Iona gave small words of explanation, but most of the time was only an intense observer. Somewhere between the repeated drenching of herself and burning of the table, the puzzle piece clicked into place. With excitement tinged with exhaustion, she suddenly *knew* how to do it! She sat back, opened her eyes wide and stared at Iona. Without blinking, she lit the candle and then put it out with a perfect single drop of water.

"Good, Chile, good! I knew you'd get it! Don take as much effort as you thought, hee, hee, hee!"

"No, it doesn't! I understand the process, I think. I'm not asking the elements to *do* something; I'm giving direction to what they do because it's their job! All I'm giving is direction and guidance!" Soraya explained.

"Excellent! We kin go up an have supper nah, Hee, hee, hee!"

Soraya was thrilled. The concept was so easy it was almost embarrassing that it had taken her so long to *get* it.

By the time Iona called it a day, Soraya's body hurt and her eyes were as bloodshot as if she'd spent the day drinking instead of studying. She wondered if working magic was always so exhausting, because if it was, she vowed that she wouldn't be using it unless she absolutely had to.

As they climbed the stairs to the kitchen, Soraya couldn't believe how hungry she was! Ravenous was more the word that fit her appetite. She quickly downed a dinner of grilled cheese and tomato soup which was quick, hot and filling. But Soraya didn't even remember what she'd eaten by the time she was in bed. And she was asleep almost as soon as her head hit the pillow.

The dream started immediately. Soraya checked herself and strangely didn't feel any of the exhaustion she'd gone to bed with, but she knew she hadn't been asleep very long either. She just stood still for a moment trying to get her bearings and figure out where she was. Using her tentative control over the elements, she asked for her location to be revealed, and the Earth came forth with the answer faster than she'd expected. Chicago again. Why did Chicago seem to be the focal point for what was happening to The Circle?

This time she was on the sidewalk in front of one of the skyscrapers downtown. She didn't recognize the building, and it was quite a distance from Zacharias' shop, so why was she here? She looked up at the building she was standing in front of and saw the name "DNAgen Biolabs" in lights at the top. It meant nothing to her. She'd never heard of the company before. As she stood there bewildered and confused, she saw a group of people arrive in a large van. There were at least twenty of them, and they caught her attention because they were all dressed in the same black cloaks.

I wonder what kind of uniform that is? She walked up to the main doors to the building after the group had gone inside and peered into the lobby. Other than the people who had just entered, there were very few other people around.

Soraya was so intent on the why of her being there that she missed it when one of the cloaked figures turned towards the doorway just as she shrugged and walked back out to the sidewalk where she'd started. There didn't seem to be anything else happening; and while she wasn't as tired as she should have been, she was weary. She yawned and the city faded to dark.

They both slept without further interruption that night; and Soraya woke early, grabbed her notebook and started writing. She wanted to write down the dream she had and the questions that she didn't get a chance to ask Iona the night before.

Iona came to the door and peeked in. "Thought I heard you stirrin' in here. No dreams las night, huh?"

"Nothing serious last night, for a change. It was nice to be able to just sleep for a night."

"What chu'workin on, Chile?" Iona said as she squeezed into the room and sat down.

"I want to keep track of things, my questions, my dreams."

"Ohhh, a journal. Das a good idea, Chile, put things down in ya'own words. Tis a bit repetitious, but if'n dat makes you feel better, dat's ok." She sighed loudly, "Nah," Iona slapped her leg for emphasis and reached to give Soraya a hug before standing, "You feel like eatin somethin dis mornin?"

It was just then that Soraya realized she didn't smell the customary bacon frying for breakfast. The thought of greasy food made her stomach do sluggish flips, "No, I think I'll just have coffee this morning, thank you."

"Ah thought so! Coffee comin right up!"

Soraya crawled out of bed as Iona left the room. The shock of the cold wood-slat floor did more to wake her than a cold shower could ever accomplish.

Between the cold of the floor and the splash of water from the washbowl, the shock started her mind working again, "Why is it so easy for these people to get to The Circle? How did they find us?" Her heart began to race with all the questions spinning in her head. She threw on some clothes and sped into the kitchen. There was a cup of coffee already waiting for her on the table. She sat across from Iona, who was nibbling on some toast. It reminded her of the night before, after they'd come up from the workroom. Iona didn't eat with as much relish as usual, and it made her questions resurface. "Why is it I was so hungry and you were barely eating last night?"

"Chile, you did more work than I did! You supose t'be hungry. You used a lotta energy tracin dem energy cords n'patterns. Ah jus followed what'chu was doin'."

"Does it always do that to you-make you hungry and tired, I mean?"

"Ever'thing has a price, Chile. Usin power costs jus like walkin n'talkin, sometimes more. What'chu pay with depends on what'chu callin an what'chu doin with it."

"So, does that mean that whenever I use it I'll be starving and exhausted afterwards?"

"Well nah, you'll always feel it, Chile; but da'more you use it, da longer it'll take to tire you out."

"Tell me why you all, I mean The Circle, don't seem to be using the power much at all?"

"Teachin you gon be fun Soraya; you sharp Chile! We's done got tired, like mos ol'folks. Ah guess we ain't had no trouble til nah, so we let da tiredness git us."

Soraya nodded. Complacency, apathy, whatever you wanted to call it, had finally seeped in and laid them to rest, literally. They were so used to *not* having to do anything other than *be*, that they had almost forgotten what they were about.

"We need to fix this, Iona. We *have* to fix this, and fast. Whoever our enemy is will continue to take advantage of us until we can fight back and mount an offensive."

"Dat's why you here, Chile! Dat's why all you young'uns is comin nah! Hee, hee, hee, a lil' fire, tha's all we needed!"

"Iona, cut that out! This is serious!"

"I know, Chile. I know it's serious. But you cain't stop an ol'woman fer gittin 'cited! Been a long time since any us had reason t'be 'cited bout sumthin!"

Soraya just couldn't feel the same spirit that Iona had. Things weighed too heavily on her. "Well, it would've been a lot better and a little more fun if people weren't dying," she said, shaking her head.

"You right, Soraya. I'll keep it down… Hee, hee, hee." Iona couldn't seem to keep the smile off her face, or the giggle out of her voice, but Soraya's next question wiped it away.

"Can we put the computer on the counter near the back of the shop?"

Iona grimaced when she answered, "Sure Chile, wherever you want it. What we gon do wit it agin?"

"We're going to get the whole Circle hooked up on the Internet so we don't have to use phones, and only do a sending when it's an emergency. Then we'll be able to monitor every shop, and vice versa, for trouble."

"If we kin do dat, cain't dey do it too?"

Soraya paused. This was the part of her plan that she hadn't quite worked out yet. "It's possible, yes. I'm hoping that we can set some safeguards against that before they figure out we're looking for them."

"An, how we gon' figger out who *dey* is?"

"When they try to make the next hit, we've got to track the assassins. Or maybe I should say *I've* got to track them."

"Das gon be a long time on da plain, Soraya. When you plannin on makin dis here trip?"

"When they make the next attempt. That's why we need to link up with everybody this morning."

"Wit dem puters?"

"No, not yet; we won't be ready for that until tomorrow afternoon. I need you to show me how to *send*."

"How bout after dat beau o'yours comin wit da puter gits here."

Soraya looked at Iona and felt heat rise up in her face, "Miss Iona!"

"Hee, hee, hee, don be so flustered, Chile! Dere ain't nuthin wrong wit likin sumbody! Yo mama had dat same look when yo daddy show up, hee, hee, hee!"

The next words Soraya was about to say almost choked her trying to hold them back. She took a slow deep breath and just watched the old woman laughing herself hoarse. Then the statement Iona made suddenly registered, "Iona… you knew my father?"

Making an effort not to laugh anymore, Iona said, "Yes, Chile, yo father wasn't here long, but Ah guess t'was long nough!"

"Tell me about my father, please? Mama didn't ever volunteer very much information about him."

"Well, dat's not s'prisin, she was purty tore up when he lef."

"What happened? Who was he?"

"Ok, ok. I'll tell you what I know, Chile, jus a minit!"

For some reason, Soraya knew this information was important to her. Even though she had accepted her *destiny* as far as the Circle was concerned, she still wanted to know why *her*."

After pouring them both another cup of coffee, Iona's voice lowered to almost a whisper as she spoke. "Some us born wit jus da seed fo da power, Chile. Yo Mama is one dem. Da seed not nough to use it, but it's nough to pass it on. Prentices chosen from chil'ren o'dem carryin da seed."

"Yes, but my father was special Iona. I can feel that he was… I know this."

"Yeah, he was special awraght. Da Histry say we was gon need sumone strong. I tol you how I was chosen?"

Soraya nodded.

"Well, da book tol us dat when da time was raght, my prentice had to be strong; not jus a seed to be taught, but a sprout, if you will, t'be nurtured."

"So, my father was… chosen?"

"Yo father was chosen to quickin da seed yo mama carried. I tol you, we was joined by da cord afore you was born, Chile."

"So, who was my father?"

"Man was a trav'ler from da mother lan. Only here fo a li'l while, but I guess it was long nough."

"Who was he though?"

"Jus a man, Chile, nobody too special."

"But special enough for me to be born your apprentice."

"Well, Ah guess thas purty special at dat!" Iona smiled.

"Was it preordained or something that he meet my mother?"

Iona sighed, "Chile, dere was a need fo me t'have a prentice. It was writ in da histry dat da time was nigh. I tol you many born wit da seed. Yo mama was strong, Chile. Tha was ne'sary, an here you are." Iona's brows furrowed with frustration at the question.

Soraya nodded again, realizing Iona was finished with her narration. There wasn't anything else to tell. "Is it recorded in the History?"

Iona smiled again, "Of course it is, Chile."

They both stood to head down to the workroom, "I need to make a phone call before we go down. Is there a phone down there, Iona?"

"Hee, hee, hee, Chile, you sumthin else! Ain't no phone down there, but we kin take one if'n you think we need it."

"Please. I'm thinking I should pick up a cell phone, as much as I've tried to avoid them; looks like it's necessary to have one now." She picked up the kitchen handset and dialed Marceme's Computer Store. "Marceme? Hi, it's me, Soraya."

"Ooooo, twice in one week! I am lucky!" Marceme replied.

"OK, stop it!" she laughed, "Could you do me a little favor?"

"Name it, Sugar, if I can do it, I will!"

"I just need your delivery person to call before they come. We might not hear the door, and the shop isn't going to be open today."

"Huh… Miss Iona's shop not open? Ok, if you say so. Not normal, that she ain't open, but if you say so. I'll have him call first. No problem. Anything else?"

"No, that's all Marceme, and thank you again!"

"You are most certainly welcome, Miss Soraya!"

Soraya shook her head as she hung up the phone; and she turned to see Iona standing at the top of the stairs that led down to the workroom, watching her, a crooked smile creasing her lips.

"The delivery of the computer is all set, and they'll call first."

ELEVEN

As they descended the stairs to the workroom, Iona said, "You blush when you talk t'dat fella, y'know dat?"

"I do not!" Soraya replied too loudly.

Iona snickered, "Hee, hee, hee, you do! But I won tell, hee, hee, hee ."

Soraya did blush then. She felt the heat rise in her face, and hoped that Iona didn't notice as she stepped off the stairs onto the dirt floor. She took a deep breath to calm herself as Iona followed her into the room. Soraya pulled the trapdoor shut behind them, looking up to watch the steps nestle themselves into the ceiling.

"OK, what do we start with today?"

Iona was at the worktable, her back to Soraya. "We's gon' work dis lessun an git whut you need t'know t'fect da plain."

"OK, what do I do?"

"Fust, jus set on dat dere stool. We's gon' do a castin. Dis here what dem witches you was talkin bout calls a spell. A castin takes power from you and whut's roun you."

"Does the balance of power come from you or from your surroundings?"

"If'n I hear yo question right, mos o'da pow'r come from you. Whut you take from roun you is t'keep you anchored here. Da forces we's messin wit strong nough t'take you out, Chile. You hear? Don second guess'em!"

Soraya nodded and watched everything Iona did with the intensity of someone entranced. Iona lit candles and began to chant.

"What is it that you're saying while you do this?"

Iona laughed, "Sorry Chile, not used to havin someone watch, let lone someone learnin! Da chant is a simple prayer. The Almighty guides and pr'tects us. We don' wanna invite no evil in what we do, so we ask for da light t'cover us. It's bad nough we's got t'open da gates dey kin git through. Don wanna call dey tention t'us while we got'em open."

"I don't like the sound of that! What do you mean *open the gates they can get through?*"

"We's dealin wit magic… ol' magic. Fo ere'thing good and clean, dey is a opp'sit. If'n we's call on sumthin good t'come and help us, sumthin bad kin squeeze through da door wit it. Likewise, dem's dat work da evil side has a equal chance o'gittin sumthin good dat works agin whut day be tryin't do."

"Equals, like Yin and Yang, or Newton's theory. Everything has an opposite," Soraya said nodding her head.

"Don know who *Newton* is, but soun like you git it, Chile."

Iona stopped and started lighting the candles in the tiny room as she was answering her questions, before she went back to the ritual. Soraya asked, "Why do you light the candles by hand rather than using the elements?"

"Das a good quesion, Chile… Why waste energy dat might be portent fo sumthin else?"

Soraya nodded, the explanation being so simple she felt foolish for asking; and watching Iona finish lighting the candles, she concentrated on trying to relax. She knew from her last visits to the workroom that she needed to be as calm as possible to be receptive to whatever was going to happen.

Iona finished with the candles and turned to face Soraya. "Nah we start! Close yo eyes, Soraya. Kin you see it?"

"Uhhh, see what Iona? What am I looking for?"

"It's a thread. Might be silva, mebbe gol. Should be hangin cross dis room."

Soraya searched the blackness behind her eyelids for the thread Iona described. She was just about to confess her inability to see it when she caught a glimmer to her right. She focused on the tiny flash of brightness until she could see a thin ribbon of gold flailing in the darkness.

"I see it!"

"You soun surprised, Chile! I tol you it was dere! Nah, follow it. I want you t'see the kinnections."

Curious about what Iona meant by connections, Soraya followed the wisp of thread and was surprised to find one end connected to herself! She rushed along it to the other end to see it attached to Iona, which is what Iona described."

"It's connected between us!"

"Dis is a thread of pow'r. Nah, afore you came t'me, it was faint an almos colorless. Watchit, and tell me wha'chu see."

Soraya closed her eyes again and concentrated. "It pulsates and the golden color dims between beats."

"Good, good. Whut else?"

"My end is… stronger, thicker…" she trailed off and opened her eyes wide to stare at Iona.

The old woman was nodding vigorously. "Very good! Mah end is waning, yours is on the rise. Da link was stablished shortly afta yo birth, Soraya. Dere should be lines jus like dat hangin out dere where Zacharias, Willamae an Walterine was, only not as bright cause one end is broke."

Iona was silent, like she was waiting for Soraya to say something; so, clearing her throat nervously, she said, "So, what does that mean, Iona?"

"Chile, sumtime you is so smart, and t'other's… tsk, tsk, tsk. You got t'find dem threads!"

Soraya sat straight up on the stool, "Oh! I understand, sorry. Guess I'm a little slow on the uptake!"

"Only sumtimes, Chile, only sumtimes, hee, hee, hee!"

"OK, so how do we do this? The threads can't reach all the way here…"

"No, you gotta go dere, on da plain."

Soraya was suddenly overwhelmed by feelings of dark foreboding. How was she going to be able to do this? So far, the only location she knew she could get back to easily was Zacharias' shop in Chicago. The shops in DC and L.A., well, she'd only been there once and didn't go on her own because she was drawn the first few times. And once there, what would she do? "Iona…"

"Oh, Chile, you kin do dis! I'll be here t'help. Nah, close dem eyes agin."

Sighing, Soraya closed her eyes and concentrated.

"OK, we's going to Chicago fust. Zacharias been gone da longest. We need t'catch up his thread fust. Pitchure da shop, dat's where t'start."

Soraya went back in her memory to the night Zacharias was killed to pull a complete picture of the shop. Once she saw it in her mind, she was there. Only this time, it was empty and dark. Someone had boarded it up leaving everything in its place, as if waiting for someone to come along and claim it all.

"I'm in the shop. It's empty."

"Oh, it ain't empty, Chile. Look closer. Kin you see da thread?"

At first Soraya couldn't *see* anything. Even the shadows didn't really have any definition. But the longer she searched the darkness, the more things came into focus. There were the counters and cabinets filled to brimming with the clutter she had come to expect. She was just wondering whether each of the twelve had a copy of the history when she caught the flicker. It wasn't bright gold like hers, but more of a coppery color and very dim. "I see one! It's kinda orange."

She heard Ioan sigh heavily. "Praise Him, Da Creator, he always provides! Folla it, Chile, folla it afore it fades completely! The color don' matter right nah."

Soraya began to follow the thread moving as fast as she could. Iona was right. It was fading fast, almost as if now that she'd found it, it was running away. "This is difficult, Iona, it's fading almost as fast as I can move to follow it!"

"Da link is dyin. Hurry, Chile, hurry!"

Soraya dove at the thing, watching it writhe as if alive of its own volition. She travelled for what seemed like miles when she realized that the color was getting brighter. "I think I'm getting close. It's gaining strength."

"Thank goodness we's not too late!" Iona breathed.

Soraya passed through a final door to find the end of the copper thread wrapped around the soul of a young man curled into a tight ball of anguish. He wasn't much older than her, but scared to death and still feeling the physical shock of Zacharias' death, made worse because of no understanding. "Iona, I need your help here. He's a mess!"

"OK, dis gonna take some strength. I gotta touch 'im through you, Chile. You gotta make room fo me to git to'im."

While Soraya had no real idea of what Iona had in mind, she knew she didn't have time to ask for detailed explanations. The man was too close to giving up. Soraya made herself small. She crawled into a corner of herself leaving room for Iona to use their thread and travel to the cold room in Chicago's east side where Randall Stevens was about to find his purpose in this life.

Soraya watched as Iona flew past her and reached toward Randall. She touched his head with gentle fingertips at the temples. "It's all right, Chile. You ain't crazy, and wha'chu feel is grief fo yo mentor's passin."

Randall started to cry, and Soraya could feel the grief he released like it was a tangible thing hovering in the room with them. Instinctively, she added her own comforting hands to Iona's. Iona seemed pleased at her response.

"Sho him where the shop is Soraya. He need t'go home; it's his home nah."

Soraya gave Randall the picture of the shop, including directions on how to find it from where they were. His tears finally dried up. He responded with a hunger so strong it rocked both Soraya and Iona in its intensity.

"He'll make it nah." Iona said. She sounded satisfied with her work and slowly withdrew back the way she came along their thread.

Soraya stayed just a little longer to leave one last message. "We're in Harlem. Use the Net. Call *Home*."

Randall nodded once, and then left the little room where Soraya had found him. She watched to see that he was headed in the right direction and then went home herself. There were still two more to go.

The second one, Willamae's apprentice, wasn't as difficult to find. The girl, she wasn't much more than that at the age of sixteen, had such a strong thread that Soraya saw it as soon as she entered the shop in Washington DC. Talavera Prentice was gifted and knew it. It seemed to Soraya that Willamae's death had only increased the girls' awareness. Iona watched from a distance this time; and taking what she had learned from watching her with Randall, Soraya took the girl in hand and sent her home. She left her with the same message she gave to Randall.

The third one, Walterine's apprentice, was a bit of a struggle. In comparison, as strong as Russell's denial of his gifts, which sent him into despair, Kenyatta Griffen was defiant, but he was also angry. He'd spent the last few days doing everything he could to suppress the visions and feelings he was receiving because of Walterine's death. He argued with Soraya and didn't want any part of what was being offered, and she again asked Iona for some intervention. Iona touched his forehead with her fingertips which calmed the storm in his mind. He had been fighting with himself so hard to stop the magic that he was making himself sick. Once his mind was quiet, Iona moved aside and let Soraya come back in to finish her instructions and give the directions to the shop. This time, when they left, Kenyatta was resigned but not totally accepting of what lay ahead. Soraya told him she knew how he felt because she felt the same way in the beginning. "Just give it some time, Kenyatta. I promise you won't be disappointed."

Soraya ended with the same instructions she'd given Randall and Talavera and then returned home. When she finally opened her eyes again, she was exhausted and sitting in the dirt on the floor again. Iona stuck a wooden cup to her lips, and she drank without thinking about what it might hold and was grateful for the taste of clean, cold water that hit her tongue.

"You done well, Chile! Exceptional well! We's dun caught all three dem threads and tied'em back t'da circle!" Iona stood and offered Soraya a hand up.

"We's still twe've. Dey ain't licked us yet!"

"No, not just yet. But we still have a long row to hoe!" Soraya said.

"Yup, you got dat right! But… we's planted some new seed, an da stock is strong!"

The phone rang and Soraya looked at her watch. It was already 3:30! Not only did this *magic* take every ounce of energy she could muster, but it took all the time away from a day whenever she worked with it! There just had to be a better way!

"Soraya, it's fo you, Chile. Dat young man I think, hee, hee, hee."

Iona handed her the phone then turned to pull the stairs down.

"Hello?"

"Hello, Miss Soraya?"

"Yes, this is Soraya."

"I got a d'livery and setup scheduled for you this afternoon, and I'm about ten minutes away. Is somebody there?"

"Yes, I'll be here."

"OK, I'm on my way!

"OK, thank you!"

She stood and brushed the dust from her clothes. "Iona, they're coming to setup the computer. We need to clear the space for it."

"I got a idea. Come on up and git sumthin t'eat and we'll git a place ready," Iona said as she ascended up the stairs.

Soraya put out the candles and went up the stairs behind her. As little time as the old woman had been in the kitchen, she already had chicken salad sandwiches and lemonade on the table. Soraya shook her head in bewilderment. "How do you do that?"

"Do whut, Chile?"

"Nothing. Nevermind. So, can we put the computer on that end of the counter I pointed out earlier?"

They chatted while they ate, and then Soraya went to the front and cleared the end of the counter off so the computer would have enough room.

There was a knock on the door, and Soraya went to let the computer delivery man into the shop.

The young man who delivered and set up the computer was engaging and seemed to know computers well. Iona just watched as he and Soraya talked about the network she was trying to get hooked up in the other shops.

"So, Kevin, do you think you can get all the others installed and hooked up by tomorrow evening?"

"Sure, Miss Soraya. We don't have stores in all the cities you named, but we can work with other companies to get it done."

"What do we need to do to arrange for payment?"

"Well, each delivery will need to be paid from the store that receives it, so I think payment will have to happen separately for each store."

"Ok. If you send me the list of computer stores, I'll make sure each of the shops has payment ready. And, I'll also give you the names of the shop owners."

"That's great, Miss Soraya. We'll get this all done for you!"

Kevin did a few last minute checks on the computer software then left. "Thank you for all your help, Kevin."

"My pleasure. Have a great day Miss Soraya!"

Soraya turned from the door to see Iona poking at the computer with a look of mistrust on her face.

"So, dis thing gon make us be closer?" Iona said, her voice full of distrust.

Soraya took a deep breath, "Iona, we need another way to communicate. Telephone wires can be cut, and cellphones are most likely beyond most of the Circle members ability to learn and keep track of. The computers are too large to lose, are always connected and don't need wires to *be* connected. They also don't use any personal power to speak with each other."

"Ok, Chile, *OK*! I give!" Iona threw her hands up in the air and waived off the computer as she walked back up the hallway.

Soraya shook her head and picked up the phone. It took her about an hour to call all of the other shops. There was no trouble with the three new apprentices, but the others presented a challenge. They all had the same attitude as Iona. Most of them had their apprentices in place so she was able to get things arranged through them. But three of the shops were still waiting on their apprentices to arrive. She decided to hold off on getting those deliveries arranged until the apprentices got there. Hopefully, another couple of days wouldn't be too dangerous. At least she prayed that would be the case.

Hanging up the phone, she sighed and headed to the kitchen for the discussion she knew was waiting for her. When she stepped into the room, she took a deep breath and marveled at the aroma of the tuna casserole that was baking in the oven. How is it she didn't smell it before she got to the kitchen?

"That smells absolutely delicious, Iona!"

"Nuthin special, Chile, be done in a bit," Iona said as she sat in the chair. She was sipping what looked like ice tea.

"Any more of that?"

"Sure, Chile, in'a fridge."

"Iona…"

The old woman looked up from her glass and met Soraya's gaze. "Iona, I know you don't like the idea of the computer. I know it's new and that you disagree with the need for it."

Iona just looked at her, not saying a word, and not giving away any of her feelings through her expression.

"We *need* to do this, Iona. We are not dealing with only old world powers here. I feel that there is something… something evil working at the edges of the Circle. But, there's something else there too. Something, I don't know… something that is rooted in today's magic. We need to build up our defenses on the Plain, in the Power and in today's technology. We have to be ready on all levels, not just one."

Soraya was breathing hard and took a long swallow of her tea. She waited for Iona to say something, anything. It didn't take long.

"Soraya, it's OK, Chile." Iona sighed, "Chile, Ah may not unda'stan what'chu tryin t'do here, but Ah do git dat we's vuner'ble. We's a target; an cause we ol, we's easy targets. Ah mit, Ah don like it, but Ah ain't gon argue wit'chu bout it. You gon take mah place here. Dat means thang's gotta change." With that, she shrugged, took another sip and stood to open the oven and take the casserole out.

They ate in almost total silence, which was unusual for Iona. Soraya knew she was still upset by the installation of the computers, but she didn't know how to alleviate her fears. This was a needed and necessary upgrade to The Circle's communications. Learning how to use the magic was so tiring for Soraya, she knew the other new apprentices would have as much if not more difficulty harnessing the power and being able to use it as quickly as the need was going to be. She was especially worried about the three who had no mentor in place. They would have a much more difficult time of it than any of the others. She decided to just change the subject.

"Iona, how substantial is the dreamworld I walk in when I sleep?"

Iona paused, fork halfway to her mouth. She shook her head before eating and swallowing the mouthful prior to answering. "Chile, jus whut is you askin?"

Soraya looked Iona in the eyes, not sure how to react to the tone of her voice. She restated her question, "When my dreams take me to the other shops, I don't have any substance, can't touch anything, no one can hear me. Will the elements do my bidding in that state? Will I have the same… control I have in the waking state?"

Iona pursed her lips, "Mmmm hmmmm, Ah think Ah see where you goin wit dis. You power is t'direct, not control, da elements. It does cross over, but not da way you thinkin."

Soraya gathered the plates and utensils and started washing the dishes.

Iona cleared her throat, "Da elements will do yo biddin' in a'dream state, but it's only dem thas dere."

"They aren't all present everywhere?"

"Well, yes an no. They're presence is always possible, but in a'dream state it's dem you kin see dat you kin direct."

Soraya thought about this for a minute, and drying her hands, joined Iona back at the table. "So, if there is no flame in the room, I can't direct fire?"

"Das right, Chile! You cain't conjure up flame from nuthin when you in a dream, cause you ain't physical dere."

"That puts some limitations on how much effect I can have in a dream."

"Yes, thas true. But dey is a reason fo it."

"Go on, please."

"In a dream, you kin direct what you see cause yo vision is yo power in dat state. Folks'd be directin an leavin' da elements t'do dey biddin whilst dey go off somewhere else'n be causin' trouble. Elements have no mind, so once directed, if nobody stop'em, dey jus keep goin!"

"I see. So, my being able to see the element is important. Once it is no longer in my sight…"

"It stops whatever yo direction was'n goes back to it's normal state. You set Fire to burn a board and leave it, it will burn the board to ash, and anything else it comes in contact with."

"How fast is the reaction time? Does it slow down any because of the dream state?"

"No, Chile. It's da same no matter it be nah or in a dream."

Soraya was quietly contemplating just what that would mean. If she'd had the power to direct the elements in her vision of Zacharias' death, could she have stopped it? She shivered. More importantly, would she have the courage to direct the elements to stop it from happening again?

Iona yawned loudly bringing her back to reality. "I'm sorry Iona, we should go to bed! You've been up as long as I have and working as hard!"

"No worries, Chile. Ah be fine!" Iona smiled, but quickly yawned again.

"It has still been a long day. We can pick this up in the morning."

"G'nite Chile." Iona yawned hugely and headed to her room. Soraya turned off the lights and went to her own room. She hoped sleep would be uninterrupted tonight as well.

Iona had a visitation that night. Zacharias came to her in *her* dreams. "Iona, dat boy yo gurl seein was t'be mah prentice. Name be Shawn. His aura be dark nah, not mah prentice nah."

"Zacharias, I knows dis. We foun'da one be yo prentice. He at d'shop nah."

"Dis be good, but dat boy Shawn an yo prentice share sumpthin. Cain't see whut tis but tis sumpthin. Dat gon make a difernce."

"Thank you, Zacharias. Ah miss yo bein roun," Iona said with deep sadness.

Zacharias answered, his voice fading, "You be here soon. We's gon catch up on all'a stuff we miss."

TWELVE

When he made it up to his penthouse, Shawn paced his living room, his mind a jumble of bright flames, clear water and the voices of all those he'd spoken with during the day. Even with all the speeches, presentations and announcements of the day, he kept circling back to the fire and water. He quickly realized that the whole fire and water exercise was a total lesson in control. Things would do his bidding. It was only a matter of how to make them do it when *he* wanted them to.

He wasn't hungry, but the more he moved through his home, the more food kept interrupting his chain of thought. Shawn pulled the cart over to the sofa deciding he probably needed to eat. He ate dinner without seeing or tasting it. If anyone asked what it was, he wouldn't have been able to answer. He was mentally exhausted and physically sore, like he'd run a mile in the fastest time ever recorded. After eating, he pushed the cart back into the entryway and staggered into the bathroom to take a hot shower. As he dried off, he heard a knock at the door.

When he answered, he was surprised to see it was Ray. "You're still here? I thought you went home."

"I did, but I came back. When I went to check on you in the sub-basement, I saw the cart was gone; after speaking with Madeline, I figured you'd taken it with you when you left."

"Ray, you continue to amaze me."

"Nothing fancy, Sir. I called and asked if anyone had seen you. When nobody had, I thought I'd come and check."

"I appreciate all your concern for my well-being, Ray; but I *can* take care of myself you know."

Ray's voice held a note of panic when he said, "Hey, boss, I know that. I just take my job of being your assistant *very* seriously!"

"It's OK, Ray. I said I appreciated it!" Shawn said, the exhaustion coming through in his voice. He wobbled, and Ray grabbed his elbow and steered him back towards his bedroom.

Shawn was pleased that Ray visibly relaxed. He wasn't in the mood and didn't have the energy to stroke his lapdog at the moment. He was also slightly perturbed that he needed Ray's help to navigate his way back to his bed. "So, did I miss anything important this evening?"

Ray stepped back from him and said, "No Sir, nothing you'd be interested in hearing any way."

Wearily Shawn said, "Ray, I'm interested in *hearing* about everything. Whether I choose to react is a different matter." He swung his legs up onto the bed and pulled himself onto the pillows, looking expectantly at Ray.

Ray started to babble about mundane employee issues and late night workers while Shawn closed his eyes and listened. After the first few sentences he was nodding his head, but his mind was elsewhere. He was thinking about what Madeline had said as he left - that his dreams were important. He started thinking about the dreams he'd been having over the last few days, specifically the one with the girl in it. He sighed and interrupted Ray's diatribe, "Ok, Ok, I get it. Nothing important happened, Ray."

"I tried to tell you, Sir."

"And so you did.

Abruptly Shawn asked, "Ray, when the boys hit the shop in Chicago, did they mention seeing anyone?"

Ray was dumbstruck for a moment because he'd been talking about employees' complaints about not being able to use the sub-basement conference rooms. "Uh, not that I remember, Sir. Only on the third mission was anyone reported. Has someone come forward as a witness?"

Shawn was annoyed at the alarm in Ray's voice. That shop was the first hit and *the boys* were no longer around either. Even an eyewitness would be hard pressed to make a connection to DNAgen. "No Ray, just a feeling I have about the place. Don't worry about it."

Ray sighed in relief.

Shawn asked, "The girl from mission three... what'd she look like?" He was hard pressed to keep his annoyance at Ray's panic out of his voice.

Ray sighed again then proceeded to repeat the same description he'd given Shawn during the mission debrief. "They said they saw a ghost-like girl. No real details about what she looked like."

Shawn was silent. Ray waited a few minutes and then picked up right where he left off in the dissertation of the evening's events.

Shawn quickly stopped him. "Alright, that's quite enough, Ray. I will take the employee complaints into consideration. See you in the morning."

Summarily dismissed, Ray turned the lights down as he left, "Goodnight, Sir," he said, grabbing the cart on his way out the door.

Once Ray left, Shawn turned the bedroom lights off and went back to studying the girl in his dream. He wondered who she was and if she was what Madeline meant by his dreams being important. He went to sleep thinking of her face; so when she reappeared in his dream, he wasn't surprised. He was in the Chicago shop again, and at first he was alone. He poked around at a few things, but there was really nothing of interest to him in the shop itself. *It feels... different this time.*

Then two things happened; first he saw his full given name, Shawn Alexander Kites, written in a scrawly handwriting at the top of a page in an ancient looking open book sitting by the cash register, and then *she* materialized. He was so startled by the simultaneity that he woke up, sitting straight up in bed. Looking at the clock, he saw it was five a.m.; and try as he might, he couldn't get back to sleep after he lay back down. He decided to write down the dream so he could share it with Madeline. Maybe she could shed some light on why the girl, and he himself for that matter, kept going back to that shop. And who wrote his name in the book?

Why did the shop feel so different this time? He got up, showered, dressed and went down to his office. When he crossed in front of the credenza, he felt a sudden pull from it. Facing it, he slid open the door and his eyes fell on that box he'd picked up from his mother just days ago. Feeling an odd sensation of electricity as he touched it, he pulled it out and put it on his desk.

With more reluctance than he'd felt in years about anything, he slowly opened the box. The contents were all still the same as when he last looked at them with Madeline, except they weren't glowing anymore. The small items did have a different feel to them. They now felt strangely, personally significant. The seven items in the box, each one still wrapped in tissue paper, looked innocent and even more worthless than before. Shawn examined them each again anyway: first the black and white picture of two black men standing in front of a store. He looked closely at the break pattern in the broken glass in the frame; and then he examined the picture; as he stared at it he suddenly realized the photo was taken in front of the Chicago shop. The revelation gave him the chills.

He instinctively knew that one of the men had to be his father, even though he'd never laid eyes on him. He recognized his own features in one of the men's faces. The other man had to be the now dead shop owner. It disturbed him to know that his father had known the man. He was reminded of his name being scrawled in that book on the counter and shivered again. He put the picture down and reached inside the box again.

Each piece was wrapped separately. The paper was old and thinner than he expected. The second item was a small ivory carving of an animal. At first glance he thought is was a deer, but realized it was a stag. The horns had been broken off into tiny fragments leaving the head bald except for nubs and ears. The breaks were clean, and looked as if each point had been deliberately broken off one at a time because the breaks were all angled differently. The pieces of the horns weren't in the box.

The next item was a watch that didn't work. The hands were frozen at twelve after midnight on March 21st. The date meant nothing to Shawn. The fourth item was really three: three small, red, flat stones with carvings in them. The symbols were vaguely familiar, but he had no idea what they meant or where he might have seen them before.

The fifth was what looked like a very smooth piece of black glass. If not for being slightly transparent and having no edges, he would have thought it was obsidian. It was oval in shape and had no flaws he could find, but it did have some weight to it. It was heavier than it looked. The sixth item was a small vial of what could be water, except it was cloudy.

The final object was the weirdest of all. It was a circular symbol, intricately designed and engraved in detail with twelve symbols hanging from a chain clearly made of high quality gold. When he held it, it started to get warm in his hands. He turned it over a couple of times before dropping it back into the box. It didn't burn him, but it felt like it would have if he'd continued to hold it.

He shook his head in bewilderment. What could these things possibly mean? He could feel a connection to them, albeit very vague in some cases, but they were each meant for him, and only him. He knew this as well as he knew his name was Shawn Alexander Kites.

A knock at the door broke his concentration, and he quickly scooped all the items back into the box, putting the photo on top. He shoved the box under his desk as Ray came through the door.

"You're here early, Ray! I thought you'd sleep in this morning. Don't you ever spend any time at home?" It was only six and it felt like it had only been minutes since he saw the man last.

"I knew you had a full day and thought I'd get an early start too. Have you had breakfast yet?"

Shawn shook his head no.

"Thought not. How about bagels and lox?"

Ray pulled a bag from behind his back, and Shawn was surprised he hadn't noticed it. *More preoccupied than I realized.* "Thank you, Ray. You're always so thoughtful. Have a seat!" Shawn watched as Ray meticulously laid out breakfast in front of him and then sat down. He picked up a bagel and began slathering cream cheese on it.

"So, what's my agenda filled with today?"

"Well, Sir, there is the Bifadene press conference at ten and a pre-conference meeting with the Chicago Tribune. Then you have a meeting with the White Wing Sovereign at noon."

"Who's catering lunch?"

Ray flipped through his notepad and answered, "That would be Gertsmier Delicatessen"

"Good. Go on."

Ray cleared his throat, "Your mother called again last night. I told her you were tied up, but she insisted I get a message to you by this morning."

"And that is?"

"That she needs to see you one last time…"

"One last time? She said that?"

"Yes, Sir, she did."

One last time… what could she mean by that?

"Those were her words, exactly, Sir. And she refused to elaborate."

Ray spoke as if Shawn had voiced the words instead of just thinking them. He grumbled under his breath, "I don't have time for this!"

"Sir, you could make it over there and back in an hour. I've already got a car standing by."

"Damn that old woman! I was just there a few days ago! What could she possibly have to add to our last discussion?!?"

Ray remained quiet, just waiting.

"Oh all right! But I'd better not be late for the press conference, Ray."

"Absolutely not, Sir."

Ray thought to himself, *I wonder why he has so much hatred for his mother. It's his mother! You only get one of them, and his seems OK, if not a little feeble and weak-minded. At least she ain't mean!*

When the car pulled up in front of his mother's house, Shawn hesitated before getting out. The driver glanced at him in the rear-view mirror, then looked quickly away. He finally sighed and opened the car door. When he entered his mother's house, it was very quiet inside. So quiet he could hear the old grandfather clock ticking in the living room. "Mother?" he called. A feeble voice answered him coming from her bedroom. He circled through the lower floor, walking through the kitchen, past the living room and back to the stairs, which he climbed to her room on the second floor. "Mother? What's wrong with you?" His voice was full of annoyance and disdain.

She said, "Did you look in the box?"

He caught his breath. How could she know he'd only looked in the box this morning?" "Yes, I did."

"Good," she coughed, bringing up phlegm, and her chest rattled loudly. "You needed to see what was inside," she said weakly.

He pulled a chair over to the bed and sat down. He couldn't help how he felt. His whole being was full of pity and loathing. "Why was my seeing the contents of that box so important to you?"

"Not to me, but *for* you. *He* said you had to see it before anything important happened. I was hoping that I didn't wait too long to give it to you."

"Wait, was there a time limit on it? How long did you have it?" Shawn asked with genuine interest, but it was hard for him to keep the contempt he held for her out of his voice. "I thought you'd only just received it when you called!"

"I'd only had it for a little while when I called you. And he just said, *Before anything important happens to the boy.*"

Full of skepticism he asked, "And what made you decide now was the time?"

She had another coughing fit before she could answer, "Just a feeling," she sighed. "Something's going to happen. It's big, and it involves you. I don't know what you've been doing, except for what shows up in the paper, but I have a feeling."

Shawn sat there for a moment staring at the frail old woman in the bed. The emotions were roiling in battle within him: Anger, pain and disgust fought against the pity, regret and shame that he always associated with his heritage, a heritage that was *her* fault. Shawn felt like he was going to explode and needed to get out of there. He rose abruptly, pecked her forehead and walked out without saying another word. Her *I Love You, Shawn* followed him down the stairs.

Shawn knew his emotions were irrational. He had never told his mother anything about his work, his company, nothing. He somehow felt cheated that she'd waited so long to give him the box. "I don't understand the significance of those seven items, but I know I should have had them a long time ago," he hissed. "Stupid old woman! I wish she'd just die and leave me alone!"

He dove back into the limo and the driver pulled off at a fast clip. Shawn didn't know who he was angrier with, himself or his mother. He fumed all the way back to DNAgen headquarters and had to pull himself together before he was presented to the press. Then there was the reception for the Sovereign after that. He wouldn't be able to sulk and fume again until just before his witch lesson.

Shawn caught Ray's eye as he entered the building, "Everything all set, Ray?" Even he could hear the tension in his voice, and he took a deep breath to calm himself.

"Yes Sir. They are being seated in the auditorium and will be ready for your entrance in a few minutes."

"Good, I just need a couple of those minutes to freshen up, then I'll be ready."

"You've got it, boss!"

Shawn walked into the men's room and it cleared immediately. Alone now, he stared at himself in the wall mirror over the sinks. Except for his color, he looked OK. The red in his face and neck would have to go though. He took some deep breaths blowing out slowly, splashed some cool water on his face and used a paper towel to dry up and cool his neck line. He looked at himself again... passable. Tucking his anger into a corner of his mind for later, he left the restroom and put a smile on to perform for the press.

Shawn waded through the people milling around in the hallway in front of the auditorium. Nodding and smiling, he made his way through the doorway and then up to the stage. Ray was waiting off to the side on the edge of the stage and went to meet Shawn, "Hi, Sir. You all set?"

"I'm good Ray, I'm good. Everything ready? Everyone we expected here?"

"The papers are all here, and the news cameras are all setting up over there on the left. They said they'd like to ask some questions at the end."

"OK, that'll work. I'll make sure to address their reps when it's time."

"Alright, Sir. Please step to the podium, and we'll get this rolling once I get the ready signal from all the stations."

"Thank you for coordinating all this."

"No problem, Sir. The ladies in the admin pool helped, along with Vicki, your admin assistant."

Ray turned and finished directing the foot traffic giving Shawn the opportunity to focus on his speech, which Ray had placed on the podium. He read through it once, and then looked up to survey his audience. The room was almost full, and Shawn couldn't help feeling a little full of himself.

Finally, everyone was seated and the lights went down on the audience and came up on the stage. Ray signaled to Shawn from stage right, and the spotlight came up on Shawn.

Shawn stood up taller and ran his fingers through his hair before he spoke. "Good morning, ladies and gentlemen. Thank you for joining us here at DNAgen Biolabs for a monumental, life changing announcement for those who suffer the genetic possibility of the devastating birth defect,

Spina Bifida." The applause was a crescendo that included whistles, and shouts.

Shawn stepped back and smiled broadly, basking in the adulations. He stepped back to the microphone, gesturing for the audience to quiet down. "Thank you, thank you. We are as excited as you are and very humbled by the blessing that Bifadene will be to millions of families the world over." Another round of applause met those words as well.

"Thank you again. Now, if there are any questions?"

For the next forty-five minutes, Shawn fielded various questions about the new drug, Bifadene. Most of the questions were routine: cost, availability, trial study results. Ray had the doctors on stage in their lab coats to answer any of the technical questions; and through hand signals, kept them from going on and on about the research. By the time it was over, Shawn was exhausted, but exhilarated. Once the last news van was packed up and moving out of the parking lot, he was ready to just sit for a minute.

"Ray, how much time before the Sovereign arrives; and is there anything else that I must attend to today, or can I veg out for awhile once the Sovereign leaves?"

"You've got about forty-five minutes before the Sovereign arrives, and other than your trip to the sub-basement, which is scheduled for five today, you're free."

"Excellent! I'm going upstairs for a few minutes. Please notify me when the Sovereign arrives."

Shawn went up to his suite and took off his jacket and tie, splashing cool water on his face again. The meeting with the Sovereign would be short, but he knew there would be questions about the Melacrit. He wasn't ready to answer them all, but felt he could divert his attention, at least for this meeting.

He lay across the bed and closed his eyes meaning only to rest for a few minutes, but he fell fast asleep. He was out for about half-an-hour when the phone rang. "Yes, Ray?" he yawned.

"Sir, the Sovereign has arrived. He's just getting out of his car."

"Thank you Ray. Please set him up in the first floor conference room."

"Already arranged, Sir. And lunch is already set up in the room."

"Thank you Ray, I'll be right down."

Shawn rolled over and stretched before standing. He put his tie and jacket back on and, stopping by his office to grab the Melacrit report from his desk, he went straight to the conference room. Smiling as he entered, he said, "Good afternoon, Sovereign. Thank you so much for taking this time out of your busy day to meet with me."

"Your invitation was such that I felt it well worth the time to come visit with you, Shawn."

"I hope you haven't had lunch yet?"

"As a matter of fact, I have not!"

"Wonderful! Ray, would you have the servers come in please?"

Ray moved to the door and gestured for two men, white this time, to come in and serve lunch. Shawn seated the Sovereign on one side of the conference room table, and he took a chair on the other.

Once they both had plates in front of them, Ray dismissed the servers and nodded to Shawn as he too left the room.

The two men chatted while eating hot pastrami sandwiches with coleslaw, the meat piled so high you had to use a knife and fork to eat them.

As the Sovereign finally pushed his plate away and reached for a slice of cheesecake, he spoke of the reason for the meeting. "So Shawn, what is this breakthrough you alluded to in your invitation?"

"Ah, so I did! Sir, I'm sure you've seen the announcements regarding the release of Bifadene to the market?"

"Yes, yes, I have; and while that is surely a triumphant milestone, it hardly brings me any personal joy."

"No, no, that is to be expected! What was not announced is the second milestone we have reached here at DNAgen."

Shawn stood and pulled the Melacrit fact-sheet from his portfolio and handed it to the Sovereign with a flourish.

The rest of the meeting was filled with *ooohs* and *aaaahs* and exclamations of disbelief as the Sovereign read through the Melacrit report and proposal. By the time he left, Shawn knew he had him in his hip pocket and that he would provide all the distribution support he needed.

After the Sovereign left, Shawn went looking for Ray and found him at the main guard station. "Would you come up about 4:30 just for a few minutes? I need to have you take care of something for me."

"Sure, Boss. See you then."

Shawn took the elevator back up to his office and poured himself a tall scotch before he sat at his desk and pulled the box from underneath it. That reminded him of his mother, and he swallowed a big gulp of scotch, grimacing as he put the glass down. *I wish she'd just hurry up and die,* he thought for the second time today, lifting the lid on the box again. *She's never been anything more than a pain in the ass! Whinin, and hobbling around... And now she's laid herself up in bed like an invalid!* He took another swallow, *What am I going to do with her! I just don't have time to deal with her right now. I wonder...* his raging thoughts were interrupted by a knock at the door.

Ray stuck his head in and asked, "I know I'm a little early, but can we talk now? I've got an appointment myself this evening and need to get across town during the rush hour."

"No problem, Ray, come on in. I'm hoping you can help me with a little... problem."

Ray walked over and sat in the chair. "Would this have anything to do with your mother, Sir?"

Shawn was taken aback. "How could you ever know that?!"

"Oh, Sir, perhaps I've just been working for you long enough to know you. I saw your face when the car dropped you off this afternoon. I kinda figured it didn't go well with her?"

Shawn sighed and finished the drink before he answered. "Oh, it went as well as it ever goes when I visit with her. She was bundled up in blankets and lying in the middle of the bed looking pitiful, as usual."

"Was she ill? Running a fever or something?"

Shawn snorted in disgust, slamming the box down on the desk. "She's always sick! Something is *always* wrong with her, Ray!"

Ray didn't say anything and actually leaned back in the chair from the vehemence in Shawn's words. "What can I do to help, Sir?" he quietly responded.

Shawn shook himself; and taking a deep breath, looked at Ray seeing the horror in the man's face at his response. "No, Ray. Sorry, it's just..." he was searching for some words to change what he saw in Ray's expression, and relaxed as he found the right ones, "Ray, it's... I don't know... it's just that every time I go over there she's weaker, sicker, and I know the doctors haven't a clue what's wrong with her. I don't know what to do with that!

How do I deal with something unknown! I solve problems! But I have to know what the problem *is* before I can solve it!" Ray visibly relaxed, and Shawn was pleased that he'd hit the right combination of words to change the man's demeanor.

Ray said, "Sir, I'm sorry. I know it's difficult to watch a loved one suffer, but she is getting on in age. Maybe it's just her time?"

"Her time… would that it were, Ray, would that it were. You hit the nail on the head, her suffering… it's her *suffering*, Ray." Shawn felt this was an Oscar worthy performance, and was hoping that it would be enough to get Ray to do what he was going to suggest next. "Ray…"

"Sir, what do you need?" Ray was suspicious; and the hair on the back of his neck was raised and staticky, a feeling he didn't like much."

"Ray, if I ask you to check in on my mother, just a few times a week, would you do that for me, Ray?"

Ray swallowed and reached up to run nervous fingers through his hair. "Sir, if that's what you need me to do, I'll do it."

"Well, I think that's what I need you to do. At least for a week or so."

"OK, sir," Ray answered as he stood and turned to leave the room. "Is there anything else I can do for you tonight?"

Shawn sighed, dropping the act and letting his weariness show. "Please order some dinner for me, your choice. I'll eat whatever you have delivered."

"When do you want it to be here?"

"I suppose nine will do. I'm heading downstairs now, so I should be back by then."

"You got it Sir."

As Ray left the room, Shawn exhaled sharply. *Wow, didn't realize I was holding my breath.* He shook his head, *I can't have the man doubting me now, not when I need him to carry out orders without question.* He looked at the box and decided to put it away again until later. "I'll play with the trinkets during dinner."

Ray stood outside the door for a few minutes, listening. When he didn't hear any footsteps, he went on to his office, mumbling to himself along the way. "I don't know what's going on, but Shawn is just acting weird now. For a minute there I thought he was going to ask me to off his mother! I know the woman is a whining harpy, but… it's his *mother*!!! And who doesn't have issues with their family!" He shook himself and ordered dinner for Shawn before he resumed his personal conversation. "I swear the man had murder in his eyes; tried to cover it up too, with all that fake *I care for my mother* crap. But I ain't buyin' it. I know he can't stand her; and while I don't know all the history, I know his hatred is over-the-top when it comes to her. Poor thing, she can't help it if she's sickly! And it ain't like he's got brothers and sisters to take up the slack. I'll check in on her. Don't mind at all, and I know it's more that he'll ever do for the old woman."

Ray cleared his desk off and made his final rounds of the day, planning to stop by and check on Chrystal Kites before he went home.

THIRTEEN

Shawn sat for a few more minutes just trying to clear his head. Between his mothers' perpetual weakness, the pressure and excitement of the press conference, the curiosity of the things in the box, and the excitement he felt at having his next lesson, he was jittery as an alcoholic needing a drink. He took a deep breath and stood up, deciding to do just what he told Ray he was going to do. He went to the bathroom, splashed cold water on his face for the third time today, and after drying his hands and face, left the office to head down to the sub-basement and his next lesson in being a witch.

When the elevator came to rest and the doors opened, Shawn was surprised that Madeline wasn't there to meet him. He stepped off the elevator and looked up and down the hallway. He could hear the murmur of the chanting coming from the room where the working was going on. He could also feel the power. It was like static electricity, only stronger. It crawled over his skin like water pouring over the rocks on a cliff. Shawn inhaled deeply, like he was absorbing a favorite fragrance. He closed his eyes and felt like he could almost see the power as it coursed around him.

"Shawn? Are you alright?"

Madeline's voice startled him out of his reverie. "I'm fine, Madeline. I was just…"

"Enjoying the power flows?" she smiled, and laughter danced in her eyes.

For the first time, Shawn realized that she had beautiful red hair and that her eyes were a vivid green. He smiled back, "Yes, I guess that's what I'm doing. It's intoxicating."

Madeline laughed again, "Oh, Shawn, you are such the typical initiate in so many ways." Then her demeanor abruptly changed. "But you are anything but typical. Come, its time for your next lesson." She turned and walked toward the room they had used for his first lesson.

Shawn only hesitated for a moment, wondering at her words and her attitude, then followed her down the hallway. They went back to the same room as before, and Shawn asked, "How is the working going? The buzz in my head isn't as strong as last time I was here."

Madeline sat amongst the cushions, "Oh, it's going fine. We've given many a chance to rest during this reprieve you've given us because we feel that the next mission will require more strength than the last ones combined."

Shawn's attention piqued at her words. "Oh? What is it you are... feeling?" he joined her on the cushions.

She smiled widely, "One of our seers feels that the next mission will be the center of the power source we are fighting against."

Shawn's pulse raced at hearing this. It took a measure of control to keep calm before he asked his next question, "Can you see where it is focused?"

Madeline's red hair danced around her head as she shook it, "No, we can't see exactly where, only that it lies north of where we are."

That information took Shawn aback. There was only one location on his list that was north of Chicago, and that was in New York. He had been planning it for later because it was so close, and because they had already done D.C., but this changed things. He chose his next words very carefully and said, "What exactly was seen, and do you know for certain that this is the focal point?"

Madeline smiled again, "Here, let me show you!" She took his hands in hers and lowered her voice. "Close your eyes, breathe slowly, deeply; calm the chatter in your mind and put it aside for later. Whatever thoughts are spinning in your head, let them rest and go to your center. This is the place from where you can see everything whirling around you like a storm; but you are in the calm center, like the eye of a hurricane." She felt Shawn's grip on her hands relax and nodded. "Now that you're centered, I want you to look around. What do you see?"

Just listening to Madeline's voice was soothing, and Shawn was not only aware that he was indeed at the center of the storm of thoughts in his mind, but that he could actually see them! "I can see my thoughts! They are like pictures or movie frames spinning wildly around me."

"Good, good! Now, lets go from looking at those pictures to looking beyond them. What else do you see? What does the space look like?"

Shawn was fascinated with the pictures whirring by but pulled his attention away from them to focus on Madeline's voice and her suggestions. "Ok, I see… colors, colors against darkness, but the darkness isn't… solid."

"Good! The colors are unimportant at the moment. Focus on the darkness, especially the parts that appear less solid."

Shawn chose the first lighter area to what felt like his right and focused on that spot. "It looks like there's something there. Like a beam of soft light."

Madeline laughed aloud as she said, "Wonderful Shawn! What you're looking at is a power flow. The more you focus your attention on it, the more solid it will get. I need you to tell me what color the flow is. This will tell us what the power base of the flow is, and then we can trace the direction it is coming from." She had to physically calm herself down. The fact that Shawn could see the power flow and found it so easily was amazing! He was indeed a very powerful warlock. She needed to control her emotions so she could keep control of him as long as possible.

Shawn stared at the area where the power flow was located and concentrated on what he was seeing. "The lighter area I'm looking at has a bit of a glow to it, kind of gold in tone. But it's moving, or it appears to move, like there's a breeze here, although I don't feel anything."

"Things can move of their own volition, Shawn. There doesn't have to be a breeze," she said matter-of-factly.

Shawn frowned, "So, you're saying it's alive?" he had trouble keeping the sarcasm out of his voice.

Madeline ignored it saying, "Alive in a manner of speaking. Let me ask you a question. Can something have life but not be *living* as we define life?"

Shawn was quiet, thinking hard about how to answer her question. "I believe I understand what you're asking." He focused again on the now writhing, tubular shape that was clearly hanging in the lighter area of darkness in his vision. "The answer is, yes. Something *can* be alive but not be *living*. An example would be an electrical wire," his voice was now smug in his revelation.

"Very good example, Shawn." She paused a few moments to emphasize her next words. Watching him carefully she waited until he began to fidget with impatience before she spoke again. "You see the power flow, right?"

"I do," he said, almost baring his teeth with the words.

"By now it should be more solid."

"It is."

"Can you tell where it begins and ends?"

Shawn inhaled sharply. This was not the next question he'd anticipated. "No, there really isn't a beginning or an end. It just kinda fades into the darkness around it." He was truly perplexed. Where he thought he understood what he was looking at, he now realized he hadn't a clue as to what was going on.

Madeline nodded, "What you are seeing is the part of the power flow that intersects with our location. It wouldn't have a beginning or end, as you would expect with a piece of rope or wire, because those two reference points are far from where we are."

Shawn exhaled with more force than he intended, not realizing he was holding his breath again. "So, what does that mean? How can we trace it to where it's coming from?"

"Now that gets tricky. You realize that this flow is not tangible, it's not something you can stand up and grab?"

"Yeah, I get that."

"So, to find its origin, we need to leave this place." She ended her sentence with a finality that she purposely pitched to get a reaction out of Shawn. And it worked. He immediately opened his eyes and stared at her.

"You mean we need to physically follow it? How in hell do we do that when we can only see it while…" his voice trailed off as the answer dawned on him. His eyes widened in amazement as he leaned forward and whispered, "We do it on another…"

Madeline finished for him, "Plain. Yes, that's right. We follow it on the ethereal plain, rather than hopping into a car, which incidentally wouldn't work for this kind of treasure hunt."

Shawn was excited again. He had questions about the ethereal plain that perhaps would get answered during this exercise. "So, what do we do? How do we follow the flow?"

His eagerness delighted Madeline, and she smiled. "Ok, lets go back to where we were when you saw the flow." She wanted to see how fast he could do it without the play-by-play instructions.

Shawn closed his eyes and concentrated on where he'd seen the undulating tube of energy and was surprised he was able to find it so fast this time, "I have it! It seems brighter than before and it's moving faster."

Madeline involuntarily inhaled. The speed at which he'd located the flow was incredible! "OK, good, Shawn. Now, we're going to try and trace it to its point of origin."

"We can do that? I thought this was… you called it *old magic*. Wouldn't that mean the point of origin would be somewhere in the past?"

Madeline smiled again, and Shawn could hear it in her words, "You're right, Shawn. It is old magic, and it's point of origin would be somewhere in the past, however… In order for it to be so strong here in the present means that it is being used right now, in our time. That usage has a point of origin that we should be able to locate."

Shawn exhaled noisily, again not realizing he'd been holding his breath. "I see. Following the trail should lead us to the origin of its current use."

"Yes, that's it." She closed her eyes and concentrated on the flow so she could locate it and join him in the journey to find the current usage point. "I'm going to join with you to follow the flow. If you see anything that you find familiar, please let me know."

Shawn wasn't exactly sure what she meant by that, but decided not to ask. "OK, let's go!"

Together, Shawn and Madeline began to follow the writhing tube of raw energy that coiled itself up and away from them into the blackness beyond their sight. Shawn felt like someone was holding his hand and realized that Madeline had a tight grip on his. He vaguely wondered at that, since they really had no physical bodies while in this place. But he put that thought aside for a later question, and concentrated on following the tube of energy.

They seemed to float in sheer blackness for a long time before he began to see anything he could put a name to other than the tube of energy. At first it was only the *feeling* that things were whizzing by them at a high rate of speed. Gradually, he was able to make out actual shapes; but they were mostly shadows rather than anything solid. Everything was flying by before he had more than a second or two to identify anything for certain.

169

And then suddenly, it all just became clear. The picture clarified, colors were now normal, the shadows all gone. He could see clearly that they were traveling north, and recognized New York City when they arrived. It was like watching a movie, only he was *in* this movie.

They began to slow down, and now he recognized that they were in Harlem. He'd only been there once when he was younger, and he didn't like it. Too many of *Them* in one place for him. As their rate of travel continued to slow, he saw the shop. The *Home* shop. He stopped, pulling Madeline to a stop beside him.

"Don't you want to see who's inside?"

Shawn shuddered, "No. I don't need to see who it is. In fact, I think it's better if I don't."

"So, what do you want to do, Shawn? It's clear that this shop is the center of the power source. I think we should look inside."

"No, Madeline. We're leaving."

Shawn frowned at her, but she didn't see it. She was too busy craning her neck towards the shop. "We don't need to see the face of the person inside. Makes it too personal. We've got the location. That's enough. Let's go, Madeline."

He tugged on her arm and turned back towards Chicago. It was difficult to concentrate on the trip home because his mind kept trying to focus on and to think about the shop and who was inside. For some reason, he'd always thought the shop in Chicago was the focal point, and the picture in the box from his Mom had made that assumption feel right. Now, he was… confused. The sight of the *Home* shop made him uneasy.

They slowed down every time he began to contemplate who could possibly be inside the *Home* shop. Consequently, the trip home took longer than the trip to Harlem. Once they *landed*, he released Madeline's hand and opened his eyes. A wave of vertigo hit him so hard he slammed his eyelids shut again and gasped aloud.

"Take a few slow, deep breaths, Shawn. You can't come in from a trip like that and just stand up and leave the room. You've got to give your body and your mind time to re-assimilate into normal surroundings. Especially on your first time out!"

Shawn did as instructed and took a long, slow, deep breath; and then another, willing his rapidly beating heart to slow down. Rolling his shoulders and stretching his body, he slowly opened his eyes, blinking and looked around, almost surprised that they were still in the tiny room at the end of the sub-basement hallway. When he finally looked at Madeline, she was smiling broadly. "What?" His voice was raspy, as if he hadn't spoken for hours, which he hadn't.

"I'm just so pleased with your progress Shawn. You are truly a very powerful Warlock. To be able to travel such a great distance on your first journey on the dream plain is simply... impressive!"

She was absolutely *gushing,* and Shawn found it absolutely annoying. "Well, it really isn't my first trip on the dream plain, Madeline." He was rewarded with her startled expression. "Yes, I've been there before. Not on purpose, you know, but by accident. I've been to the shop in Chicago a couple of times via the plain. Didn't really understand what was happening, but now I do."

Madeline recovered quickly, but the shock of his statement was still in her voice when she spoke, "You've been there before? Well, that explains it!"

"Explains what?"

"It explains why you seemed to be such a natural at traveling! Once you found the flow and were able to see it's path, we literally flew to the location of origin. A total beginner would never have been able to achieve such speed on their first trip. Well done, Shawn!"

She clapped him on the back and it sent a shiver down his spine. "So, what I did tonight was unusual?"

"Oh, Shawn, unusual is much too tame a word. Your performance tonight was stellar!" She took a deep breath and said, "Now that we know where the origin is, what will you do about it?"

He answered with a smirk in his voice, "Oh, my dear Madeline, I think you know what we will do about it!" The smile he returned was so full of malice that Madeline's breath caught in her throat.

Seeing the distress on her face, Shawn abruptly changed his demeanor. He'd forgotten that this woman had no idea what her coven was helping him achieve. He quickly answered her question, "We'll be changing our next target Madeline. Our new target is the Harlem shop."

Madeline nodded her head, not surprised with his answer, but still very concerned about what she'd seen in his eyes only moments before. "Well,

I think that's enough for this lesson. I will change the focus of our intent and assume that you'll give the new orders to Mr. Crosser?"

"Yes, that will work just fine. And, yes, I'll take care of Ray. Thank you, Madeline. I'll see you tomorrow?"

"Oh, absolutely, Shawn. Same time?"

"Yes, same time. Have a good evening."

"Thank you, and the same to you."

Shawn rose, albeit a bit unsteadily, and stretched before leaving the room without another glance toward Madeline.

Madeline just sat there for a few minutes mulling over that last exchange with Shawn. *This is very disturbing,* she shook her head, *and the hatred I saw in his eyes was soul-deep. Up until this very moment, I haven't had any reason to know, or want to know, why we are targeting these people. But now I do. And his reluctance to go into the shop and see the people in it... there was such vehemence in his response. We must know what we are helping him do.* Madeline shook her head again and stretched before rising. She was truly perplexed about Shawn's behavior, but felt a dark foreboding in what she'd seen today. She left the little room and went in search of Eric to inform him of the change in plans on their next target. It wouldn't be any easier than Miami, and in fact might be even more contentious since Harlem was the power focal point, but she knew they could handle it.

Shawn was tired but exhilarated. He felt like he'd found the secret to the reason the shops existed because they'd located the origin of the power flow. "If I can get rid of whoever is in that shop, I'll be victorious in everything else I have planned!" He was giddy with excitement at the prospect of having no resistance when he launched the Melacrit. When he got off the elevator on the main floor, he went looking for Ray and was rewarded with finding him at the security desk in the lobby. "Ray, I need to speak with you."

Ray looked up as if startled. "Sir, is something wrong?"

"No, no, nothing wrong. Just some new information I need to impart to you. Would you come up to my office as soon as you can?"

"Sure, boss. I'll be right up."

Shawn smiled and spun around heading back to the elevators. Ray watched him and the hair on the back of his neck stood up on end. *What the hell does this mean? I don't know what he's gonna tell me, but it ain't gonna be good. I can tell. He's way too happy, and nothin good for others ever makes him happy, so it's gotta be somethin nasty.* Ray shook his head and called the guard off his break so he could get upstairs as fast as possible. When he got up to the top floor, he could see Shawn's office door was standing open. He straightened his shoulders, took a deep breath and stepped through the doors.

"Oh, good, good! I was hoping you wouldn't be too long!" Shawn said from behind his desk.

Ray's hair stood up again and he reached up to scratch his neck as he answered, "What's the problem, Sir?"

"Like I said, no problem. Just a change in plans. I need you to call off the crew in Miami and get one together in Harlem." Shawn watched Ray closely to see what his response would be to the news. Ray looked bewildered, but other than that, Shawn couldn't guess what the man might be thinking.

Ray said, "Harlem? You really want to call off on the Miami target?"

"Just postpone it for a bit. I have new information that indicates we will gain a better result if we hit Harlem now."

Ray sat down scratching his head. This was just unbelievable! They had Miami ready to go! They had been ready to pull the trigger tonight! "Sir, you do realize that this means we can't strike for at least a day. I've got to make some calls and get a crew together, case the shop…"

Shawn waved off his concerns, "None of that matters! Have the Miami crew just hold off for a week. We'll hit that one next. Right now, we need to hit Harlem and as soon as it's possible."

Ray shrugged, "Hey, it's your party, Boss. I'll inform the witches they can stand down for a day or so."

Shawn cut him off, "I've already told Madeline of the change, so they just need to know what the new timetable will be." He leveled his gaze at Ray and said, "Ray, I know this is not the way you like to do business, but it's how it needs to be. Please just get it done as soon as you can. Let me know when everything is ready. Thank you, Ray." Shawn grabbed the stack of printouts and started reading, summarily dismissing Ray without another word.

Ray stood and left shutting the office doors behind him. He went to his office and started dialing. He called Miami first and put them on ice. Then he reached out to a colleague in New York who could help him get a crew together for the Harlem job. *Guess I won't be going by to see 'mom' tonight! She'll have to wait until I get her baby boy's orders taken care of.* He hung up the phone and lit a cigarette. Ray was just amazed at how much Shawn didn't think about his mother. "Poor old woman. Glad I'm not related to him!" he growled to himself.

The next several hours in the sub-basement were spent changing the focus of the working. They had been pushing toward Miami, and had to do a 180 flip to swing north to Harlem. Nobody asked any questions, but Madeline was ready with her answer just in case. She thoroughly expected Eric to begin plying her with complaints as soon as the shift was completed. After checking on the flows to be sure that all the focus was now on Harlem, she retreated to her makeshift study. As she entered the room, she heard footsteps behind her and knew it was Eric.

"So, what happened, Madeline? Why the switch? I thought we had a definite pattern to hold to."

Madeline sighed, "I've been tutoring Shawn in his understanding of his power. He is a remarkable student. He's already traveled the dream-plain, and this evening we followed the flow to the source." She sat in a chair as she finished, and Eric almost pounced on her.

"He's been on the plain? You followed the flow to the source? How can he possibly be that, that… advanced in just two days?"

Madeline gestured for Eric to take a seat, "Eric, just take a deep breath. I told you he was very strong in his power. I didn't realize just how strong until tonight. He is exceptional. A prodigy, if you will. It won't be long before he will exceed what I can teach him, and he'll need a much more advanced mentor. We need to think about that, very carefully and very soon. We have to be ready for that transition."

"You really believe he will pick it up so fast that *you* won't be able to contain him? Madeline, you are the strongest witch I know, and he's a newbie!!"

Madeline sighed again, "I know Eric. I'm as amazed as you are. And, yes, he is just that strong, and he takes to the power as if his spirit has just been waiting for someone to unlock it and provide the opportunity to soar."

Eric sat speechless, his mind moving at a million thoughts a minute.

"What are you thinking?" she asked.

Eric leveled his gaze at her. "You said that you followed the flow to the source. So it's a single source? We'd always thought it was a combination of earth power and something else, not a single source!"

"I know Eric, I know. And I still think it's a combination of the earth powers involved, but there is a definite focal point for the power and it is definitely directed from this single source."

"And this focal point is in Harlem?"

"Yes, it's another one of those shops, but this one has a very powerful aura around it."

"Did he identify the aura or is that your observation?"

Madelene noted an element of fear in Eric's voice when he asked the question. "No, it was what I saw, Eric."

Eric breathed a sigh of relief, "At least that's something."

"Yes, it is *something*, but I hope it's enough. If there is any type of backlash from attacking this shop, we need to be ready. Please alert the workers to strengthen their personal shields, and then you tweak our coven shields as well."

"Our coven shields? Do you really think there is that much power there?"

"Oh yes, and probably more than we can imagine. This is *old* magic, Eric, and I try to *never* underestimate *old* magic."

Nodding in agreement, they walked down the hallway to the working room to inform the Oak Vein and White Oak coven members of the changes.

Up in the penthouse offices, Ray was beginning to sweat. Not only did he never make it over to see Mrs. Kites, which was making him feel guilty, he was stretching his network tight in order to put a kill team together so fast. As he sat drumming his fingers on the desk, he wondered just how long it would take the witches to change their focus. "That ought to give me several hours, considering how long it takes them to build to their peak," he said aloud to himself.

Ray picked up the phone again and started dialing then abruptly hung it back up. "I've got to know how much time I've got!" He stood and went to the elevator going straight to the sub-basement. When he stepped off the elevator he could hear the muffled sound of the chanting coming up the hallway. He took a few steps, and then Madeline came out of one of the doors.

"Hi Ray, can I help you?"

"Hi, Madeline. I'm sorry to bother you, but I know you know that Mr. Kites has changed our target, and I need to know how much time before your folks will be ready?"

"I've been expecting you, Ray. I thought you might need that information. What was your original time-table?"

Ray fidgeted. Being down here and talking to this woman gave him the creeps. "We were originally scheduled to go this evening, but I need at least another day."

"I think I can help you with that. We need at least 12 hours to fully redirect, and then we will refocus on the new target. Also, due to the strength of the new target, can you be ready to go in 24 hours?"

Ray sighed aloud, "24 hours would be great! That should give me the time I need to make the arrangements."

"Fine, then 24 hours it is. We'll be ready to rock this time tomorrow!"

"Thank you again, Madeline," and he turned and almost ran back to the elevator.

Madeline smiled as she watched his retreat.

Ray got back to his office and was almost out of breath. "Geez, that woman just makes my skin crawl! If it wasn't for that, she'd be some piece of ass to look at!" He sat behind his desk and picked up the phone, dialing the number he'd started earlier. "So, it's me. How're we doin on pickin the drones?"

The voice on the other end of the line was muffled, "I'll have'em in place by this time t'morrow."

"You got somebody there... you can't talk?" Ray's frustration was palpable. He didn't need any hangers' on knowing about what they were doing.

"Nah, jus me," the speaker said, but he sounded funny, and Ray didn't believe him.

"You know I can reach out and touch if this ain't right…"

The speaker's voice now had the appropriate quiver and volume in it when he answered, "No sir, not necessary. Ever'thing'll be in place, no problem."

"Alright. Better be up'n up. Don't need no extra complications now."

"We good, sir, we good."

Ray hung up the phone feeling only mildly assured. "Just don't like using folks I don't know myself. Changing the target messed up my game plan!" he growled.

The 24 hours was flying by. Ray finally had everything in place, and the New York mission was a go. Shawn had stayed out of his hair for most of the day busy pouring over a stack of paper of his own making. And then he'd gone down to where the witches were.

Ray just sat for a few more minutes, staring into space. Then he decided to go home and catch a few hours of sleep. *Maybe I can stop by and see Mrs. Kites in the morning.* Yawning, he stepped into the elevator heading down.

FOURTEEN

Soraya woke up with a feeling of foreboding hanging over her like a rain-laden cloud. She listened for Iona but didn't hear anything and that made the feeling worse. Rolling out of bed, she stretched, splashed water on her face and dressed quickly before crossing the few steps to Iona's door. Just before she knocked, she heard muffled snoring and decided that she would surprise the old woman and fix breakfast for her for a change.

After pulling all her ingredients together, Soraya began to cook what she considered a good, healthy breakfast, adding some bacon, since she knew Iona favored a little pork in the morning. She was just turning the second veggie omelet onto a plate when she heard the door to Iona's room creek open.

"What'chu doin', Chile? Dat bacon I smell?" Iona said as she came into the kitchen.

Smiling broadly, Soraya answered, "Yep, thought I'd cook for you this morning!"

"Hee, hee, hee, can't b'lieve dis here! Nobody cook for Iona in a long tahm!" Iona shook her head in disbelief as she sat in one of the chairs. "Whut got inta you dis mornin', Chile?"

"Nothing special. I just figured that since I beat you getting up this morning, you must've been more tired than me last night, and it was an opportunity to do for you for a change," Soraya grinned as she put one of the plates in front of Iona.

Iona spied the plate and looked up with surprise on her face, "Bacon an Grits?! Chile, Ah jus cain't b'lieve dis here!" she said as she picked up her fork and started eating.

Soraya sat down and picked up her own fork, but watched the old woman eat a few bites before beginning to eat herself. The fact that there wasn't much talking was a testament to breakfast being good, and she smiled as she ate.

Iona finally put her fork down and looked Soraya in the eyes. "Dat whus d'licious, Chile! Din't know you could cook too! Ah been missin out!"

Soraya grinned back, "Well, you didn't really give me a chance to show you! Mama made sure I can cook at least a few things."

"Hee, hee, hee, keepin you ready for dat man to come inta yo life, hee, hee, hee! She done a good job too!" Iona continued laughing, while Soraya blushed and cleared the dishes.

Clearing her throat and changing the subject, Soraya asked, "So, what are the plans for today? Just more practice?"

Just as Iona was going to answer, the phone rang. Iona didn't move, so Soraya went to answer. "Oh! Is she alright? How long will you keep her? Thank you, Doctor, I'll be there just as soon as I can!" She walked back into the kitchen trying hard not to look upset.

"Whut's wrong, Chile?"

Soraya tried hard to keep fear out of her voice, but wasn't very successful. "Mama's in the hospital. She's had a stroke. The doctor said she's all right but I didn't like the tone in his voice. I need to go to the hospital, Iona, I'm sorry." She trailed off, taking a deep breath to hold back tears.

"Chile, no need t'be sorry. Dat's yo Mama! You go take care her. We kin pick up when you git back." Iona grabbed her hand and stood to give her a big hug.

Soraya packed a small bag and left. She drove by her Mom's house first to pick up some things to take with her to the hospital. All the while she was torn in her emotions. Her mother could be dying, and she was really worried about that, but there was something else. Iona had given her a hug like it was the last time she would see her, and *that* worried her almost as much as her mother being in the hospital. She tried to shake it off. "Soraya, you're being silly. Iona was just expressing her sympathy for your Mom!"

Soraya took a deep breath and tried to calm herself as she turned into the hospital parking lot. She was mildly amazed that she made it so quickly and hoped she hadn't run any lights because she had no memory of the whole trip.

As she walked into the hospital, the smells accosted her nose and made her nauseous. She stopped at the information desk to ask for the room number. "I'm looking for Constance Rawlings?"

The woman behind the desk had large-rimmed glasses that made her look like an owl in one of her old children's books.

"She's in ICU on the second floor. Only family visitors allowed right now."

"I'm her daughter." The woman nodded and pointed to the elevators. Soraya's heartbeat became rapid, and she had to make a conscious effort to keep the tears at bay. Her mother hadn't been in ICU when she spoke with the doctor earlier. She was physically gulping air when she got onto the elevator; and when the doors opened onto the second floor, she took one more deep breath and stepped into the hallway. Winding her way to the ICU nurses station, she asked for her Mom again, "Hello, I'm looking for Constance Rawlings? I'm her daughter."

"Miss Rawlings, your mother is in Room 2-B, over there." The nurse pointed to a room to the left of the station.

"When will the doctor be around?" she asked, her voice shaking a little.

"Dr. Draper is on the floor. I can tell him you'd like to speak with him?"

"Yes, please. Thank you."

Soraya walked over to the room and peeked inside before pushing the big door open to go in. "Mama?" she said, her voice just above a whisper. There was no answer. She walked up to the bed and tried to ignore all the tubes and wires attached to her mother. Tears welled up in her eyes again She didn't realize how fragile her mom really was. It's not how she saw her, and the reality made her question all of her decisions over the past few weeks. "Mama, it's me, Soraya," she said as she grasped her hand.

Contance's eyes fluttered open and she tried to smile, but her mouth only moved on one side. "Hi baby…"

"It's alright, Mama, you don't have to talk. I know it's not easy."

Constance swallowed, and tried again, "Ah'm K. Don hut much", she said.

Soraya leaned over and kissed her Mom on the forehead, tears now falling gently down her face.

Constance tried to frown. "S'all raght, baby, s'all raght. Ah's gon'b jus fine…" she squeezed Soraya's hand, but it wasn't her normal strength.

Her eyes fluttered closed and she drifted back to sleep just as the doctor stepped into the room. He met Soraya's gaze and gestured for her to step outside. "Miss Rawlings?"

"Yes, Sir. And please call me Soraya. What happened Doctor? When I spoke with you on the phone earlier, she wasn't in ICU."

"No, she wasn't, Miss… Soraya. Your mother took a turn for the worse, I'm afraid. We have been unable to stabilize her blood, and the clots keep forming. She isn't responding very well to any of the medications we've tried so far."

"Do you know what triggered this? She's never had any problem with her blood before. I don't understand what's happening."

"I understand your frustration; but in folks over sixty-five, things can just happen, especially strokes. Do you know whether she had a recent fall or anything?"

"I'm sorry, I haven't been home to see her in several days or so. But she didn't tell me anything had happened. I just… but she was fine when I saw her last," Soraya sobbed.

"Now don't go blaming yourself, young lady. These things happen! And, it probably would have happened had you been there or not," Dr. Draper admonished her.

Soraya dried her eyes on her sleeve, and the doctor handed her a tissue. "Thank you," she sniffed. So, what will happen next?"

"Well, we will monitor her closely for the next several hours and try to get her blood to the right consistency. At this point in time, we're just hoping for the best."

"She seems so weak."

"Yes, well, she's on a great deal of medication: some to make her comfortable and some to get her blood to the right consistency. Hopefully, we'll be able to reduce the amounts she's getting by tonight. You're welcome to stay with her."

"Thank you, I'd like that." Soraya shook his hand and went back into the room. Constance looked more peaceful and relaxed now than when she first arrived. She hoped it was her presence that was making the difference. She put her things down and pulled the chair closer to the bed. Then she went into the bathroom and called Iona.

"Hello?"

"Hi Iona, it's Soraya."

"How's yo Mama, Chile?"

"She's not so good, Iona. I'm not sure what's going to happen, but the doctor sounded hopeful. I think I'm going to stay here with her for awhile. Is that OK?"

"Oh, Chile, course dat's OK! Like I said, dat's yo Mama! You need t'be dere. Jus lemme know when you comin home."

"OK, I will. Thank you, Iona."

When she hung up the phone, she got that funny feeling about seeing Iona again, but shook it of. *I need to concentrate on Mama. Besides, I'm probably just mixing up what I'm feeling for my mom with Iona.* She stepped over to the sink and splashed water on her face and quickly dried off, then went to sit with her mother. She started talking, recounting her days spent with the old woman; and it seemed to make her mother relax even more, so she kept it up for several hours. She dozed off for a bit and was startled awake by a nurse coming in to check on the tubes and take Constance's vitals. Soraya decided to take a few minutes and move around, her arms and legs were stiff from sitting in the same position for so long. "I'll be right back, Mama."

It was almost three o'clock; and once Soraya started moving, her body reminded her that she hadn't eaten since breakfast. She went down to the cafeteria and grabbed some coffee and a sandwich. Not the best fare, but it was better than nothing. She ate fast, and as she walked back into the room the nurses were just finishing with her mother and she was actually awake.

"Hi Mama, how are you feeling?"

"I'm al-raght, baby. Jus tired, real tired." Constance reached for Soraya's hand with her good arm. "You OK, baby? How long you bin here?"

"I'm fine, Mama, and I've been here since not too long after you got here this morning. I'm fine. It's *you* I'm worried about!"

"Nah, nah, don you b'worrin bout me. I'm gon'b al-right. S'good t'see ya, baby. I know'd you got t'be learnin wit Miss Iona, but Ah do miss ya bein roun."

"I know, Mama. Maybe I'll stay awhile when you get outta here and go home."

"Nah, s'all right baby. You is grown nah, don need be roun yo mama all d'time."

"It will be no bother, Mama. Now, let's not talk about that anymore. What happened this morning?"

"Oh, well, I wuz making brekfust and got real dizzy. I fell out d'chair an pushed dat button you got fo me awhile back. Den, I was in da amb'lance... Don member how I got dere..."

"OK, I get the picture. Sure glad you let me put that system in the house."

"Yes, Lawd, dat was a good deed you done!"

They sat quiet for a few moments, Soraya running the story through her head adding all kinds of imagined possibilities. Then Constance interrupted her thoughts by squeezing her hand. "Soraya, baby, you know Ah love you, raght?"

Soraya looked at her mother, shocked at the question. "Of course I know you love me, Mama! Why do you ask?"

"Ah jus makin shore you know Ah love you. You is my everthang. An everthang I ever done wuz fo you, baby girl. Jus want make shore you know dat."

"I know, Mama, and I love you too." Soraya hugged her as hard as she dared, only pulling back when she felt her relax and heard her breathing slow. Constance had fallen asleep in the arms of her daughter. It wasn't long after that before she went home to be with Jesus, as the old folks say.

Soraya was still sitting in the parking lot at the hospital when the sun came up. She was all cried out, or so she thought. Her mother passed at about two a.m., and she'd spent the next few hours filling out paperwork for the hospital, coroner and the funeral home. She was exhausted, in shock, and still sitting in the parking lot because she didn't know where to go. *I can't go back to Mama's house yet. I can't do that right now. So, Iona's it is.*

Soraya started the car and drove back to the Home Shop. Her head was empty. She was trying hard not to think about anything. The closer she got to the shop, the rawer her nerves were getting. *What is happening to me now!*

As she turned down the street and passed in front of the shop she suddenly felt icy cold. *Why's the door standing open? Iona never leaves that door open...* Panic began to set in. She pulled around back and parked the car, almost forgetting to turn it off as she jumped out and ran in through the back door. She got halfway up the hallway when she stopped, that icy feeling freezing her feet to the floor. Laid out before her eyes was a scene she had seen three times before, only this time she was awake. *Iona* lay crumpled, bleeding and lifeless in a pool of her own blood on the floor in front of the counter. The door was open, and the morning sun was just creeping through the windows.

Soraya couldn't move. The only sound she heard was a far off wail that sounded ghost-like and eerie. It was several moments before she realized that the sound she was hearing was coming from her. Somebody was standing just outside the door with a cell phone to their ear, "Hello, 911? There's a lady dead here and another one who looks like she's in shock! Yeah, I'm in front of the old Home Shop on 125th? Yeah, that's the one. Sure, I can stay here 'til you get here. Yeah, I'll stay on the line…"

Soraya shut her mouth. clamping down on the sound escaping from her, as the words the woman outside the door said registered on her consciousness. She continued to just stand there because she just couldn't think of what else to do.

The lady at the door spoke to her, "Hey kid, you OK? Police are on their way. Just hang in there kid, they're coming."

Somewhere in her head, Soraya knew she shouldn't touch anything, but she also felt like she was going to pass out at any minute. She opted to grab the counter, looking first to make sure there weren't any marks in the dust where she put her hand. Then the tears started. The lady at the door looked sympathetic, like she wanted to come in and give her a hug, but she didn't move either.

"The kid's crying now," the lady said into the phone. "Can't I just step inside? Ok, Ok, I'll wait! Yeah, I hear'em now. About damn time!"

The lady was clearly angry at having to wait so long for the police response. Soraya was just grateful to finally hear the sirens. She stood there, counting in her head, "One, two, three, four, five, six…" She felt like she was a time bomb and the seconds were ticking away before she exploded. "Seven, eight, nine, ten…"

"Yeah, they're close now, about damn time!" The lady said again, shaking her head.

Suddenly the police arrived and the surreal turned into chaos: sirens blaring, men and women running in all directions, shutting down the street, one man was pulling that yellow *Caution* tape across the front of the shop, another whisked the lady who had been standing in the doorway away, and she was replaced by a woman in a suit who first peered in the doorway, then gingerly stepped over the threshold, careful to avoid the footprints on the floor.

"Hello, Miss?"

"Soraya," she was surprised that her voice came out in a choked, cracked whisper. She cleared her throat and tried again, "My name is Soraya..."

"I'm Officer Crabtree. And who are you to the deceased?" the woman was now standing beside her and grabbing Soraya by the elbow and led her back down the hallway, away from the grisly scene that she had been frozen to for nearly an hour.

"I'm Miss Iona's apprentice."

"Apprentice? Hmmm, don't hear that term used too often today. Apprentice to what?"

"Her apprentice... to running the shop." Soraya decided that to be totally truthful would end with her sitting in a white room with a straightjacket on.

"You related?"

"No ma'am, just her apprentice. She needed someone to leave the shop to, and without any children of her own, she asked my mother if it was OK for me to be her apprentice." the tears started falling again, this time with big, audible, sobs to accompany them.

"There, there, kid, it's gonna be alright," the officer said, clumsily patting her on the back.

"No, it's *NOT*! I've lost *EVERYTHING* today!!! First my mother and now Miss Iona," she wailed, her voice rising in pitch with each word she said."

The policewoman's eyes grew big, and she grabbed her walkie-talkie. Can I get a shrink in here please? This kid's gonna need somebody to talk to and it ain't me!" she said emphatically, squeezing Soraya's hand while she spoke.

The voice on the box squawked something that Soraya didn't understand, and the woman answered, "10-4", and began pulling her towards the kitchen.

185

"Come on, have a seat kid. There's a doctor on the way, and I'm not gonna ask you anything else right now."

Soraya sat in the chair and slumped forward, tears still streaming down her face, but no longer wailing aloud. The officer gingerly held her, nervously patting her on the back while they awaited the arrival of the doctor she was expecting.

Sitting up from leaning on the officer's shoulder what seemed like hours later, the tears were finally waning. Muffled voices reached Soraya's ears from the shop. She couldn't make out exactly what they were saying, but she could guess at the content. Iona was dead. The blood and dust of the gruesome scene would be forever imprinted in her memory. She felt totally drained of energy, feeling and emotion.

The sound of footsteps coming down the hall made the woman sitting with her visibly relax, and she mumbled, "Took'em long enough! I'm not trained for this kinda trauma."

Another woman in a suit came into the kitchen, and Officer Crabtree stood and whispered something quickly to her. "Soraya, I'm going to leave you in the very capable hands of Ms. Whinston now, but I'll be around if you need anything from me.

"Hello, Soraya. I'm Agnes Whinston."

"Are you also a police officer?" Soraya said, her voice dry and scratchy.

"I'm a victim's advocate and psychologist," Agnes said as she turned the water on and pulled a glass of water from the sink, handing it to Soraya. "I understand that you've had a very difficult morning. Can you tell me about it?"

Soraya swallowed some water and then drained the glass. With all that crying, she knew she was dehydrated. "I think so. Where do you want me to start?" She took a few deep breaths trying to prepare for what this part of the ordeal would be like.

"My dear, why don't you start where this all began?" Agnes said as she sat down.

"Ok..." she gulped air trying to hold back tears she didn't think she had, "as I told Officer Crabtree, I am Iona's apprentice. I woke up before her this morn... oh, wait, it was *yesterday morning*!!!" she gulped air again, and Agnes grabbed her hands.

"There, there, honey. It's OK, slow down, take your time..."

Soraya was shaking, and she wasn't sure she could even say a word at the moment. She took big gulps of air, trying to get control of her emotions. She knew she had to tell the woman this; she had to get the story out of her head...

"Ok, ok, I'm sorry..."

"That's OK, honey. Take your time, we aren't in any hurry here."

Agnes patted her hand, and it made Soraya want to jerk it away because she could feel the insincerity in the woman. To Agnes, this was just her job. To Soraya, this was her life.

"Ok, yesterday morning, I woke up before Iona..."

"So you live here?"

Soraya fought the urge to narrow her eyes at the woman, "Yes, I lived here with Iona. She felt it was necessary for my training as her apprentice that I live here."

"Ok, go on," Agnes took out a notebook and began taking notes.

Soraya sighed and started again, "Since I woke up before Iona, I fixed breakfast. Just as we finished, the phone rang and it was the hospital calling about my mother..." she almost choked on the words as the picture of her mother lying in that hospital bed flashed before her eyes.

Agnes patted her hand again, "it's OK honey. Go on..."

Soraya gulped air again, "Mama had a stroke, and she passed away last night... I mean, early this morning..."

"It's OK, honey," Agnes said while she kept patting her hand.

It made Soraya want to jerk her hand away again but she didn't. "I left the hospital after finishing all the paperwork and came straight home, I mean here..." she gulped again and then said with ferocity in her voice, "Home. That's when I found Iona, and I just froze..." The tears began to well up and pour down her face again. "The lady who had been standing outside the door when the police arrived called you..." her voice trailed off in despair.

Agnes stopped writing and put her pen down, grabbing both of Soraya's hands again. "Honey, is there somewhere else you can stay tonight? I'd hate for you to have to be here all alone."

Soraya looked at her and just blinked. There was nobody else, nowhere else to go. Whether she stayed here or went to her mother's house, she was facing the same exact things... being alone and having to deal with both of them being gone. "No Agnes, there isn't anywhere else for me to go. I don't have any other family left…" She choked on those last words for how empty they sounded in her ears.

Agnes held her hands tighter and Soraya pulled away. It just didn't feel… real. Agnes was just doing her job. Soraya watched her as she ducked her eyes and picked up the pen again.

"I'll just note here that you are alone. Someone from the precinct and the coroner's office will be in touch." Agnes reached for Soraya's hand again, and this time she didn't jerk away deciding that if she just cooperated, this woman would finally leave.

"If you need anything, anything at all, you just call me, and I'll come. That's my job, to be here if you need me." Agnes finished with a final pat to Soraya's hand and began to gather her things.

Soraya watched Agnes in silence. She marveled at how much one person could babble on about nothing. When she had finally packed away all of her pens and pads, Soraya rose to walk her to the door.

"Oh, Honey, I can see my way out. And I'll flip the lock on the door. You might want to think about adding some security to the shop, too. I'll call you tomorrow, just to check on you."

And then she was gone. Soraya sat staring at the now empty kitchen table, just listening to the now very quiet shop. She took a slow, deep breath. "I'm really alone now." she said out loud, her voice cracking. Soraya stood from the chair, just needing to move, trying desperately to keep more tears at bay. Part of her wondered how she still had any tears left to shed, but she knew they were there, just waiting to flood down her face again.

She slowly walked down the hallway to the main shop area. The only light now was from the little naked bulb hanging over the counter, since the sun had set. Soraya inhaled slowly as she surveyed the room. "If I had been here, could I have stopped it from happening? Would it have even happened if I had been here?" she thought to herself.

Then the rational part of her mind kicked in. "Soraya, even if you had been here, it would have happened. You would have been asleep." She answered herself saying aloud, "But I would have *been* here!" her voice sounding ragged as tears started to fall again. She looked around the room, her eyes stopping at the spot on the floor where Iona's body had been. Idly, she wondered at who would have tried to clean it up. The police normally don't do that, but she could tell that somebody had done a cursory job of removing the blood, although there were still traces. And, she would still have to hire someone to professionally clean it.

Soraya tearfully turned from the room, flipping the light switch to off as she went back down the hallway towards her room. She was exhausted but didn't feel that she could sleep… at least not yet. She stopped in front of Iona's room. The door was partially open and putting her palm flat against the wood, she pushed it open, and stepped into the room.

She'd never been in Iona's room, she felt like a child sneaking into her mom's room… but it was hers now. The whole shop was hers. She shook her head as if to lose that thought, and she focused on the little room instead. It was larger than hers, but not by much. There were old photos on the walls of people she didn't know and probably would never know of. The bed was neatly made; and she went and sat on it, looking around the room from where she imagined Iona would have sat each night. The dresser was filled with trinkets and mementos, and the bedside table also had its share of tiny items, all neatly placed. There was no dust in here, which was such a strong juxtaposition to the shop that Soraya smiled.

The room gave her a warm feeling, a comfortable feeling. It was almost like Iona was sitting beside her on the bed. It didn't feel like anything creepy, just warm and welcoming. Soraya ran her hand over the pillow and heard a crinkly sound. Reaching under the pillow, she found a note addressed to her. Her breath caught in her throat when she saw her name scrawled in Iona's handwriting. She sat there just looking at it for several minutes, afraid to open it. Taking a deep breath and sighing heavily, she unfolded the piece of paper.

"Soraya, Chile, I is sorry I ain't dere; an I know dis here is hard, but I also know you kin handle it. Chile, you is strong in yo pow'r, and cain't nobody take dat away from you! Dere is so much I di'nt git a chance t'tell you bout, but I b'lieve I lef nough fo you t'find whut you need. Da book'll hep, an I'll do much as I kin from here. Nah, I know tis late an you ain't slept none, so you do dat nah. It gon b'ok. Da Circle is wit chu!

All my love, Iona"

Soraya lost it then and collapsed on the bed crying the last of her tears into Iona's pillow. Curled into a fetal position, she did sleep, soundly… until the dream started.

FIFTEEN

Ray woke up the next morning feeling almost as tired as when he'd hit the sack the night before. Dressing quickly, he headed for the Kites' house before going to the office. When he spoke to the driver, he could hear the rust in his own voice from not speaking more than a couple of words so far this morning. "Just hang, I shouldn't be but a few minutes."

As Ray walked to the door of the house, he suddenly had a feeling of dread come over him. "Now what… I don't need this day to start off crappy cause the rest of it's gonna stink on its own!" he said to himself.

He unlocked the door and stepped inside. "Mrs. Kites? Hello? You OK?" there was no sound coming down the stairs. Nothing! No radio or TV noise, no water running, and he couldn't hear any breathing either.

"Aw, man, this ain't no good. C'mon ol' lady, please be alright…" He stopped on the landing and listened before going into the room. The odor hit his nose before he got the door all the way opened. "Damn it, this bitch done died! Damn it, damn it, *DAMN* it! Just one more piece o'shit to add to this day."

Ray dialed Shawn's number as he walked to the bed, "Hey Boss. I stopped by your mom's on the way in."

Shawn's voice was annoyed when he answered, "What is it Ray? I've got more important things on my mind this morning."

"Sir, I think you need to get over here."

"Ray, just what is it? Can't you take care of whatever it is? You're there already…"

"Sir, your mother's dead. Looks like it happened sometime last night. I haven't called 911 just yet."

There was silence at first, then, "Shit... Shit! Ray, make the call. I'll be there as soon as I can get it together. Oh, and thank you Ray."

Ray went back down the stairs as he dialed 911. He dismissed the driver telling him to bill the account and then went back inside to wait for the paramedics.

Shawn was wide-awake after Ray's call. He sat on the edge of the bed and stared into space, his mind on over-drive. "She's dead? She's really dead? Wow... I mean, *Wow*! The rational person in his head said *you did wish for that just the other day, didn't you? And now you've got it. So, what'cha gonna do with it?* He shook his head, saying aloud, "I just don't know. This is so unexpected. I'd better get over there." And with that, he stood and dressed quickly, calling a car on his way down to the lobby. The day was certainly starting off... interesting.

Shawn found Ray sitting on the front steps smoking a cigarette. There were police cars and an ambulance blocking the street when he got there, all with their lights going.

"Ray, so what happened?"

Ray stubbed his butt out as he spoke, "She was gone when I got here, boss. Smelled'er before I got into the room."

"So how long..."

"I dunno, but they was askin for you a few minutes ago. They might be able to answer your questions. Oh, and as soon as they'll let me, OK if I head to the office? I've got some more calls to make."

"Oh, sure, sure, Ray. You go ahead. I'll be there as soon as I can." Shawn turned and slowly climbed up the steps into the house. Ray watched him for a few minutes, then sat back down and waited for the cops to come back out so he could leave.

Shawn could hear voices when he went in the front door. There was an officer just inside "Sir, are you Mr. Kites?"

"Yes, I'm Shawn Kites. I understand my mother is..." His voice faltered, which surprised him. He really hadn't thought about how he *felt* about her being dead.

"Sir, s'all right, sir. Just come on in here and have a seat please. I'm sorry for your loss, sir, but we do have some questions we need to ask you."

"Sure, of course! Uhhh, can I go see her first? I mean..."

"Oh, Damn! Of course, sir; hang on just a minute." And he left the hallway going into the living room.

Shawn followed him and then heard some other muffled voices coming from the dining room, and then the officer came back into the living room where Shawn was waiting. "I'm sorry, sir. My name is Jenkins. They said you can go on up if you'd like."

Shawn turned and faced the stairway. It felt like he was looking at a mountain. He began to climb the steps and it felt like he was walking through quicksand. There were several officers standing at the top of the stairs, and they parted to let him by. One of them spoke in a quiet voice, "We are so sorry for your loss, sir. The coroner has been called and should be here within the hour."

Shawn turned absently to him and said, "Thank you." And then he went into the room. The other people in the tiny bedroom cleared out when he came through the door. And there she was. She looked frail and tiny, lying in that bed with all those pillows around her. He thought about the last conversation they'd had and shook his head again. *How could I know that would really be the last time I spoke to her? This isn't my fault!* As he looked at his mother, a sour mixture of regret, remorse and loathing pity began churning in his stomach.

Chrystal's face looked so serene. No trace of the pain he'd seen on his last visit. Part of him wanted to pull away the blankets the paramedics had tucked around her, and grab and pull her into his arms. But as soon as he had that thought, his calculating coldness kicked back in. *No, you don't want to do that. C'mon… when was the last time you gave her a hug? Showed her any affection? To do that now would be a wasted gesture"* And as fast as he'd had the urge, he dismissed it as folly. So, he just stood there looking at her dumbly. Shawn searched his feelings trying to decide what it was that he felt while looking at her. After a few minutes, he decided he didn't feel anything. No heartache, no coldness, just… nothing. He suddenly thought about that box she'd given him when he saw her last. Those seven confusing little objects that he now wouldn't be able to ask her any questions about.

Just outside the door someone cleared their throat. Shawn sighed and turned to the door. "Ok, I guess you guys can finish whatever you need to do," he said, his voice shaking just a little. He was surprised that he didn't need to embellish it in any way; the emotion was genuine. He just didn't *feel* anything!

"Yes, sir. Thank you, sir," and the officers moved past him into the room. They began cataloging her medications that were sitting on the dresser, and Shawn left them to it saying, "I think there are also a couple of bottles in the bathroom," as he headed back down the stairs.

"Thank you, sir, we'll get them."

When Shawn reached the landing, Ray was there waiting for him.

"Sir, I think you're going to be awhile here, but they've dismissed me to leave. I'll head to the office. Is there anything on your calendar this morning that I should cancel?"

Shawn answered, "I think it was clear until 11, so just warn the 11 o'clock appointment that we may need to reschedule, and I'll call you by 10:30 if I'm still tied up here."

"Ok boss, see you later. And, I'm sorry about your Ma."

"Thank you, Ray," Shawn said as he turned to go into the living room.

Ray almost ran out the door and down the steps. He turned, walked to the corner and called for a car as he headed up the block in the general direction of the office. The car service didn't take long to locate him and pick him up. He sat in the back seat and went back over everything that happened so far this morning. "What an effin' mess. Boss'll be trippin' for days about this. I know he always acted like his Ma didn't mean nothin', but sheesh, she was his Ma! I just can't believe he's that cold… but guess he could be." Ray shook his head. "Yo!" he called to the driver, "Let me out a couple blocks from the building. I need a smoke before I go inside."

"Sure thing, Mr. Crosser."

By the time the coroner arrived, Shawn was pacing the living room impatiently. The cops had called a victims advocate, but he'd dismissed the woman almost immediately after introductions. He didn't need any sappy female sitting in front of him trying to figure out what he was thinking. The coroner arrived and questioned him again and then did his *investigation* before bagging her up and wheeling her body out of the house. They left him with cards and a packet of documents with instructions on how to claim her body and suggestions for funeral homes. Once they all left it was almost 10:30, and he decided he really didn't feel like trying to keep that 11:00 appointment. He called Ray and had him cancel it and then just sat in the living room for a bit.

Shawn was amazed at how quiet the house was. Not that there had ever really been any noise in it when he visited her, but he could tell… could feel that something was different… missing. *I wonder if that's what life feels like…* He stood and walked through the house making mental notes of things he would need to address: cleaning out the kitchen, her room, packing up her things. He set the thermostat and shut most of the lights off, leaving the porch light on. He told himself he'd be back soon to go through everything.

Ray must've sent a car over, and it was sitting out front when he walked out the door of the house. On the way back to the office his mind was blank. *Shock, that's what this is… shock.*

When he entered the lobby, several people spoke: "Sorry for your loss, Sir."

"If there's anything I can do to help, Mr. Kites, please don't hesitate to ask."

Shawn just nodded as he walked to the elevators. Once inside, he took a deep breath not realizing that he'd been holding his breath while he crossed the lobby. As he reached to push the button, his hand hesitated, and then he pushed the 'S' for the sub-basement rather than the 'P' for the penthouse. When the doors opened, Madeline was standing there.

"Shawn, you've had a very bad shock. Would you join me for some tea?" He took her offered hand and let her lead him up the hallway to the room where they had been meeting for his lessons. He was mildly surprised that she hadn't started with the normal *sorry for your loss* rhetoric, but was glad that she hadn't.

After they were seated she asked, "So, were you and your mother very close?"

The question startled him. No one had ever asked him that before. "No, not really; I'd always felt she was more of a nuisance than anything else."

"I see. Was she mean? Or abusive?"

"Oh, no, that wasn't it. She was just… inadequate. I've never held her in very high regard for anything. I was almost sorry that she was *my* mother." The voice in his head snickered, *Why lie about it? You WERE sorry she was your mother!*

Madeline nodded, "So you didn't respect her?"

"Humph, respect her? No, I didn't respect her. I didn't agree with her life's choices. I didn't like how weak she always was, and how much weaker she had become. I hated who she chose to be my father. No, I didn't respect her at all." Shawn put the cup down because his hands were shaking, and he wanted to throw it against the wall. He had to slow his breathing and close his eyes to get his temper under control.

Madeline put her cup down as well, and then said, "Shawn, she's dead now. You have to do something with all that anger towards her or it will cause you problems. Your power is such that if fueled by anger, it will become uncontrollable and will consume you."

Madeline's matter of fact way of addressing the problem made Shawn realize that he'd been staring at his fists as he clenched and unclenched them while she spoke. He deliberately unclenched his hands and placed them palms down on his lap. "What do you mean *consume* me?" he barked. "Am I going to flame out like that super hero dude, or just explode?" he said laughing tightly.

Madeline narrowed her eyes and answered with no hint of joviality, "It would most likely be more of a spontaneous combustion: very hot, fast and nothing but ashes left."

Her seriousness got his attention. He uncurled his hands, which he'd clenched again, and dropped them back into his lap with a heavy sigh. "Ok, so just tell me what I need to do. I am spinning and I... I don't know... I don't know what I feel. I'm not thinking straight. I'm angry... I just don't know what to do with this..." He slumped forward in a very uncharacteristic posture.

Madeline nodded her head again and reached for his hands. He flinched at her touch but didn't pull away. She held his hands in hers and pulled him up to look at her. "Shawn, you are strong enough to handle this. A loss like this can be a building block rather than a destructive challenge. All you have to do is focus your intent."

"Focus my intent... what does that mean Madeline? What is my intent that I'm going to focus on?" He hated how pitiful he sounded, but right now it was how he felt. He was scared, angry and confused by her words.

"Your intent is to use this to build your resolve and fortify your strength and power, rather than allow grief to consume you. That fortification and strength is your focus. Your power, that inner flame that we identified yesterday, that is your target." She squeezed his hands, "Close your eyes Shawn. Find your flame, and concentrate on it."

Shawn closed his eyes and looked inward, focusing on his life flame, the source of his power that he had located in their last session. Once he locked onto it, his breathing became more rhythmic, and he visibly relaxed.

Madeline felt the tension leave his body and knew he was where she needed him to be. "Now, take the anger and feed the flame with it. Careful, don't dump it all at once. Feed it in a steady flow."

Shawn felt totally undone by all the emotions churning in his head. Madeline's touch was an abrupt point of calming coldness in the heat of his whirling anger and frustration. He relaxed and let her voice guide him through the exercise. As he focused on the flame of his power and began to feed it, he watched as the characteristics of the flame changed. He wanted to just dump it all and be done with it, but her voice kept him on task, and he was able to create a steady flow into the flame. The anger burned red hot making the center of his power almost too bright for him to look at, but he kept looking. The flow of the power into the flame was mesmerizing. It ate his anger voraciously, and eventually, he actually *felt* the difference.

Madeline's voice intruded on his solitude. "Now, let's change to one of the other emotions that is brimming over. You don't want to drain any one of them off completely because there is always a measure, a seed, of these needed to keep you in balance. Which will you drain off next?"

Shawn didn't speak but switched his focus to his despair. His curiosity was piqued at the change in color! This was blue, and the flame of his power burned bright blue with a white-hot center. This flow didn't take as long as it did to siphon off his anger, and now that he had the gist of what he was doing, he cycled through all of his emotions. Each one had a different color, but the one he was the most surprised by was love. The flame burned with a soft green, and there was very little to feed. Somewhere within him this registered as disturbing and wrong, but he was too focused on the actual process and the exhilarating lift in his spirit that siphoning off the emotions gave him to pay more than cursory attention to that mental twinge.

Having reached the last emotional bucket, Madeline spoke up again. "Now you need to examine your work, Shawn. See that your power is enhanced and strengthened by what you have fed into it. Remember that your power base now has a vast and almost limitless degree of variation, because all emotion works together to form what is the center of your being, and now the center of your power. You will want to examine this thoroughly and learn where your weaknesses lie. Those are the chinks in your armor. Those are the points from which someone of equal or greater power will be able to attack and harm you."

Shawn frowned at this news. "Is there no way to protect against an attack like that? Surely there must be a way to guard against such a breach?"

Madeline sighed, "Unfortunately, there has been little in the way of progress in determining how this could be done. Your best protection is to know where you are vulnerable and be prepared for an assault."

Shawn pulled away from his center and opened his eyes blinking rapidly to focus and look at Madeline. "Thank you for doing this for me. I don't know what I would have done without your guidance."

"You're very welcome. I do hope that you'll now have a bit more control over your emotions when they head towards a fever pitch."

"It is a lesson well learned, Madeline. Thank you again." Shawn shifted and made ready to rise from the pillows when he noticed that Madeline had not moved. "Is there something else?"

Madeline pursed her lips before responding, and then decided to just dive in. "Shawn, this… target for the next working…"

Shawn sat back down and shifted his attention to focus on her words. "Yes… is there a problem?"

"I wouldn't call it a problem, but a concern."

"OK, a concern…"

"This *target*. Do you actually know who this person is?"

Shawn was surprised by the question. "No, no I don't. Why do you ask?"

Madeline held out her hands, "Please take my hands. I need to show you something."

Totally intrigued, Shawn took her hands and closed his eyes. He felt it when Madeline joined him and she took him into the room where the coven was attending to the work. "When we shifted our focus to Harlem, there was a distinct, recognizable flavor to the power we are assaulting. Do you feel it? Better yet, do you see what I'm talking about?"

Shawn was trying hard not to be annoyed by what he felt was an interruption to his train of thought. "I'm not sure I understand what you're asking me, Madeline." He sighed, "Please explain what you mean."

Madeline cleared her throat and squeezed his hands harder. "Shawn, this power is somehow linked to you." She let her words float in the air between them.

Shawn did a sharp intake of breath before he spoke, "I see it. The... flavor, has a commonality to mine... what does this mean? How can this be?"

"The connection is weak, so I'm not sure if it's coming from the occupant of the shop or from someone else. But there's no mistaking it, you are connected."

Shawn studied the flow, tried to get a feel for what he was seeing. Then he released her hands and opened his eyes. "Does this mean I will feel something when the mission is completed?"

Madeline stared back at him with that total calm and innocence that incensed him. "I can honestly say I don't know, Shawn. It's possible you will feel something. Most likely, you won't. Since we don't know exactly what the connection is, I can only guess."

Shawn stared at her for a few moments then said, "Well, I guess we'll just have to wait and see what happens. It is certainly curious... but at this point I can't worry about it too much. The wheels are already in motion and I won't stop it just because of a possibility."

Madeline shrugged, "So be it." She stood and motioned towards the door, "I suppose I won't see you later?"

Shawn stood, "No, I need to take care of some other things this afternoon, and won't have another opportunity to come down again today. Tomorrow you'll be available?"

"Of course! I'll see you at our regular time?"

"Yes, I'll be here. Thank you, Madeline."

They left the room together, turning in opposite directions as they stepped into the hallway. Shawn walked to the elevator quickly, his mind humming with new questions and the growing list of things he had to do. Madeline paused to watch him board the elevator. "I wonder just what that connection is. This man is much more dangerous than any of us realizes. The only consolation is that *HE* doesn't know how dangerous he is." She continued on to the room where the working was continuing to build. They would peak tonight. *It will be interesting to see what direction he goes in when this one is done. I would wager that he'll dismiss us because the power level will drop significantly, but it will be premature... very premature.*

Shawn wasn't sure whether he was excited or just pumped with the new-found source of power: his own emotions. "What an exhilarating feeling to know that I can use all of that useless energy rather than be at the mercy of it!" He laughed aloud as he stepped off the elevator and walked into his office. Ray looked up from his desk, but Shawn didn't even acknowledge him. He just walked right past him to his desk. He was almost giddy with the possibilities!

Shawn sat at his desk and then saw the stack of paperwork that must have been dropped off by the driver that brought him back from his mother's house. "Ray must be totally confused. I should be torn up from this morning, and had a smile on my face, laughing even, when I got off the elevator and walked past him. Humph, I'd better remedy that or it'll be all over the building by quittin' time."

"Ray, can I see you for a moment?" he said into the intercom. Ray was at the door almost before he let go of the button.

"Yes sir?"

"You cancelled my appointment from this morning, right?"

"Yes, sir. Under the circumstances, I didn't reschedule it."

"Oh, no, that's fine. I'll call and reschedule it for next week. Have a seat, Ray. I need to ask you a couple of questions."

Ray seemed nervous but sat in the chair in front of his desk and tried to look relaxed.

"Tell me, Ray, when you arrived this morning, exactly what happened?"

Ray did relax now. The question was the one he expected. Shawn turned and poured a cup of coffee to cover the smile that tried to escape. He was still amazed at how Ray always knew when he was coming so that the coffee was brewing when he got to his desk. He turned back to face Ray expectantly.

Ray cleared his throat. "Well, it's what I said this morning, sir. I got there and it was real quiet. I called out, but it felt… different. As I went up the stairs, I knew something wasn't right and then I found her. I didn't touch anything, sir. I turned and dialed your number as I walked back down the stairs. Then I called 911 and the police arrived, and then you."

Shawn blew on his coffee before taking a sip. His mind was oddly blank after hearing the recitation again. Because he couldn't think of anything to say, he swiveled his chair around and looked out the window.

Ray perched on the edge of the chair not knowing what to expect next. He'd never seen Shawn so rattled. And to be honest, he didn't expect him to react this way, knowing how he felt about his mother. Again he wondered what that witch in the basement had said to him when he got back from his mother's house. Ray knew that's where Shawn went when he didn't show up in the elevator after being notified by the car service that he had returned. Ray tried to relax and anticipate what Shawn's next words would be.

Shawn took the few minutes of staring into the blue nothingness of the Chicago sky to get his thoughts together before turning back to face Ray's expectant face. "Ray, please go ahead and make the funeral arrangements as soon as the coroner releases her body. I believe she had some kind of plan with one of the funeral homes here in town."

"You don't know which one, sir? There are a lot of them," Ray said apprehensively.

"No, I don't know which one, Ray. But it was one nearby. Hopefully that will narrow it down a bit." Shawn recognized dismay on Ray's face at the prospect of trying to figure out what funeral home would have the paperwork. "You know, I think there is a box over at the house with what she used to call *important papers* in it. Maybe what we need will be in there?" He looked at Ray, hoping the suggestion would change his demeanor, and it worked. The man visibly relaxed, if only a little.

"OK, I'll go by tomorrow morning and see what I can find."

Shawn raised an eyebrow at the delay.

"Sir, we have that project running tonight, so I need to be here."

Shawn sighed, "Oh, yes, that's right. How could I have forgotten! Alright, tomorrow morning is soon enough. By the way, how are the plans for tonight?"

Ray was taken aback by how quickly Shawn dismissed his mother's arrangements for the murder they were putting into place. "It's going as planned, sir. The team will be ready to dispatch at the usual time tonight."

"Excellent! I'm hoping that this one will give us the space to proceed with the Melacrit launch." Shawn said, rubbing his hands together in anticipation.

Ray was sickened by the display but quickly put his poker face in place. He didn't need to upset the man, especially when he was so... unbalanced. "I'll just go get things moving, sir."

"Oh, by all means, Ray. By all means! Let me know when we're ready to rock!"

As Ray stood to leave, Shawn turned back to look out the window. Ray almost ran from the room. *I really don't like how he's acting. He's almost manic! Maybe I oughtta go see the witch about him.* He sat down and went over the itinerary one last time just to make sure he hadn't missed anything important. When the desk intercom sounded, he jumped because it had been so quiet. "Ray, I'm going to lie down for a bit. I just need to..."

"No explanation needed, sir. It's been a very emotional morning for you. I'll see that you aren't disturbed."

"Thank you, Ray."

Good, he'll be outta my hair for awhile, Ray thought. "I think I will go down and see what witch Madeline can tell me about his state of mind," he mumbled as he slipped into the elevator and left the floor.

When he got to the basement, Madeline was waiting for him.

"How is Shawn?"

"How did you know I was coming?" The alarm in his voice was almost embarrassing. He cleared his throat and said, "You always seem to know when I'm coming down here, and that's just creepy lady!"

"On the contrary, Ray. You came down an elevator... we can tell it's coming from the noise it makes. We can tell it's either you, or Shawn from how long it takes. His office is in the penthouse, right?"

Ray nodded.

"So it's either you or him when it takes more than thirty seconds. And since he's already been down here today, and I know he isn't planning on returning, it had to be you." She smiled broadly, and that only added to her creepiness.

Ray shrugged it off and stepped off the elevator as it started to complain at being held open so long. "Can you tell me what's up with the boss? He's… trippin'. I know his Ma died an all, but he's…"

"Not behaving as you would expect?"

Ray nodded again.

Madeline turned and started walking towards her workroom, and Ray fell into step with her. "Shawn is… as you say *tripping,* as well you would expect, all things considered. But he's suffering from guilt, I suspect.

"Guilt?"

"Yes, well," she stopped and turned to face him again, "He didn't really get along with her? His mother?"

"I don't know if *get along* is the right words, ma'am. He didn't *like* her. And, I think *she* knew that."

"Hmmmm…" Madeline turned and opened the door, gesturing for Ray to have a seat.

Ray thought the room was claustrophobic, but he sat anyway. He didn't like having to be so close to this woman, but he needed his questions answered.

Madeline sat across from him in the tiny room and asked, "Tell me about Shawn's mother, Ray. What kind of woman was she? Did you know his father?"

Ray quickly realized he'd walked into a trap. He thought carefully before answering her questions. "His Ma was an old woman when I met her. She seemed to really care for her son. I don't know a thing about his father," he stated, rather flatly. He hoped she'd get the message and stop the cross-examination. She wouldn't be gettin what she was lookin for from him! He followed up his answer with a question of his own. "What did you and Shawn talk about when he came down here today? He's always a little weird when he comes up from being with you people, but today he was more than weird."

"Is he OK?" she leaned forward in her chair with real concern.

Ray waved her off, "he's fine. He's lying down. He'll be available this evening if we need him for anything once things get going. But you didn't answer my question."

Madeline leaned back and narrowed her eyes at Ray. "We discussed his mother's passing. He was… confused by his feelings about her dying. I just helped him put them into perspective…"

Ray didn't believe a word she said. But, he also didn't have any grounds to state his disbelief. "Ok, well, I guess that's it then."

"Oh, no more questions?" Madeline smiled again.

"Not at the moment. If I think of anything else, I'll let you know." Ray stood, and after shaking her hand, he almost ran from the room, and he pushed the elevator button more than once, as if that would make it come faster. "I really hate being so close to that... witch!" he shook himself when he got on the elevator as if he could shake off his feelings about Madeline.

When he got back to his desk, he buried himself in the minutia of the rest of the day, still trying to forget about his encounter with Madeline.

Shawn heard Ray when he came back into his office. He had the urge to call him in and bombard him with questions but decided against it. It really didn't matter where he'd disappeared to once Shawn went to 'lie down'. But he did wonder. Lying down hadn't done any good. He was just as disconcerted as he had been when he came up from the basement. His emotions were swinging wildly between glee and despair. He wondered if everyone who lost a parent had the same feelings. "Well, that would certainly make you *normal* wouldn't it."

As he paced back across the room towards his desk, his mind began to race again. "What did she mean that I am somehow connected to the power flows coming from that shack of a shop? How is that even possible?" He walked behind his desk, and as he sat in his chair again, his eyes caught a flicker that appeared to come from the credenza cabinet. Pulling the key from the top drawer, he opened the cabinet and saw a faint glow coming from the box of crap his mother had given him on his last visit with her. "What the hell is that!" he said as he pulled the box out.

When he opened it, there was a flash, as if something had been let out. It happened so fast he dropped the box onto the desk cursing and pushed away from it, his chair rolling backwards. "What the..." Slowly, he rolled back to the desk and peered into the box. Nothing in it was glowing anymore, and looking around the room, he hadn't a clue where whatever it was had gone. He reached into the box and picked up each object, holding it for a few seconds before returning it to the box. The pendant he picked up last. It was the one that had gotten warm before, so he half expected it to burn him now. But this time it was cold, almost too cold. And the chain looked dull, almost tarnished. He put it back and just sat there staring at the pieces, bewildered. Nothing was missing, no new breaks on anything... so what was it that escaped? Shaking his head, he closed the box back up and shoved it back into the credenza.

"All that did was make for more questions!" He tried to concentrate on some of the paperwork on his desk, but after just a few minutes, he gave up. He picked up the phone and called Ray. "Hey, Ray, how about something to eat? I don't think I've eaten today and should at least try to eat something."

Ray responded with his usual attentiveness, "Would you like a dinner selection, sir, since it's so late in the day?"

"Sure, Ray, sure. You pick something, you know what I like."

"I'll take care of it."

Ray hung up the phone feeling bewildered, "He's hungry? Wow, he is a piece o'work!" he grumbled as he dialed the take out service. He ordered dinner for the two of them because he hadn't eaten today either. When it arrived, he debated whether to take his in with him when he delivered Shawn's or just leave it on his desk for afterwards. Shrugging, he decided to take it in. If he had just found out his mother died, he wouldn't want to eat alone.

He knocked on the door, and then quickly picked the boxes up off his desk, entering Shawn's office as he spoke. "I ordered your favorite and thought I'd join you, unless you'd rather eat alone tonight?" He began setting up dinner on the coffee table, grabbing the trays that were tucked in the corner.

Shawn watched the man scurry around the room in apparent agitation and wondered what had him so wired. He suddenly realized he hadn't answered Ray's question. "Sure, I'm glad of the company, Ray. Don't really think I want to be alone right now," he said, trying to keep the emotions out of his voice, but failing miserably. Shawn shook his head. He just didn't get all the feelings! He wondered if it was all really wrapped up in his mother's death or if something else was at work. He stood and went to the sofa to sit again. Trying to sound like he had enthusiasm he didn't feel for the food, he said, "So, what's for dinner Ray?"

Ray stopped and looked at Shawn with a look that was almost shock. He quickly changed his expression and said, "Nothin' special, Sir. A steak dinner with all the trimmings," he said as he finished setting things up and sat down himself.

As Ray began to eat, he noticed Shawn was just staring at the plate. He said, "Sir, you know, I think it's pretty normal if you aren't hungry."

Shawn looked up and for a moment didn't realize what Ray was talking about. "Oh! I'm sorry, Ray. I guess I'm not really hungry after all", he sighed and leaned back into the cushions, closing his eyes.

Ray put his fork down and was lost for words. He didn't know whether to finish his meal or clear the table and pack it up.

Shawn helped with the answer when he looked up and said, "I guess I just needed somebody here to talk to. Don't stop eating on my account!" Shawn said as he closed his eyes again.

Ray shrugged and picked up his fork again, trying to start a conversation. "So, the hit is a go. Everything's in place, and if the others are any indication, this should go without a hitch."

Shawn winced. "I wish you wouldn't refer to it as a *hit*. Not sure what you should call it, but hit is so... gangster-like; and I don't consider myself a gangster, Ray." He said, eyes still closed.

Ray chewed quietly for a few minutes before he replied, "Sir, we can always postpone this one for tonight."

"Oh no... no; Just because I'm a bit out of sorts is no reason to change the schedule," he said, leaning back into the cushions.

Ray was now shoveling his food in an effort to get this agony over with. Between mouthfuls he said, "Will you be joining the witches for this one?"

Shawn opened his eyes and looked at Ray, maybe for the first time that evening, "Ray, I really don't know what I'm going to do right now. I am off kilter. This whole thing with my mother has thrown me for more of a loop than I ever thought it would. Please just bear with me, and try to keep me from stepping into anything that I'll regret later."

Ray swallowed the last bite and said, "You got it boss. I got your back." And he stood to start clearing the meal away.

"Why don't you leave the steak at least; I might regain an appetite later."

"Sure thing, Sir."

Once Ray was gone, Shawn stood and walked over to the window, looking out as the sun was setting. *I have got to get myself together! Maybe*

I should go down while the… 'hit', is being carried out. Might explain how I'm connected to this power source.

Meanwhile, Ray was trippin. *The man is off all right. I sure hope he gets himself together. We can't afford any mistakes I'll have to clean up! Tomorrow I'll get that funeral planned and set. Maybe burying the old woman will make a difference.*

With that, Ray left the floor to walk the labs before the appointed hour. It always cleared his head to put some miles on his shoe leather.

When Shawn heard the elevator, he waited a few minutes for Ray to leave, then left to go to the basement. He took the box of strange objects from his mother with him, not exactly sure why, but hoping that maybe Madeline would be able to shed some light on what they were.

Madeline was waiting there when the elevator door opened. "Hello, Shawn. I thought you might come back down tonight."

"Well, I guess you were right! I am still unsettled about all that happened today, and I have some questions. Do we have time before the coven reaches its peak?"

"Of course! It might be a good idea that you're here when they do so we can observe your connection to the power source when the mission is completed."

Shawn nodded, and they headed down the hallway to the little workroom. After sitting, Shawn produced the box from under his arm and extended it towards Madeline. She looked at the box and then looked at Shawn.

"I don't think it's a good idea for me to handle that Shawn. If there's something in it that you want me to see, would you please take it out for me?"

Puzzled by her reaction, he sat the box on the floor between them and opened it. He was astonished at what he saw. *Everything* in it was glowing! Some items more than others, but every piece in the box was glowing with a soft bluish-white color. When he reached for one of them, there were tiny sparks created that jumped from his fingertips to the object he meant to pick up, and he jerked his hand back. It didn't hurt, but it didn't feel good either. "I don't understand! I've handled all of these things over the last few days, and that never happened before!"

Madeline looked from the contents of the box to Shawn's face. "So tell me, when did you come by this box and who gave it to you?"

Shawn sighed, shifted the box on the floor so it was directly in the middle of the space between them. "My mother gave it to me one of the last times I saw her before she died... so just a few days ago."

"Before we quickened you?"

Shawn frowned, thinking, "Yes, I think it was the same day. I looked at and touched everything in the box, trying to figure out why she gave it to me, and what they meant. They weren't glowing like this, but they were... different."

"And when was the last time you opened the box?"

"This morning, after I returned from her house. Everything in it was... kinda dead... like her." He realized that he was leaving out seeing the spark that seemed to fly out of the box when he'd opened it earlier, but something made him feel that she didn't need to know that.

Madeline inclined her head. "What do you mean, 'everything was *dead*?' Did the pieces have *life* of some sort? I don't understand."

Shawn sighed, "Maybe *life* isn't the right word, but yes, they appeared to have some life to them."

Madeline stared at the items in the box and had a million questions going through her head. *What about these things makes me so uncomfortable? It just looks like a box full of somebody's keepsakes, but that glow... they are charged. What could that possibly mean? Especially if Shawn doesn't know why they were of such significance to his mother.*

Shawn interrupted her train of thought, "Well..." he sighed, "I'll put these away for now, we can discuss them later."

"I think that's a good idea, Shawn. At least for now. We can tackle the importance of the box later. What else did you want to speak about?"

Shawn closed the box and slid it behind him. "Madeline, what do you think the connection is? Am I in any danger because of who we've got targeted tonight? Do I need to be worried?"

Madeline was relieved to hear the question. This she could deal with! "Shawn, I don't know. I don't have a definitive answer for you because I can't tell you what your connection to the power source is. I can tell you that it's not a very strong connection, but it's there. Will it affect you in any way? That remains to be seen. If you'd like..." she paused, meeting

Shawn's gaze, "You can, and probably should, be here when we peak. That way I can observe you. We may be able to figure out your connection and whether a successful mission makes any visible difference to you."

Shawn was quiet. Madeline thought he looked rather like a deer in the headlights.

Alright, I'll stay for the peak. I won't be missed upstairs anyway," he sighed again, weariness weighing on him heavily.

"Excellent! We'll move to the room before they set the wards for the building."

"Wards?"

"Oh, don't worry, it's just a precaution. This… *target*, is such a strong source of the power flow we are interrupting that we are setting extra protection for the space, just in case of backlash," she smiled as she stood and extended her hand to Shawn.

Shawn ignored the offered help and stood, grabbing the box from the floor.

"Oh, I think that should stay outside the room Shawn - maybe leave it in here. We don't want anything to interfere with the working, and I think that box would do that."

Shawn looked at the box vaguely wondering why Madeline was so afraid of a box of junk, even if it was full of glowing objects. Then he shrugged his shoulders and sat the box on the table, following her out of the little room. Madeline closed the door behind them throwing a quick containment spell on the room after it closed. She knew it looked like paranoia, if he noticed, but something about that box made her too uneasy to ignore it.

They walked in silence to the workroom, Shawn deep in thought and Madeline watching his every move. He stopped short, just before the door and looked up, almost confused.

"What is it Shawn?" she said, watching his hand poised over the doorknob.

"I… I'm…" he cleared his throat, feeling uneasy and embarrassed at his reluctance to enter the room. It made him angry, this feeling of not being in control! "I'm fine! How about you go in ahead of me?" he growled.

Without a word, Madeline nodded, and moved in front of him to open the door and step through.

Taking a deep breath, as if about to dive into water, Shawn followed her through the door. The sensation of the power flow was almost overwhelming! He worked hard at keeping his feet under him, and almost reached out for Madeline's shoulder.

Deftly aware of how unsteady Shawn was becoming, Madeline stepped close to him grabbing his elbow in an attempt to keep him on his feet. "Let's move over here," she whispered, pointing to a pile of those large pillows in the southeast corner of the room. She chose that corner because it was away from the path the power flow was going.

Shawn held his own as they moved to the pillows, but almost collapsed into them when they got there. He could feel the power mounting and began to sweat, wiping his brow and forehead with his sleeve. His mind was humming in tune with the chant, and in rhythm with the power that was pulsating through every person in the room, including himself. He saw Madeline's eyes close as she began to sway with the force of the power flow. He closed his own eyes glad to have the calm of the blackness behind his eyelids rather then the cacophony of whirling energy in the room. He began to hum, quietly at first, and then louder as the power began to peak. His body vibrated with the power of the energy that was now flowing through him as his energy rose to meet it and was joined to the working. He knew when they peaked. He could feel the difference in the power source they were targeting. He knew the attack would be successful. Unexpectedly, he knew that he would also lose his connection to the power source they were defeating. That knowledge saddened him, but the triumph of his plans coming to fruition outweighed that sorrow, so he buried it for examination later. Instead, he reveled in the glow of fulfillment, his mind racing with all of the potential that this one final mission's completion would allow him to achieve.

Madeline, eyes open now, was closely observing Shawn as the working subsided. The mission was now complete, and she could tell by his aura that his tie to the power source they had been working against was irreparably severed. She wondered what that would mean for him and vowed to be around when the answer was presented. Meanwhile, she waited for his euphoria to subside. She knew that the first time participating in a power flow of this magnitude would be almost toxic in the level of energy he absorbed. When his breathing became more stable, she touched his arm, "Shawn, are you present?"

Shawn heard Madeline's voice but didn't want to answer. He didn't want to be *present* just yet, but he also knew it was time to come back. Taking a long, deep breath, he said, "Yes, I'm here, Madeline. No need to worry about me."

She laughed, "Oh, I wasn't worried, but I remember my first participation in a power flow; and my desire was to stay in it, even though that wasn't possible," she smiled as she spoke.

Shawn could *hear* her smile, and finally opened his eyes to meet her gaze. "I can certainly understand that! It was…"

I know. Words aren't enough to describe it. But, you will remember it, always.

Shawn nodded and smiled. Suddenly realizing that the others were leaving the room, he asked, "Why are they leaving? They've not all left after a completion before?"

Madeline stood and stretched. "They know that this was the focal point of the power source they've been working against. The others are irrelevant. Without the focal point, they are all but useless."

"Ahhh, I see." He stood, thinking hard. "So, I suppose that means that our current contract has come to a close," he said, staring her squarely in the eyes.

Madeline sighed. She knew this would be his response, from the moment they'd located the focal point. "Yes, I suppose you are correct. May I have time for my workers to rest before we have to leave?"

Shawn smiled again. "Oh, most certainly! I know it took several days for you to get things set up down here, so it only makes sense that it would take several more to break things down. Please, take the rest time you all need, but I will expect you to have vacated the premises by this time, next week."

"And your training sessions? Will you continue them?"

Shawn stopped as he was headed for the door himself, "We will continue until I feel that your guidance is no longer necessary. However, rather than meeting down here, you can come up to the penthouse suite. I'll have Ray provide you with the proper ID so you can come up unaccompanied. Oh, and, business attire, please."

HARLEM ANGEL

With that, he was out the door. She followed behind him quickly and dropped the shield on the small room where they had been working as he touched the doorknob. He felt the shield come down and smiled wickedly thinking, *Afraid of my little box, huh... note to self...* He scooped up the box, turned and bid Madeline farewell, and left for the elevator. She didn't follow him this time, which almost made him skip down the hallway.

Midnight came and went when Ray's phone rang. "Yo, man, this is JuWan. It's done, man."

"Good. Make sure the follow-up is also taken care of."

"Sure, sure, no problem. When can I 'spect delivery?"

"It'll be there as promised. Take it easy man. I'll be in touch on the reschedule."

"Cool, man. Later."

Shawn showed up a few minutes later, and Ray watched him cross to his private elevator. "You all right, Sir?"

Shawn looked at Ray, startled. "I'm fine, Ray. Is something wrong?"

"No, sir. The mission was a success, and we're all clear."

"Good, that's good, Ray. I'll see you in the morning."

"In the morning, sir."

Ray shook his head, that was the shortest, most unusual conversation he'd ever had with the man. *I guess losing your mother, even if you hate her, is still traumatic.* He went up and closed up his office and headed home. It was a good end to a long and stressful day.

EPILOG

Soraya walked the dream plane in a fog. Both her surroundings and her mind were full and hazy. There were no buildings, people, signs, smells, sounds; just dense, wet fog. It felt like a mirror for how she felt inside: alone and adrift with no guidance or destination. She wanted to cry, but had no more tears. She wanted to sit and bury her face in her hands in despair, but there were no chairs either, and she didn't trust that she was actually standing on anything substantial. So she just stood there, the fog swirling around her, endless, grey, quiet, and wet.

Then she heard something, very faint and far away. At first, she thought it was just her imagination. Then she heard it again, still faint, but clearer. It was a voice. A familiar voice, but one she never thought she would hear again. It was her mother's voice. Constance Rawlings was calling her name from somewhere behind her... behind her no matter which direction she faced. Spinning in circles; and even though she thought that she had no more tears, they began to roll down her face again.

"Mama? Mama?" Her voice sounded raw and pitiful. She didn't like the sound of it, so she stopped calling out. Standing still again, she just listened. The sound of her mother's voice was joined by the voice of another... Iona's voice, faintly at first, then both of them became strong, ringing through the fog like the horn from a lighthouse. Suddenly, they were there. Both of them, standing in front of her, arms outstretched. She reached for them and was surprised to touch flesh. Warm arms encircled her, and she let them hold her, crying out the very last of her tears.

After what felt like hours, she stepped back from them to see them smiling at her. But even though the tears were finally gone, she didn't feel like smiling... not yet.

"You're both gone! What am I going to do without you!" she said in anguish.

Constance looked at Iona and nodded. Turning back to Soraya she said, "Baby, dis how it suppose t'be nah! You is suppose to be da leada nah! You kin do dis, baby. Ah know you kin do it!" And she smiled again.

Soraya looked at her mom and realized that there was no pain in her face, and her eyes were at ease. They were filled with the love she always felt when Constance's eyes met hers... before she died.

Iona spoke up next, "Chile, dis here what we wus gittin you ready fo! You been in despair, but you need t'git yo'self ready fo da next battle. Dis here ain't gon end jus cuz Ah's gone! You know dis... Ain't nuthin you don't know bout what Ah'm sayin."

Soraya looked at them both. Her mama's love being mixed and mingled with Iona's love and strength of conviction. "But, what do I *do*? What's my next step?" She looked up, suddenly realizing that there was a third person hanging in the background. "And who is that?!?" Her guard up, she reached for Constance and Iona and pulled them behind her while she confronted the tiny old white woman who had suddenly appeared. "Who are you and what do you want?" she demanded.

The woman timidly stepped forward, and she spoke with a frailty that was defied by her appearance, "Hello, my name is Chrystal Kites, and I don't know why I'm here, and I don't know where *here* is!" She stood, wringing her hands and looking for all the world like she was afraid one of them was going to hurt her.

Soraya relaxed knowing that Chrystal wasn't a threat, but she noticed that her name made Iona stand at attention, and her mother nodded her head. "Do you know this woman, Mama? Iona? Why is she here?"

Constance spoke first. "Hello Chrystal, you is okay bein here. You suppose t' be here too!" she smiled.

Iona sucked her teeth. "Chile, dis here woman is 'potant. An, her bein here mean we's connected. Ah know dat name..." Iona shook her head like she was trying to remember something.

Soraya thought, *Should I know her name? Chrystal Kites... Kites, there is something familiar about that name...*

Chrystal hadn't moved while they were talking, but then she looked up like she heard something none of the rest of them heard. "I have to go?"

she said, still looking up. "Ok, I'll tell them," and she looked back at the three of them standing in front of her. "I've been told that it's time for me to go. There's an angel here to take me somewhere…" and her voice faded off as she looked up again.

Soraya quickly said, "Chrystal, was there a message for us?"

"Oh! Yes! Silly me, I almost forgot! I need to tell you that you and my son, Shawn, have something in common. And that it is important that you know this for the choices you will have to make later. I'm sorry, I really don't understand what that means," her face was saddened, and it added to her look of frailty. She looked up again and smiled, and her smile was beautiful!

Soraya said, "I'm sorry you didn't get the chance to use that lovely smile more often! Goodbye Chrystal, go with love and light!"

Chrystal looked at her and said, "Thank you, Soraya, and please don't blame me for what my son has become. I didn't understand… I did the best I knew how," and with that, she raised her hands and floated up into the fog, disappearing.

Soraya stood staring up into the fog for a moment before she looked back at Iona and Constance. "What on Earth did that mean?"

Iona snorted, "Earf dint have nuthin t'do wit dat!"

Constance looked between the both of them and just shook her head, "I got nuthin t'add t'dat."

Soraya was totally confused now, not that she hadn't been confused before Chrystal showed up. "What do I do with all this information?" She looked at Constance who looked up like she was listening, much the same as Chrystal had done. "Oh, no! Do you have to go too, Mama?"

Constance looked at her daughter. "I'm sorry, baby. It looks as if I do. But, I'll be watchin out fo you! Dey cain't keep me from watchin out fo you!"

Soraya grabbed her hands and pulled her in to hug her tight. "I know you'll be watching me, Mama, I know. And I'll call out when I need you!"

"I love you, Baby! And I know you kin do whatever it is you need t'do!"

"Thank you, Mama, I love you too!" And then Constance looked up again, reaching, and she disappeared just like Crystal did. Soraya looked at Iona now. "I guess you'll be leaving next?" she said, almost choking on the words.

"Hee, hee, hee, well Chile, Ah don think it gon be dat quick fo me! Hee, hee, hee! Ya see, it wasn't mah time t'go, so Ah'll be here fo awhile yet."

Soraya didn't know if she was happy to hear that, or dismayed because of what it meant for Iona. "Well, I hope I can help with whatever you left unfinished so you can join them," she said as sincerely as she could, which didn't feel very sincere, all things considered.

"Oh, Chile, don worry, you will! You will! But, right nah, you gotta git you sef up and git da word out. Things gon be hoppin afore you know it! You still my Angel, Chile. Hee, hee, hee, mah Harlem Angel!" That said, Iona faded back into the fog, but she didn't go up like the other two.

Soraya checked her surroundings. It didn't feel as empty as when she'd first arrived. In fact, there were people and things fading in and out of her vision all around her now. The dream plain was a very busy place.

She wasn't sure of everything that she was facing, but she knew she wasn't alone, and she knew she still had access to Iona and her wisdom. For now, the tears were done. Her mind was filled with possibilities and spinning with potential strategies to further protect the people she was now responsible for. Her sorrow notwithstanding, she knew *The Circle* would continue!

The End

Printed in the United States
By Bookmasters